CHAPTER ONE

VIGGO RASSMUSSEN

Call this a party? Where's the virgin's blood you promised?

Vampire Falls. Season one, episode three –
"Better Late Than Dead"

If I do a little squint, he kind of looks like Kit Connor.

I close one eye and peer at the blob in front of me, then try through the other eye. Yes, see? Boy shape, hair on top. Basically, Kit Connor from Heartstopper.

"Um, what are you doing?" Kit Connor asks.

"I'm looking at you through my beer goggles," I giggle, holding empty Corona bottles up to my eyes like a pair of binoculars. "Like, literally. Look!"

The bass of the party thuds through my skull and my ears ring from all the shouting and whooping. *So* much whooping. The party is literally bursting with whoopers. I wonder what the appeal is? Maybe I should try it.

"WHOOOP!"

Kit Connor looks alarmed but apart from that, wow, fun! Whooping is so much fun that I stumble back and steady myself against the fridge, like the whoop actually propelled me backwards with its whoop energy. The power of the whoop, am I right? I put down my beer goggles, grab my red cup and drink, drink, drink.

Look, I know I'm drunk, OK? I never get drunk, so it's allowed (total lie, I get drunk oftentimes. Yeah. It's a word). I've had a several few more than I actually should because . . . well, there's a reason that I'm not entirely clear about now but it definitely warranted several thousand alcohol units in a very short space of time. But I'm having a good time, which is why I came. I think.

I look at my fellow party bros and hoes (ew, did I say that? It's because of the whooping, I'm sorry). I recognise most of them even though this isn't a party genre I've ever been to before. Oh, I've been to parties – just more interesting ones where we watch the season finale of *Vampire Falls*, but this isn't too bad. And yeah, I know, watching *Vampire Falls* with your bestie isn't technically a party but it's a party in my heart, OK? A hearty party. Ha!

These party people are Instagram clones, I'm telling you. Like, the girls get their hair and make-up and clothes done at the same place, and the boys do lifting to get amazing shoulders that . . . oh, wait. I see someone. Him. I remember now. That's it. He's it. He's why all the beer beverages.

Charlie Chamberlain swaggers past me into the long hallway, his followers (Awfuls, I call them) flocking round him like brain-dead flies on well-coiffed shit. He high fives them because, you know, bros, then leans against the banister and looks down the hallway, right at me. Honestly, I think he might have a wind machine app or something because his hair looks like it's moving in a gentle summer breeze. Not that I care about his hair, but he obviously got ready in a hurry because that tuft behind his right ear is sticking up. Couldn't wait to make his grand entrance, I guess.

I tuck my own greasy curls behind my ear and watch him pretend he hasn't noticed all the *I-had-a-wet-dream-about-you-last-night* looks. He doesn't break eye contact with me, and I'm not looking away from him. Why should I? I was here first. In the kitchen, I mean. And no, I didn't have a wet dream about him last night.

I feel hands around my shoulders and look round. Oh yeah! I'd forgotten about Kit Connor. He pulls me up from my actually quite comfy leaning-on-the-fridge position. Once I'm upright again, I scan the kitchen for more of those lovely jelly shots. I mean, *just lovely.* You should try them. They make your tongue go all red.

"Now what are you doing?" Kit Connor asks.

"Huh?"

"Why are you sticking your tongue out like that?"

"Oh, ha!" I snort, looking cross-eyed at my tongue. "Look, it's all red!"

"OK . . ." he says, frowning and looking around. "Where did you say your friend was?"

My friend? Roxy! Oh, my goodness, I forgot Roxy was here! At the party. Here. With me. I love Roxy. I take another slurp of my drink.

"Where's Roxy?" I say, whirling around.

Someone bumps into me and makes me spill my drink on them. Rude.

"Yeah, that's what I was ..." starts Kit Connor, but the best thing has just happened and I can't listen to him any more.

"Roxy! My Roxy!" I exclaim, as my very best personal friend comes through the back door.

I give her the best hug; you know like when there isn't enough hug for someone you love *so much* and you have to squeeze their breath out, so they know how much you truly love them? That kind of hug.

"There you are," she says. "Where did you go? Uh, you're *strangling* me. Who's this?"

"Roxy, this is Kit Connor. Kit, this is my Roxy."

"My name is actually Toby."

"Whatever," I say, letting go of Roxy and swallowing down a belch. "Kit's new so I'm looking after him, but also, guess where he's going?"

"I have no idea," Roxy says, shrugging.

"To the *Vampire Falls* convention! Where we're going, Roxy! Can you believe it? Another Faller at the party. *This* party."

"Cool," says Roxy, looking him up and down.

"But first, he wants to take me home with him. On his motorbike. A big one."

"No, I don't want to take you home. I was just ..."

"*And* he's a DJ. Look! I have his card."

Roxy plucks the card from my fingers and frowns at it.

"*Graham Flanagan. Mobile Dicos*," she reads out, and pulls a face. "Major typo, Toby."

"It's not my card; it's my dad's business. I sometimes help on weekends. I'm not actually a ..."

While Kit rabbits on, I look down the hallway and Charlie Chamberlain is still there, pointing his cheekbones at anyone stupid enough to look his way. *Vivian Erikksen* (yes, I said that in italics) sways up to him and flips her red hair over her shoulder then giggles at a joke he tells her. A joke *I* probably told *him*.

Do you know *Vivian, Queen of the Awfuls* was genetically engineered in a space test tube and sent here to make the rest of girlkind feel terrible about themselves? It's true. She fiddles with her phone, changing the song that's blaring through the speakers, and everyone whoops (not me; this music couldn't suck more). *Vivian* has control of what we listen to in the common room also. Sixth form is a dictatorship.

I grab Kit Connor's helmet (the bike kind, cheeky) and throw my arm around his neck.

"Eliza, really?" says Roxy, sticking Kit's card in my top pocket.

"*Eliza, really* what, Roxy?"

I frown at her, so she knows I'm listening really, really hard. Which I am.

"I literally went out to call my mum and I come back, and you're smashed. Remember we're driving to the convention tomorrow."

"Like I could possibly forget the best day of the year, Roxy?" I beam at her, then throw my head back. "One sleep till convention time!"

Roxy raises an eyebrow at me. She's so cool.

"You're so cool, Roxy."

"Hmmm," she says, offering me a glass of water, which

I refuse, for I am not thirsty, thank you. "You better not be an unbearable mess in the morning, babe."

"*Moi*?" I say, shocked at the accusation.

"Arguing about who's writing the sex scene in your fanfic, are we?" says one of the Awfuls as he grabs a beer from the sink.

He walks off, laughing to himself. I roll my eyes; Roxy and I have argued about that very thing before, so it's a terrible insult. Plus, although a chapter of my *Vampire Falls* fan fiction, *Never Leave,* could be found on Wattpad every Sunday night at eight o'clock for a while, I haven't actually written any in ages. Joke's on you, random Awful.

"You need to learn to hold your drink before we start at Bristol, babe," Roxy says. She looks down the hall where Charlie Chamberlain is still leaning, then looks back at me, her beautiful, pretty face sad, sad, sad. "Did the drunk happen because Charlie's here, babe?"

"PAH!!"

OK, that may have come out a little louder than I intended because the entire kitchen looks at me, plus Charlie Chamberlain and the Awfuls in the hallway.

"Pah," I whisper, hiding behind the helmet. "I didn't even know he was here. Is Charlie Chamberlain here? I didn't know that was him, Roxy, I didn't. We thought it was Archie Andrews. A brunette Archie Andrews. Didn't we, Kit?"

"Seriously, it's been nearly two years," says Roxy, sighing.

"But he left us, Roxy. He left us."

"You sound like the little girl from *Jurassic Park*," she says, pushing her long hair from her face.

"*Jurassic Park*!" I snort, throwing my arm around Kit Connor's neck. "You're so funny, Roxy. Isn't she funny, Kit?"

"You're kind of strangling *me* now," he says, also a joker it seems.

"Eliza, let go of Toby," Roxy says.

She sounds mad.

"You sound mad," I say over my shoulder as I pull Toby down the hallway. When I walk past Charlie Chamberlain, I absolutely don't even look at him, especially his face. "Don't be mad, Roxy. I'm having fun because you said to. You said let's go to the party and have fun. F-U-N. Fun."

We pile out of the front door and I trip down an outrageously uneven step, but my best friends, Kit Connor and Roxy, catch me by my elbows. Had I cracked my skull open, I could have reported this party for negligence.

"I didn't spell it out like that," Roxy says, making sure I'm vertical before she lets go of me.

"No, I know," I say, tapping her cheek as we walk down the path. "You're a terrible speller."

"If I could just get my helmet I'd like to go back inside, if that's OK? This is my first party," says Kit, rubbing his forehead.

"What's happening, nerds," says a voice that isn't mine or Roxy's or Kit's.

It's *his*. Uh. He's just *everywhere*. Why does he have to be here too?

"Not cool, Charlie," says Roxy.

"I'm just messing, Rox," he says.

I feel like someone's stuck their thumb over one of my

heart valves, one of the thick, important ones. How can he still call her that? That's what he *used* to call her.

"Where's your motorbike, Kit?" I say, refusing to look directly at Charlie Chamberlain and his conventional perfect lips and Edward Cullen hair (shut up, I know you've read it).

"My moped is there, but—"

"Sorry, Toby, there's no way she's going home with you," says Roxy.

"I don't *want* her to go home with me," groans Kit, playing hard to get. "My mum was right; I'm not ready for this yet."

"Come on," Roxy huffs. "Time for bed, Eliza."

She's so huffy tonight.

"You're so huffy tonight, Roxy."

I grab her hands and swing her round to cheer her up as she's obviously fed up with something, but then I have to stop the swinging quite abruptly. I let go of her and blink at all three of them and . . . wait. When did the three of them become six of them, and when did they sprout twins? Blurry, floating twins.

I take a long breath through my nose and look up. The man in the moon is pointing and laughing.

"What are you laughing at?" I shout. "I didn't even want to come to this party and now I've met Kit Connor and people and their cheekbones are all, like, *hey . . .*"

My mouth fills with saliva. Oh dear. That's not very promising, not at all.

"Eliza?" says Roxy, putting her hands out to me.

I take another deep breath. Good. That's good. Fresh air is good. Phew. I feel fine now. I would go as far as to say

I feel . . . effervescent. Screw Charlie Chamberlain, I'm going home with Kit Connor.

"*Vampire Falls* for ever!" I declare, then double over and hurl into Kit's helmet.

So, that lovely effervescence was actually the gallons of alcohol bubbling in my stomach, conspiring to erupt at the least ideal time possible. Another interesting sensation is a warm dampness on my legs; the visor on Kit's helmet is up so my vomit is funnelling onto my shoes, and I'm straining so hard with each *bleurgh* that my backside has decided to join in and toots every time I hurl.

From where I'm bent over, I watch Roxy's shoes rush over until her hands scoop back my hair, and even in this sorry display the love in my heart for my bestie triples. Kit's feet pace back and forth as he cries on the phone to his mum, and Charlie's feet turn away and walk back to the party.

Away from us.

Away from me.

Again.

CHAPTER TWO

VIGGO RASSMUSSEN

Your senses are off because you were in your cups last night, Juliana. Though you are more fun when you're drunk.

JULIANA THE DEMON HUNTRESS

It's the only way I can stand being around you.

Vampire Falls. Season two, episode five – "Closer Closer"

I sincerely apologise for my behaviour, but let's not dwell.

Here it is. Some people's favourite time is Halloween, aka All Hallows Costa-Spiced-Latte Eve, but this is what I look forward to three hundred and sixty-two days of the year. This is my Christmas morning, my first day of spring, my first game of some kind of sporting event tournament match.

I bustle into the hallway and knock the umbrella stand over with my bags. Excitement makes me more clumsy than usual.

"BYE!" I bellow over my shoulder.

"Was that the umbrellas?"

"No," I call back to Mum, dropping my bags and quickly rearranging the stand.

She appears in the doorway of her office just as I straighten up.

"See?" I say, gesturing at the stand as I grab my bags. "Vertical."

She rolls her eyes but steps towards me, opening her arms.

"I can't hug," I say, nodding at my bags, "I'm all balanced out."

"Sorry – mum hugs trump the laws of equilibrium, Eliza," she says, demonstrating her hypothesis by squeezing me practically to death.

I reciprocate until she releases me from her Kraken embrace.

"Eliza?" she says, putting her hands on my cheeks.

"Yes, Mother," I say, preparing myself for an emotional outpouring of how she'll miss me this weekend.

"Tell fan favourite, humanitarian and official hottest vampire actor of all the vampire actors Damon Van Schwartz I haven't washed my hand since he brushed it when I got his autograph last year."

"Ew," I say, heading to the door. "I will tell him no such thing and I hope you're joking."

A short, polite, car horn toots out the front and we both look round. I told Roxy not to come inside otherwise she'd get caught in Mum's tentacles as well and we'd never get away.

"OK, I'm really going now," I say, rushing to the door.

"Eliza?"

"I don't want to know about any more body parts you haven't washed, Mother."

I look round, my hand on the door handle. She's standing in the middle of the hallway, her eyebrows high and her arms folded.

"Have a wonderful time," she says, gently. *But,* I know there's a but coming. "But when you get back, it's decision time."

See.

"Fine," I say, turning from her.

"Sorry, hun, but you've had enough time."

"*OK*," I snap, opening the door. I take a deep breath. "Sorry. OK."

She nods at me, then her face breaks into a wide smile; she's back in bon voyage mode.

"Go. You and Roxy have the best time, but please be sensible or I'll regret letting you go on your own," she says, "and don't forget to tell Damon Van—"

"Goodbye!" I shout, drowning out her voice as I trundle through the door and down the steps.

Roxy's waiting in her car, the *Vampire Falls* theme blasting through the open window.

"Ready for Damon Van Schwartz?" she shouts over the music.

"Yes!" I squeal as I run to her car, my suitcase clonking into my heels – but I feel no pain, for this is the greatest day of the year. "Ready for SFX magazine's eleventh greatest TV actress of all time, Amber Anderson?"

"The real question is," says Roxy, getting out, "is she ready for me?"

I launch myself at her and we do a jumpy dance, squeezing and squeeing. We walk to the back of her car, still doing springy steps of joy, and Roxy opens the boot. Her suitcase is tucked into the boot among bags filled with crisps and chocolate and rosé and vodka.

Air whistles out of the inflated balloon that is my soul as the sight of the vodka reminds me of the heinous events of the party. I can still taste the vodka jelly travelling up my nose.

"Hey?" says Roxy.

I look at her. "Hmm?"

"No frowning. There's no place for frowning on convention day, Eliza Gellar." She points at my face, her finger so close to my nose I have to lean back. "What's that about?"

"Sorry, it's that," I say, nodding at the vodka and suppressing the urge to gag.

"Oh. Poor hungover Eliza." Roxy smirks. "Sucks for you."

"I'm not hungover. I'm just . . . tired."

"Right, OK. *Tired*," she says, squeezing my stuff in the boot. "But do not dwell, because even if you throw up all over yourself and fart the national anthem this weekend, nobody will care. Our people won't care."

"Our people." I smile, then look down at my outfit. I turn to Roxy and tug the bottom of my white T-shirt. "Can you totally see my bra through this top?"

"No, Eliza, I cannot see your bra through that top," she sighs, pushing on my suitcase and not even looking at me or my T-shirt. "I couldn't see it when you FaceTimed me while I was eating my Coco Pops, and I couldn't see it in the wide variety of angles you sent on WhatsApp either. Nobody can see your bra."

"But if I stand . . ."

"No more. Do not say bra." She holds her hand up to me and looks at her watch. "We need to go if you want to stop for coffee?"

"Of course I want to stop for coffee," I say, pulling the boot down. "We always stop for coffee."

"Get your arse in the car then, and let the fun commence!"

she says, clapping her hands. "My brother borrowed the car for a uni trip last weekend. Sorry if it still smells of boy."

I don't care if the car smells of boy. I wouldn't care if it smelt of rancid old cheese. I race round to the passenger door and climb in; the *Vampire Falls* theme embracing me by my ears.

"You know, next time we do this we'll probably be going straight to Bristol together," she says, pulling off the driveway. "Did you hear about your accommodation choices yet?"

I shake my head, then, halfway up the road, I gasp and turn to her.

"Did you bring the highlighters!?"

"Yes," she says, not taking her eyes off the road.

"How many?" I ask.

"Four. Two each in case one runs out."

I nod. *Phew.* One time, I lost my highlighter and had to underline the talks and autograph sessions in the schedule using a blue biro, like some kind of savage.

"Get that Haribo open," Roxy says.

Yes, Haribo for breakfast, another convention road trip ritual. I gleefully pull the pack open, take seven and give Roxy some hearts, then glance down at my t-shirt again.

"Are you sure you can't see my bra?"

"Surer than I have ever been in my life about anything," she says without looking at me.

I smile, satisfied that my undergarments aren't on show. Each of my outfits is planned down to the finest of details. Comfy onesies to roll down to breakfast in, outfits specific to the eye colour of which guests we're having photos with, and, of course, the cosplay outfits for each of the parties. The party themes for each night are as follows: Masquerade (overdone), Full Moon Diner (yes), *Vampire Falls* Zombie Apocalypse (like it, really a lot) and Ghosts and Gargoyles (meh). Four nights of cosplay, four nights of nerd joy.

"Did you watch the pilot yet?" asks Roxy, tapping the steering wheel along to the music. I look at her. "*Midnight in Portland*."

I nod and look out the window. "It was shit."

"What?" Roxy glances at me and shakes her head. "You haven't watched it."

"I have. I mean, I watched the cold open and the credits. The theme was terrible, like, kill me with a cello bow now. Depressing. And the quality was *awful*. Most of it was blurry and pixelated."

"Because it's not supposed to have been shared yet. It's a production leak," she says. "Watch it, babe, honestly. Definite *Vampire Falls* vibes, with a different angle. There's already fan fiction on Wattpad."

"I don't care about fan fiction any more," I say, bristling a little. I used to carry a spiral-bound *Vampire Falls* notepad around at all times, in case inspiration struck, but not for a while now. "And spin-offs are always shit."

"Reckon this won't be, from what I saw. I hope it gets picked up. Apparently, one of the main actor guys is in rehab or something."

"Hmmm," I say, digging a ring out of the Haribo bag.

"Your refusal to try anything remotely new is adorable, Eliza."

"I don't need to try it; I have *Vampire Falls* to fill my obsession quota, thank you."

I remember the day said obsession with *Vampire Falls* started like it was my wedding day, and I know that doesn't make sense as I'm yet to marry or even, like, *meet* someone I can stand being around, but nevertheless, it was a defining moment.

Just like every good story starts, I was skiving school due to (not-that-bad) cramps courtesy of Aunt Flo. Mum came into the living room with a hot water bottle and Marmite on toast, telling me about a new thing on Netflix. The creator was inspired by some vampire show Mum watched back in the dark ages, and she wanted us to watch it together. Too weak from blood loss to resist, I agreed.

At that point in my life, I was still searching for an Eliza-shaped space to slot into, but nothing fit properly. Or *I* didn't fit properly. School was hideous because I didn't get my peers and they didn't get me (apart from Roxy, who I believe was sent to me from heaven). Gymnastics wasn't fun any more because the girls at my club decided I wasn't worth their effort as I wasn't competitive enough, and I got kicked out of the school orchestra because I *drummed too enthusiastically* according to the music teacher.

Lila Murphy, played by Megan Nicole Jefferies, who'd isolated herself at her last school because she could speak to dead people, arriving in Vistoria Falls and finding a gang of misfits who became cooler and more attractive with each scene, *was* that Eliza-shaped space I'd been searching for. I swear, I felt my soul sighing with relief.

I was following most of the cast on Instagram before the end credits, got a Lila Murphy cut (but grew it out immediately as *bangs* only work if you have cheekbones; I looked like a doughy-faced pre-pubescent boy when I put my hair in a ponytail) and took up stage combat the following month. Roxy also fell hard after I made her watch the first episode, and Mum took us to our first convention that year. I joined Wattpad and started writing fan fiction under the username of FallerForever. I'd always enjoyed scribbling stories in my notepads, but once I discovered *Vampire Falls* I wrote words for those characters with total focus, respect and passion. Life finally felt like it made sense.

"Give me a cola bottle," Roxy says, turning into the retail park. "Not a gummy bear."

I root around the packet and stick a cola bottle in Roxy's mouth. Charlie Chamberlain's favourite are the bears. Or they used to be. He's probably too cool for Haribo now. Not one of his macros.

Urgh. Charlie Chamberlain. He just lurks in the subconscious of my Haribo packet, waiting to annoy me.

"Did you see Charlie Chamberlain yesterday with the rest of the Awfuls? I hate the way they just stand around talking to each other."

"We stand around talking to each other," says Roxy, disinterested. I should really talk to her about her tone when I've finished ranting.

"But we don't do it in a *worship-our-perfect-bone-structure-and-lucky-genes* way. I mean, that's all good looks are anyway. Luck. It's nothing to be proud of."

"You didn't think that when we were friends with him."

"He didn't look like that when we were friends with him," I say, folding my arms.

"Yes, he did."

"Well, yes, if you want to get technical, but he wasn't all groomed and in proportion, and he couldn't shave properly because of his acne."

"If you say so."

"Remember that Halloween he was so embarrassed of his acne he wore a McKinley the Pessimistic Werewolf mask to take Sadie trick or treating and then kept it on for days? He hated McKinley the Pessimistic Werewolf."

Sadie is Charlie's little sister and *Vampire Falls* superfan in training. She's seriously cute and I miss seeing her, but that's what happens when best friends ditch you and move on. They take their cute little sister out of your life too.

"McKinley's the worst," says Roxy, shaking her head at the mention of everyone's least favourite *Vampire Falls* character. "Everyone hates McKinley."

"Duh, that's why there's a song called 'Everyone Hates McKinley' in the musical episode."

Roxy immediately bursts into song.

"*McKinley, McKinley, you sing out of tune, don't blame the full moon,*" she sings, tapping her hand on the steering wheel.

I obviously must join in.

"*We know it's a curse, but your pessimism's the worst. Everyone hates McKinleeeey.*"

We finish the song on a horrific crescendo and pull into the Costa drive-thru. Roxy doesn't even pause at the menu;

we have the same thing every year. It's a tradition my mum started when she took us to our first convention five years ago. Mum always had a triple-shot of espresso in her iced mocha (we could get very squealy on the journey) and Roxy and I have since graduated from decaf. You don't mess with tradition, even when your chaperone has let you fly free. I clear my throat and continue.

"And what does he even talk to them about anyway? He can't talk to them about what we used to talk about, can he? Did he get a handbook or something when he went to the dark side?"

"He didn't go to the dark side, Eliza, he—"

"He abandoned us and started hanging out with the Awfuls: that's the dark side, Roxy," I say. "Uh, and did you see Vivian hanging off him? Made for each other in an evil laboratory."

"You just don't like her because of that time she got gold on the balance beam, and you came last."

"Because she was twice my height when we were eleven! I could barely get on the thing properly. Super-rich *bitch*."

"I don't think she's super-rich, babe," says Roxy, frowning. "Her parents run an events company or something. She's not that bad. She actually invited us to that party."

"Well, I didn't actually want to go."

"But then you would never have met Kit Connor," she says, fluttering her eyelashes.

"Don't," I say, my stomach bubbling with embarrassment. "I can't believe Charlie Chamberlain witnessed me barfing everywhere. I bet he's told everyone."

"He wouldn't."

"I bet he filmed it. Did he film it?"

"Here's an idea we haven't tried," says Roxy, showing her perfect teeth in a fake open-mouthed smile. "If you talk about Charlie again, I will stop the car."

"You brought him up, buddy, but fine with me." I peer down and pull the seatbelt tight across my T-shirt. "Are you sure you can't see my bra?"

Roxy purses her lips and raises her eyebrows at me. That's bad. We've been in the car for less than five minutes and she's already getting annoyed with me (or my *shit*, as she lovingly refers to it). I undo my seatbelt and lean over her as we pull up to the speaker thing at the drive-thru.

"Hi, Costa! Eliza here, of Eliza and Roxy."

"Um . . . can I take your order?" says a monotone voice.

Jeez, you'd think people would be aching for witty banter at this time of the morning.

"Listen good, Costa, for our order is threefold." Roxy shakes her head and I waggle my eyebrows at her. "Actually, two lots of threefold so that's . . . sixfold."

Silence from the speaker thing.

"Costa? Are you receiving me, Costa?"

Roxy elbows me back into my seat and takes control of the speaker thing, but I don't mind because she loves me again.

"Have you heard from anyone else? What time is Iris arriving?" I ask.

Iris is Roxy's girlfriend. She lives a couple of hours' drive from us so they see each other when they can. I'm happy to confirm that she's lovely and good enough for my best friend.

Roxy shakes her head as she stops at the next window.

"I wonder if Charlie Chamberlain will remember the convention is usually this weekend?"

"*Eliza.*"

Eek. Warning tone.

"Sorry. But how lucky are we? Bunking off school and leaving the Awfuls and their drama, and, frankly, the uncreative name-calling behind? I mean, Viggo the Virgin? It doesn't even make any sense. Firstly, Viggo is male, and secondly, he screwed every warm- and cold-blooded character from season one through five, and that's what they decide to call me? Like, do your research, guys. Just because they don't appreciate the genius of *Vampire Falls*, or what it means to pledge your allegiance to fictious characters, they try to make me feel bad for it? Which I will *never.*"

It might shock you to know that I'm not exactly Miss Popular at school. Apparently, being obsessed with football is totally acceptable by general society, but being passionate about a TV show is not. I still don't see the difference between wearing your team's football shirt and dressing as your favourite character. But when I came into school in full cosplay on a non-uniform day once, the rest of my year (and a couple of teachers) made it perfectly clear that there *is* a difference. I went as a Clopwyck witch from season three, so I didn't even have any weapons (their eyeballs are their weapons), but I was still told to change. That day, I graduated from being sort-of weird to everyone's favourite target, but the fandom and my love for *Vampire Falls* act like a cloak of armour. Which *is* what I wore when I was a Clopwyck witch, specifically dragon hide.

Roxy takes the drinks from the Costa guy and hands them to me. I put hers in the drinks holder and take a long slurp from mine. Mmmm. Icy caffeinated goodness. She dumps the food in my lap then pulls away from the window.

"And like the word virgin is some big insult anyway," I say. "Charlie Chamberlain should—"

"Eliza!" Roxy smacks the steering wheel. "I know it's my fault for mentioning Haribo bears, therefore referring to him indirectly, and believe me I'm kicking myself that I did, but *stop talking about him*. It makes you sulky and I refuse to have a sulky weekend, OK? If you mention his name one more time, I will stop this car and you can sit in the back where Daisy pissed all over the seat."

Don't panic. Daisy is Roxy's Labrador. But still, gross.

"OK, fine, I'm sorry. I'm just being wistful, you know?" I take the lid off my latte and give the ice cubes a good swirl around. Don't you just love that sound? "You can't look forward without looking back, Roxy – and I'm looking forward to the best, most perfect, weekend of the year and that involves considering what we're leaving behind, which is Charlie Chamberlain and the— UUUUHHHHH!"

Just so you're up to speed, Roxy has slammed on the brakes like her driving test depends on it and my entire iced latte has saturated my T-shirt, my bra and my general crotchal area.

"Roxanne Fu!" I scream, trying to keep as still as possible to not aggravate the seepage. "What the actual fucking fuck?!"

She stares at me, her hands over her mouth.

"Eliza, I'm so, *so* sorry." She grabs a tiny travel tissue and dabs at me. I smack her hand away. "Hey, I'm trying to help before it stains."

"*Before* it stains? We're a bit beyond that, don't you think?" I pull my T-shirt away from my skin. Ew. Moist. "You did that on purpose."

Roxy sighs and folds her arms.

"Not the spillage part but yes, yes, I stopped the car on purpose, after I told you that I was going to stop the car if you didn't stop talking about Charlie. I didn't know you'd taken the lid off. I mean, why would you do that in a moving car?" She looks me up and down, and her face softens. "I really am sorry, babe. Shall we go back to Costa so you can get changed?"

I am burning with absolute rage, but my entire front half is freezing cold and squelchy. It's quite the juxtaposition.

"I don't have anything else to wear!"

"How can you not? Your suitcase is bulging with clothes."

"Yes: cosplay clothes and my scheduled outfits. I didn't pack anything in case my friend drowned me in iced latte, *Roxy*."

"Sorry. Again. Truly sorry."

I ignore her and shift in my seat. Yes. Yes, it's now soaking through to my knickers. Amazing.

"Eliza?"

"What?" I snap, and glare at her.

Roxy's looking at me, biting her lip like her life depends on it, and even in my fury I can tell she's trying to suppress laughter.

"Um . . . I can totally see your bra."

CHAPTER THREE

LILA MURPHY

Why does the universe hate me?

BUD LEROY

The universe doesn't hate you, Lils. Our entire class hates you.
Maybe even the entire school, but not the universe.
The universe is incapable of hate; sixteen-year-olds aren't.

Vampire Falls. Season four, episode seven –
"What Kills You Makes You Unpopular"

There is no greater moment in a nerd's happy little life than arriving in the hotel foyer for their favourite convention. Frazzled stewards hurry about and excited attendees rush through the revolving doors, their heads swivelling around looking for friends and incognito stars. It's a perfect moment for obsessed fans. My bum twitches with possibility and belonging, and I'm in superfan heaven.

Usually. My bum *usually* twitches and I'm *usually* in a perfect superfan moment. Right now, I'm so far from convention bliss I may as well have arrived at the dentist. I do not share the buzz of my fellow attendees, nor do I care about spotting potential guests. Instead, I'm uber-grumpy in a dairy-soaked bra and Roxy's brother's horrendous T-shirt that we found in the car.

"We've arrived!" says Roxy, elbowing me as we walk through the revolving doors. I grunt. "Oh, come on, Eliza, this is your best bit."

"My best bit in my planned outfit, not dressed like some horrendous fresher boy."

"It's not that bad," says Roxy, biting her lip.

I glare at her and drop my bag on the floor, my bad mood like a forcefield reflecting everyone's euphoria. I turn to Roxy and pull the T-shirt taut so she can read the slogan properly.

"*This* is not that bad?! Your brother's stupid *I'm a Virgin* T-shirt is not that bad?!"

"It does say *But this is an old T-shirt* on the back, though," she says, pretending other people aren't watching us.

"I don't care what it says on the back! I look like a douche, and I smell like a milkmaid!"

"At least it's clean," she says. I harrumph and fold my arms. "It's not my fault you didn't pack another bra, Eliza. Stop sulking."

Yeah, so interesting discovery after latte-gate; I only brought the bra I'm wearing, the one that smells of baby sick.

"It's your fault I smell like this though," I say.

"What's wrong with you, babe?" she says, frowning.

"Er, hello?" I say, gesturing at the T-shirt.

"I get that bit, but you're just more . . . than usual," she says, pulling a face that can only be described as banshee-like.

"Nothing's *wrong* with me, Roxy, apart from *everything*," I say.

Roxy rolls her eyes and drops her bag, then puts her hands

on my face and makes me look at her, giving me hamster cheeks in the process.

"Eliza, look where we are," she says. I open my mouth to complain, again, but she squeezes my cheeks tighter. "I said, *look* where we are. We're in our best place; our people are here. Remember last year, when Derek in the fishnet stockings tripped on his whip, slipped on his spilt pint and gave himself a nosebleed with the spikes on his bustier?"

"Yes," I murmur.

"Everyone helped him up, got him another drink and carried on like nothing had happened. Nobody laughed, nobody cared. I bet if he smelt like rotten milk, they wouldn't have cared either."

I shrug. Poor Derek. But Roxy's right; nobody took the piss.

"Let's just reset, and maybe you could tone the . . . down a bit," she says, doing that awful banshee grimace again.

"Fine, but stop doing that face to describe my behaviour," I say.

"Show me excited, convention Eliza then," she says, throwing an arm around my neck, and I can't help but soften. Her hugs are literal magic. "There's my girl. Let's go register, then we'll get the rest of the stuff from the car."

We walk through the hotel foyer, nodding at attendees we recognise from over the years, some of them already in full costume. I don't know everyone, but I *know* them. I love the kindred spirits that bump shoulders at our weekend honouring our shared enthusiasm. This convention is our sanctuary from the real world, our safe room from people that make fun of our passions and mock what we love.

Roxy's right. Nothing can touch us here, smelly bra or not.

There's a bit of a queue snaking along the registration desk, so we pick up speed and stand behind a couple of Malcorr demons, leaving some space for their long tails.

"Hey, isn't that . . . ?" Roxy says, her voice trailing off as I look where she's pointing.

My eyebrows ping up.

"It's Sadie. She looks so big," I say, an eleven-year-old girl turning to look at me at the sound of her name. She waves enthusiastically and I wave back. "Who's she's here—"

My hand freezes mid-wave and my heart turns to cement. No. Absolutely, definitely, *no*. This is not happening. The revolving doors of the hotel are obviously some kind of portal into hell, because Sadie's apparent chaperone is the only person on the planet whose presence could make my perfect weekend an inferno of misery and suffering.

My hands shake and my insides rage – *rage*, I tell you – and I turn to Roxy who has taken a few steps back from me, out of my fighting arc.

"What, in the seven hells of Penumbra," I say, my voice a low growl, "is Charlie Chamberlain doing here?!"

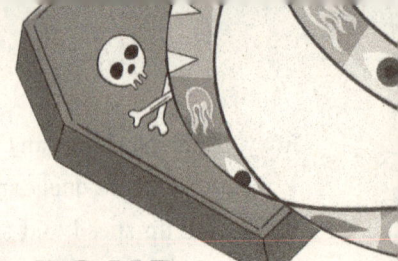

CHAPTER FOUR

LILA MURPHY

This day could not get any worse.

BUD LEROY

Really? There's an apocalypse prophesied for later, Lils.

LILA MURPHY

I stand by my statement.

Vampire Falls. Season three, episode twenty-two –
"End Again, Again"

Charlie Chamberlain looks down at Sadie, frowns, then turns to look at Roxy and me. I've read about red mist, but never really understood what it meant until the specific moment his eyes lock with mine. He runs a smug hand through his smug hair and smiles a smuggy mother-smugging smile, and then he starts walking over.

Yes, I know. He's walking over to *me* at *my* convention surrounded by *my* people. I might be turning green and bursting out of my clothes, I just don't know right now. All I can hear is my hot, angry breath whistling out of my nose.

"Eliza?" I can just about hear Roxy's gentle tone and feel her hand on my arm, but I can't move. "Eliza? Be cool, OK? He's probably just dropping Sadie off or something."

The red mist clears like a pair of curtains. Of course, that's definitely, probably it. He's dropping his little sister off at a convention for her favourite show. Why else would he be here? Eleven-year-olds go to conventions on their own all the time, don't they? Don't they?

DON'T THEY?

Charlie Chamberlain stops in front of us and puts his hands in his pockets. I get a waft of his deodorant, the spicy one that celebrity/footballer/model person he used to bang on about endorses. The smell is like petrol on the bonfire of my emotional state.

"Hey, Rox." He looks at me. "Eliza."

I manage a noise somewhere between a squeak and a groan. Roxy looks at me like I'm a child who was expecting a PlayStation on Christmas Day but has unwrapped a second-hand abacus. She frowns and widens her eyes at me, but I probably shouldn't move or say words until I know I'm in full control of myself.

"Hey, Charlie," says Roxy, then steps forward and squeezes Sadie. "And Sadie!"

"She doesn't really do hugs any more," says Charlie Chamberlain.

"Shut up, Charlie," says Sadie, pulling a face.

"How are you this big?" says Roxy, looking down at her.

"I know, I'm nearly as tall as Eliza!" says Sadie, beaming at us.

"What are you guys doing here?" asks Roxy.

"Well, Sadie wanted to come for her birthday and mum was going to bring her, but that sort of fell through. It was either lose the hotel deposit and the cost of the ticket, or guilt trip big brother into bringing her, so I figured, hey, day off school. So, here I am. Bonus."

"Here you are," I say, through gritted teeth. "Bonus."

He smiles at me, oh-so-pleased with himself, standing here ruining my life. He's lucky he's got his little sister in front of him.

"Yep," he says, doing subtle jazz hands. "Surprise."

Is surprise the word?

"You're here all weekend then?" Roxy asks, glancing at me then smiling back at Charlie Chamberlain and Sadie.

Charlie nods and rolls his eyes. "Yep, four whole nights of nerd fun."

"Hey," says Sadie, elbowing him in the stomach. Did I mention I love this kid? "Mum said you've got to be nice, and you're not allowed to say nerd or anything bad about *Vampire Falls*."

"Not even Damon Van Schwartz?" he says, bending down and making wide eyes at his sister.

"*Especially* not Damon Van Schwartz," says Sadie, her eyes misting over at the thought of him.

"I don't know why you're all piss-takey, pal; you had a DVS haircut for an entire year," says Roxy, raising an eyebrow.

"I did not," he says.

"Oh, you so did." Roxy pulls out her phone and waves it in front of him. "Would you like a little reminder, Charlie Van Schwartz?"

"Whatever," he says, then looks at me. "You're quiet. Something wrong?"

Roxy stiffens next to me. I take a deep breath, ready to launch a diatribe (*yes*, I said diatribe) into Charlie Chamberlain's self-satisfied, friendship defector face, but as I form the first word which starts with a hard F, there is a slight, but not invisible to the experienced ear, change in background hotel foyer noise.

I look around, my convention senses tingling, and I'm right. Everyone holds up their phones in the direction of the revolving doors, which means that a Convention Guest has just entered the vicinity. I grab Roxy's arm, but she's already sensed it and is looking at the same person I am.

Damon Van Schwartz, aka everyone's favourite morally grey vampire, Viggo Rassmussen, has entered the building.

CHAPTER FIVE

BUD LEROY

That looks bad. Like, amputation bad.

I think there was a medicine cabinet back there.

I'll check it out. Do you have any allergies?

JULIANA THE DEMON HUNTRESS

I'm only allergic to two things: Incubus venom,

and assholes. [looks at Viggo]

Vampire Falls. Season six, episode nine – "All Together Now"

If you think Damon Van Schwartz's eyes look blue in *Vampire Falls*, then I'm here to tell you that they are way, way higher on the blue scale in real life, my friend. Like, bluer than every expanse of water a young-adult fiction author could ever compare them to. Insanely blue. I swear a blue hue reflects across the marble floor as he strides in with a Colgate smile, phone in his hand, and an assistant picking up on his every non-verbal command.

I swallow and tuck my hair behind my ears as I watch him cross the floor, the rest of the convention attendees flocking towards him like ants to honey. He glances between them and his phone, his smile not faltering as he greets fans and nods, but not stopping for a moment in case anyone tries to mount him. (I've seen this happen once. Poor woman was so overwhelmed she started crying and tried to climb up his back. We've all been there, Marion.)

"Oh my god, oh my god, oh my god," squeals Sadie, as Damon glides across the foyer, "his eyes are *so blue*."

See?

Roxy has pulled Sadie close and put an arm around her as she slowly falls apart being in the same oxygen space as her favourite actor for the first time. It's an important rite of passage for any superfan, and honestly, I'm glad I'm here for it.

Sadie's *oh-my-gods* become more and more incoherent until the poor girl is actually sobbing. Roxy and I share a knowing smile, then we turn back to watch Damon Van Schwartz finish doing his thing, and something incredible is happening.

Damon Van Schwartz, being the ultra-sensitive people-loving person he is, has clocked the cute crying kid and is heading right for her.

Which means he's heading right for us.

Basically, right for *me*.

I quickly insert myself between Charlie Chamberlain and Sadie and put my arm around her too, so she looks like mine and Roxy's daughter and, ignoring Charlie Chamberlain's insistence that I apologise for crushing his metatarsal, look down adoringly at Sadie who is now practically hyperventilating.

"Hey kid, what's up?" drawls Damon Van Schwartz. Oh, his *voice*. "Who you here with?"

"My-my-my . . ." stammers Sadie, fanning her face with both hands.

Charlie Chamberlain steps in front of me. Wanker-face.

"Me, her brother. Sorry, Damon, I think she's a little overwhelmed."

Damon? Who the bloody hell does Charlie Chamberlain think he is, addressing Damon Van Schwartz in such a casual manner? Unbelievable.

"Oh, that's OK, we all get a little overwhelmed sometimes, right?" says Damon Van Schwartz. "What's your name, kid?"

"S-s-s-s . . ." hiccups poor Sadie.

"Sadie," says Charlie, stepping backwards and putting his arm around Sadie so I'm relegated to standing behind him and his stupid tallness.

"Nice name." Damon looks at Charlie Chamberlain. "What about you, big brother. What's your name?"

"Charlie."

"You think our Sadie's gonna be OK, Charlie?"

"She'll be fine."

I step to the side as Damon Van Schwartz beams at Sadie, well-schooled in calming down hysterical tween fans. He stretches his arm out behind, turning his palm up without even looking at his assistant who somehow reads his mind and pulls out a Sharpie and a glossy photo from thin air. She puts them in his hand, and he signs his name across the *Vampire Falls* photo and hands it to a snivelling Sadie.

"Well, I hope you have a great weekend, Sadie. Make sure you say hey next time we see each other, OK?"

Sadie manages something between a nod and a convulsion,

and Damon Van Schwartz stands up and takes a moment to acknowledge Roxy and then me. His eyes rest on my face for a moment before he looks down, and I remember with horror what I'm wearing. He reads the slogan and raises his eyebrows.

"Well, good for you, I guess," he says, then turns to walk away.

"This isn't my T-shirt!" I blurt. Damon Van Schwartz recoils a little. I guess he's always on high alert for potential *I'm-your-biggest-fan-I've-saved-my-toenail-clippings-for-you* types. "I mean, I had an accident and had to get changed and this was all there was."

"Hey, no need to explain: you do you," says Damon Van Schwartz, pressing his palms together, then pointing at me with both index fingers. "You wanna be a virgin, you be a virgin."

"No, I mean, thank you, but this isn't mine and anyway, it says *This is an old T-shirt* on the back," I say, turning round so he can read the back.

"So, you're not a virgin then?" asks Charlie Chamberlain, folding his arms.

"What? No. I mean, yes," I say, shaking my head then glaring at Charlie Chamberlain. "I mean, what's the question again?"

"So, you are then?" says Charlie Chamberlain, squinting at me and putting his thumb and forefinger on his chin.

"Not cool, Charlie," says Roxy, shaking her head. "Eliza, maybe we should register?"

"It's none of your business whether I'm a virgin or not,

Charlie," I say, knowing I should grasp Roxy's way out of this hell conversation, but you're probably not surprised that I'm not thinking straight right now.

"But you're wearing a T-shirt proclaiming that you are one, Eliza."

"But it says *This is an old T-shirt* on the back!"

"So, is it an old T-shirt then?" asks Damon Van Schwartz.

"What?" Oh please, not Damon Van Schwartz as well. I have dreamt so many conversations with him, but none of them involve discussing my virgin status. "No, no, it's not *my* T-shirt. I had an accident and had to change my clothes."

"An *accident*?" repeats Charlie Chamberlain, doing air quotes round the word.

"I didn't wet myself!" I blurt. "I spilt my drink, and this was all there was to change into. For god's sake, I wouldn't wear a T-shirt like this even if I *wasn't* a virgin."

"So, you're saying you *are* a virgin?"

"YES, CHARLIE. I *AM* A VIRGIN, OK?!"

Did someone just shout that on my behalf? No? Oh good, it was me then. Perfect.

Someone presses pause on the entire hotel, and I know without having to look around that everyone's eyes are on me, including the bluest of blue eyes of Damon Van Schwartz who is whispering something to his publicist as she places herself between him and me.

"Sorry, I didn't mean to shout. It's just . . ." I let out a breath and waft the neck of the T-shirt to let some of the air conditioning cool down my skin, "it's been kind of a crappy morning so far."

"Forget it, you guys. Go. Go have the best of weekends and enjoy . . ." says Damon Van Schwartz, then his nose wrinkles, and he leans into his publicist and whispers something about a *heinous smell*.

It's me. *I'm* the heinous smell. If I could fold myself up and put myself into an envelope and post it to Easter Island, I would, but instead I shuffle backwards as Damon Van Schwartz, and everyone in the vicinity, sniffs the air. Everyone including Charlie Chamberlain, who's taking long sniffs, closer and closer to the source. Again, me.

"Ew," he says, waving his hand across his face. "Eliza. Gross."

Damon Van Schwartz looks at me like I'm a fresh something he's stepped in and holds his hand out to his assistant again. She pulls out a small tub of mints and he takes it, throwing one into his mouth. Within seconds, his eyes widen, and then they bulge as he spins round to his assistant and grabs her shoulder with one hand and his neck with the other, a rasping sound coming from his throat as his face gets redder and redder.

He's choking. Oh, my Goddess of Rage and Jealousy, Damon Van Schwartz is choking on a mint right in front of our eyes.

"Somebody do something!" shouts his assistant in a Californian accent. "Call 911!"

I don't think now's the time to tell her 911 won't be much help in England. Damon Van Schwartz stumbles around in front of us, his arms waving and his lips turning blue, and we all just stare at him like he's doing a scene from *Vampire Falls*.

Charlie Chamberlain springs from my side and moves quickly behind him. He puts both arms around Damon Van Schwartz's chest, clasping his hands in front.

"Cough!" he shouts, tightening his arms. "Cough!"

All of a sudden, whatever Charlie Chamberlain's doing dislodges the mint from Damon Van Schwartz's throat and it flies from his mouth, hitting me directly between the eyes. He heaves a huge breath then starts coughing and Charlie Chamberlain moves to his side to take his weight. The coughing slows and he wipes his eyes, then puts his hand on Charlie Chamberlain's shoulder and straightens up.

"Man," he says, still panting hard, "I thought that was the end of the line, for sure. You saved my life, kid."

"No, you would have been OK," says Charlie Chamberlain, shrugging like he's always going round giving celebrities the Heimlich manoeuvre.

"I mean it, Charlie; you saved my life." Damon Van Schwartz grabs his hand then raises it above his head like he's just won a boxing match. "Everybody; Charlie just saved my life!"

Everyone bursts into applause, some wiping away tears of joy that their favourite *Vampire Falls* star is still alive and able to honour his convention commitments. People elbow me out of the way to smack Charlie Chamberlain on the back or high-five him, and the entire hotel chants his name.

"Your brother's a hero, Sadie!" says Damon Van Schwartz, giving Sadie's shoulder a squeeze. Sadie bursts into tears and clings to Roxy. "Charlie, you and Sadie are my guests of honour this weekend. I'm gonna get you guest passes, and tonight, I'm taking you both out for dinner."

"That's really not necessary, Damon," says Charlie.

No, Damon, that's *really* not necessary.

"Hey," says Damon Van Schwartz, putting his hand on Charlie's shoulder and looking deep into his eyes. "For the guy who just saved my life, it's a thousand per cent necessary. Now, you and Sadie come with me to the green room. I want Debbie to get all your details so we can make the arrangements."

They walk off together and Debbie (apparently) ushers Sadie along with them, who hurries after her big brother. Roxy turns to me, her mouth wide open.

"Can you believe what just happened?" she says.

I shake my head. Charlie Chamberlain has been here for twelve minutes and he's saved the star of the show's life, become everyone's hero and got an upgrade on the whole weekend.

He's also upgraded himself from being my annoying ex-best friend to my arch nemesis.

CHAPTER SIX

BUD LEROY

Just think of me as your own personal cheerleader.
But I don't, like, think you're a crackpot
like the actual cheerleaders do.

Vampire Falls. Season one, episode six – "Did You See?"

The wall feels cold and hard against my forehead. I dread to think the last time it was cleaned, but who cares if I catch E. coli from invisible handprints and die a slow, painful death. I certainly don't.

The door beeps and Roxy shuffles in with baggage slung around her like a donkey; I'm too emotionally drained to carry anything. I follow her into our room and slump headfirst onto the terracotta-coloured bedspread. Again, probably covered in bacteria invisible to the naked eye, but who cares when your life is ruined.

"Did Charlie Chamberlain just become the guest of honour at my convention?"

"What?" says Roxy. "I can't hear what you're mumbling into the bed."

Roxy hauls me over like she's pulling me into the recovery position. I mean, I don't think it'll help but I would be willing to give it a try. My head lolls round and I stare at her.

"Damon Van Schwartz knows I'm a virgin," I whisper.

"I think the entire hotel knows you're a virgin, babe."

"Uuuuh!" I throw my arm over my face. "Why? Why is this happening?"

"Get off the bed," she says. "Unpack. It'll make you feel better."

I sit up and gape at her.

"We can't stay," I say.

She looks back at me, a bag of Kettle Chips clamped under her chin and a bottle of vodka in each hand.

"Now what are you talking about?"

"We can't stay, Roxy. Not now. Not now I've humiliated myself. Not now *he's* here."

"Damon Van Schwartz?"

"Charlie Chamberlain."

She puts everything down and lays next to me.

"Why do you say his name like that?" she asks. "You always say his full name, since you fell out."

"Because it's more words to clench my teeth around and when I think of him my teeth get clenchy, Roxy. That's why."

"Clenchy teeth. OK." Roxy takes a deep breath and turns to me. "How serious are you about not staying?"

"As serious as when Cox the Observer told Whitlock Abrahams that the fate of the world rested on him giving birth. To triplets."

She whips round to look at me.

"Wow. That *is* serious." She flings her long legs up so they're vertical then does a cool sort of flip up from the bed.

"But you're overreacting."

"I'm sorry, have we only just met?" I wail. Yes, *wail*. "This is standard level reaction, neither over nor under. Standard. Level."

She shakes her head.

"No, this is a higher-than-normal response to something that doesn't have to affect the weekend," she says. "You've been on Eliza steroids since I picked you up. What's going on with you?"

I start crawling under the bedspread but Roxy dives at me, yanking the covers out of my hand.

"Hey! I need that; it's my cloak of invisibility."

She throws it over her shoulder like she's just whipped off a superhero cape. God, everything she does is so cool. Maybe because she's so tall. Maybe because she's Roxy. I look down at my (still reeking) offensive T-shirt and groan, then Jawfain, my cuddly grey bat, lands on my lap. Jawfain the bat lives in the abandoned asylum with Viggo Rassmussen and is perhaps his only true friend. Roxy gave it to me a year ago when my nanna died. It was so sweet of her, and I was such an emotional wreck at the time that I could only just manage a GIF of Viggo bowing and saying thank you.

I give Jawfain a hefty squeeze. Roxy sits next to me and starts fussing my hair.

"Look, I know this isn't exactly your ideal, but we've been planning it for months and we're here, Eliza. We're here, at the one place you love the most."

"But ..."

She folds her arms and frowns at me.

"Don't let him ruin this for you, Eliza. It's been over a year of avoidance since you . . . since he stopped hanging out with us, and you can't let him run us out of here too."

"It's not just him . . ." I sigh, my stomach churning when I think of Mum's reminder about *decision time*, earlier.

"Then what?" she says, but I can't tell her. Not now, it'll ruin the weekend – and if I say it out loud then it's really happening. She pulls me up into a half slump. "Look, babe, have a shower, like, *immediately*, because it's beyond offensive now. We'll register, then go to the opening ceremony. Let's see how that goes, and then if you feel the same way, we can leave tomorrow. OK?"

"Really?"

She nods.

"If you really can't bear it, we'll leave, but I'm not driving back when we've only just got here. Fair?"

"Fair," I say. "Thank you."

"You're welcome." She ruffles my hair. I think touching my hair might be a way to manipulate me. "OK. I will find the masquerade ball playlist and you, fair one, can get your stinky self in that shower." I give her a hug. "I am literally trying not to vomit down your back right now."

"I love you too," I say, grabbing my wash bag and heading into the shower.

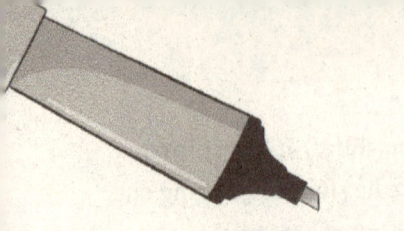

CHAPTER SEVEN

VIGGO RASSMUSSEN

People are never what they seem.

BUD LEROY

How about vampires? 'Cause, seems to me,
you're a bloodthirsty monster.

Vampire Falls. Season five, episode twelve –
"Blood's Thicker Than Disorder"

We walk into Conference Hall A, the familiar hum of the convention brightening my mood, like the irresistible minx it is. Any true *Vampire Falls* fan should have a masquerade costume knocking around, due to the season one finale, "Masquerade Brawl", and Roxy and I are no exception. My tea-length dress is emerald green, with gold piping and a matching eye mask, and Roxy's wearing a harlequin-style cat suit and eye mask. We have chosen not to drench ourselves in fake blood, but lots of others have in homage to that episode. Total bloodbath.

"Where's Iris?" I say, looking across the rows of chairs as we walk down the aisle. "Has she messaged you?"

Roxy doesn't stop or answer me.

"Hey, what's going on?" I say, hurrying to her side. Her

forehead is tight under her mask. My blood runs cold. "Oh shit, is it because of Charlie Chamberlain? Did she see him and leave immediately?"

"God, Eliza! Not everything is about Charlie fucking Chamberlain and not everyone hates him like you do." She takes a breath. "Iris isn't coming."

"*What*?" I say, swallowing.

"Sorry, babe."

"No Iris? I . . . I . . ." I drop onto a banquet chair, grateful to the person dressed as McKinley the Pessimistic Werewolf for scooching along just in time. "I thought it would be the three of us? Me, you and Iris?"

"I know," she says, biting the inside of her cheek.

Iris has been the third leg of our tripod or, more accurately, the mediator between me and Roxy when Roxy's had enough of my behaviour. I can be a bit of a handful, so it's really a two-person job. Also, Iris does our cosplay make-up.

I slump against my werewolf neighbour. The fur is comforting. Suddenly, whoever's inside clears their throat.

"Sorry," it says.

"Don't apologise," I say, looking into his vacant glass eyes. "It's not your fault she's not here."

"No, I mean . . ." He clears his throat. "You're sitting on my tail."

I roll my eyes and turn back to Roxy.

"I can't believe she's not here," I say, sinking into the chair. "Everything is changing."

"Sometimes change is good," offers Fake McKinley, shrugging (as much as you can in a werewolf costume).

Sometimes change can be good. Who *is* this joker? I glare at him then turn back to Roxy, who is patting my hand patiently.

"Sorry, babe. Just us two this time."

I look at her fingers over my own, her silver rings shining under the artificial lights, and I realise I'm looking at the lack of Iris all wrong. My heart flutters with best-friend-all-to-myself joy.

"Just us two!" I say, squeezing Roxy's hand. "This could be perfect, Roxy!"

"You don't have to sound so gleeful about it."

"Not *gleeful*," I say, shaking my head, "just . . . glee *half* full. It's like our first time here, minus my mum, obviously. It'll be amazing, Roxy. You know, sometimes change can be good."

"Right," she says, folding her arms and glancing at the werewolf I'm sitting next to.

He shrugs and Roxy opens her mouth to say something else, but the lights dim, so she shoves me into him and sits down. Red light flashes across the stage, and the *Vampire Falls* theme booms through the speakers. I love this part.

"Sorry . . ." says Fake McKinley.

"Shhh!" I hiss.

"But you're still on my tail."

"Yes!" we shout.

"I said, *are you ready to celebrate* Vampire Falls?!"

"*Yes!*" we scream.

"Then welcome our organiser, MC for the weekend, owner of Mirror Events and ultimate nerd . . . Felix Hutson!"

Felix jogs onto the stage and we don't care that he's just

announced his own self. We scream and clap for him as he stops in front of the mic and unbuttons the jacket on his signature checked suit (a blue one this year, the same colour as his hi-top fade), waving at everyone.

"Are you ready to *fall* in love with our *Vampire Falls* guests?" he asks, which is of course a rhetorical question.

The noise dials up a few notches and my palms are numb from slapping them together, but I'm soaring into such a euphoric state that I feel no pain. You can feel the good vibes bouncing around Conference Hall A, a truly mystical place.

Felix starts with the guests who are further down the alphabet than some. You know, those guys who are on the convention circuit because they've been showing up under layers of prosthetics since the dawn of time. Don't get me wrong, they have no less right to be here than the A-listers; they are the foundations on which conventions are built and Felix introduces them with the vigour they very much deserve.

First, we have Clayton Tusk, who smiles widely and blows kisses as he comes on, his long hair co-ordinated with a pair of grey cowboy boots. He has the record for most characters played in the show, appearing as Kip the Bartender, Eudoff Grost and Krugg the Scavenger.

He's joined by Sage Howard, owner of the most amazing cheekbones I've ever seen in real life, who played Goddess Bydora in season three.

Kawata Hisashi, who played the principal both before and after he was possessed by a Hangorth demon, comes on next.

Dax St. James (Whitlock Abrahams, a sorcerer and one of the vertices of the Whitlock/Juliana/Viggo love triangle) comes on next, his arms open wide making his six-foot frame even bigger. He turns a *stumble* into Felix into a *hug* for Felix, but Rxy and I share a knowing look; he's already drunk.

Orlando Wilde, who plays Lila Murphy's best friend, Bud Leroy, comes on next, waving at the audience, then hugs the other guests before he sits down.

Roxy grabs my hand when Amber Anderson strides on stage next, her legs impossibly long but the only ones that could fill the boots of Juliana the Demon Huntress.

There's just one chair left up on the stage, and I have plenty in the tank to welcome the final guest. We all do. I throw my arms around Roxy's waist.

"Thank you for making me stay," I shout in her ear. "Love you."

"Love you too," she says, putting her arm around me.

"Now . . . get ready to *fall in love at first bite*," whispers Felix, like he's sharing a secret. "Would you like to meet our final guest?"

Wild. We are *wild* with excitement, and we don't care who knows it.

"I said . . ." he says, louder this time.

Nobody can hear him as we're *screaming* for our guest and our show and our fandom and our love for it all. I can see his lips moving and 1 know when someone is saying my favourite actor's name without me hearing a word. We all know.

Felix opens his arms and steps back as Damon Van Schwartz jogs on, his black shirt the same shade as his hair.

He looks out at us with a big, humble smile on his face and puts his hands together in prayer. The screaming and clapping continue, even when he raises his hand for us to stop.

We slowly quieten down, ready to hear his smooth voice. He leans into the mic and lifts a hand to his brow, looking out at the audience. We all straighten up in our seats so he can see us properly. I'm so happy right now I could actually straddle someone and kiss them all over.

"Now, let's get down to some important business," he says, his eyes sparkling in the spotlights. "Is Charlie Chamberlain here?"

CHAPTER EIGHT

WHITLOCK ABRAHAMS

We have history, Juliana. Don't you think of me?
I think of you all the time.

JULIANA THE DEMON HUNTRESS

I don't let myself.

Vampire Falls. Season two, episode seventeen –
"Dead Moon"

I am so livid right now I could actually leap on someone and murder them dead.

"Charlie Chamberlain, I know you're out there," calls Damon Van Schwartz, his voice all sing-songy. "Stand up so I can see you, my brother."

Sometimes the actors chat with members of the crowd, or babies get attention (on my pro list for considering pregnancy in the very distant future), but I've never seen someone singled out by name. Hopefully it's because they've discovered that Charlie Chamberlain hasn't watched an episode of *Vampire Falls* since he swapped the show for protein shakes and want to expose him for the fraud that he is, and not because he was in the right place at the right time and just happened to save our favourite cast member's life.

I remember clearly the day Charlie Chamberlain's mum dropped him off at mine so she could take Sadie to ballet. I wish I couldn't, but I can. It's our origin story, I guess. He shuffled in on crutches, his leg in plaster from a bad break after falling out of a tree, and he'd used so much deodorant I could taste it in the back of my throat. He was a gangly fourteen-year-old then; his shoulders hadn't filled out and he was all Adam's apple and angry spots. I believe he would have been called a hobbledehoy back in the day, fact fans, but I was still struck by his smile.

I was kind of nervously excited, waiting for him to arrive. Our mums had met at a baby group years before, and we'd shared a birthday party once when we were pre-schoolers. Fairies and Cowboys. He actually chose fairies, and I chose cowboys. We were progressive in that way. But then we sort of drifted at primary school when he decided girls were gross.

He was nervous and polite, and I was bolshy and territorial (I know; hard to imagine, right?). We had no friends or classes in common so just sat in silence staring at the TV until my mum came in.

"Charlie, can you manage in here with your leg? Or would you rather eat at the table?"

"Here's fine," he said, his voice squeaking in that unpredictable teenage boy way.

"Good." My mum's face brightened. "We normally watch the latest *Vampire Falls* episode on a Thursday. Do you watch it, Charlie?"

Charlie shook his head and glanced at me. I could see

the discomfort in his eyes – probably the thought of eating a meal cooked by someone else in an unfamiliar house and now having to sit through a TV show he had zero interest in.

"It's kind of our little tradition, isn't it, Eliza?"

I nodded, squirming on the sofa as my mum revealed to Charlie that I actually enjoyed spending time with her. I mean, *lame*. She disappeared back into the kitchen while I lined up the latest episode of *Vampire Falls*.

"So, what's it about?" he asked.

"Vampires," I said, without looking at him.

"Right," he said, shifting on the sofa. "Helpful."

Mum brought Charlie's dinner in on a tray. His face lit up when he saw the massive plate of breadcrumb coated chicken, chips and peas, and my mum handed him the ketchup.

He smiled and drenched his chips in sauce, then I pressed play and he politely watched the pre-credit scene, his eyebrows pinching together as he tried to work out which of the two characters fighting was the vampire. Next thing, the intro music kicked in and he watched each actor's sequence, his eyes brightening when he saw Amber Anderson.

"Who's she?" he asked.

"That's Juliana the Demon Huntress," Mum explained. "An undead warrior from the Megna dimension. Her mother was murdered by vampires. She hates everything about this world, apart from heavy metal."

Mum pulled the metal sign with her fingers then did a little air guitar riff as Charlie Chamberlain blinked at her.

Amazingly, I didn't die of embarrassment. He swallowed down a chip, then cleared his throat.

"Is . . . she in every episode?"

"She first appeared at the end of season one but was so popular they made her a series regular in season two," Mum clarified.

He nodded and looked back at the TV, frowning again as he attempted to follow the storyline. He was hooked by the end of that episode, and that week he came over after school every day to watch it from the first episode. We'd watched the entire first season by Sadie's next ballet lesson.

The audience looks around, even Roxy, trying to spot the mysterious *brother* of Damon Van Schwartz. I do not move, my back pressed to my chair as tightly as my jaw is clenched.

"He's here!" shouts a very loud, very proud voice. "Over here!"

"Sadie, honey, is that you?" says Damon Van Schwartz.

"Y-yes!"

"Can you bring up that hero brother of yours?"

"Y-yes!" she manages.

The crowd erupts like Charlie Chamberlain has the chance to win a million dollars. I mean, it would feel like winning a million dollars, being invited onto the stage by Damon Van Schwartz. Not that I'm jealous. Not that I'm at all bothered by what Charlie Chamberlain does. He could trip over on the top step, fall over and smash his perfect teeth for all I care.

Roxy elbows me and I look round, horrified to see her clapping and smiling as Sadie drags Charlie towards the stage. I glare at her, and she rolls her eyes.

"Come on, ice queen. This is cool. Look how excited Sadie is."

They climb up the steps to the stage, then Damon Van Schwartz says something to Sadie away from the mic as her brother looks on. Felix brings two extra chairs on while Damon Van Schwartz says something *else* we can't hear to Charlie Chamberlain. Honestly, it was kind of cute when it was Sadie, but this is just *rude*. There's a bit of laughter and a few more words between them, then he lifts the mic and he's all of ours again.

"Friends, I want you all to meet Charlie Chamberlain."

Applause. Blah.

"You may not know this, but if it wasn't for Charlie, my life would have ended abruptly earlier today."

More applause. Eye roll.

"I want to say the biggest thank you to this hero, right here. I really thought the reaper was about to claim me, but you fought him off."

"For goodness' sake!" I say, possibly louder than I'd planned as *a lot* of people in front turn and look at me like I've broken a puppy's neck with my bare hands.

"What now?" hisses Roxy.

"We don't know he was actually about to *die*," I say, doing angry air quotes.

"Are you calling Damon Van Schwartz a *liar*?" asks a woman in a faded *Vampire Falls* T-shirt in the row in front of me.

"No," says Roxy, pulling me back into my seat. I didn't

even realise I was perched on the edge of it. "No, she's not saying that. She's just . . . excited."

Damon Van Schwartz's assistant appears with a couple of red lanyards (RED ONES, ffs) and puts them over their heads like they've just won gold at the Olympics, which they basically have because red lanyards are the best passes money can buy. I can't imagine what the extra perks would be. I heard you can only get them on the dark web. The red lanyards that is, not the perks.

Roxy strokes my head in a fruitless attempt to settle me down; red lanyards are the ultimate dream, as well as meeting Megan Nicole Jefferies who plays Lila Murphy, most Fallers' final cast member on their photo op bingo card.

"I've also arranged for a room upgrade, right here at the hotel, and we're going to have dinner tomorrow."

"*Room upgrade*?!" I blurt, this time loud enough that Charlie Chamberlain, Sadie and Damon Van Schwartz peer at me all the way from the stage.

I sink down into my seat in case the stewards try to remove me because I'm being so loud. Actually, not loud. *Emotional.* OK, fine. Loud *and* emotional, but a room upgrade *and* dinner? We all know what a great guy Damon Van Schwartz is, but this special treatment is wildly unnecessary, in my humble opinion.

"Can I hear it for Charlie and his sister Sadie, guys?"

The crowd cheers even louder, if possible, as Felix ushers them to their seats on the stage. Sadie beams at Amber Anderson who high-fives her as she sits down, while the rest of the guests lean forward to welcome them.

"You OK?" asks Roxy.

I gape at the stage, and then at Roxy.

"Am I *OK*? Do you even *know* me?"

"Fair. Just try and screw a lid on it before one of the stewards throws you out."

"Pffft."

Yes, I pffft-ed. My heart and soul pffft-ed for my little convention.

CHAPTER NINE

COX THE OBSERVER

Just look at the clouds clearing.
Things are never as bad as they may seem.

BUD LEROY

Unless there's an elemental witch in the
next town over, getting all her clouds in
a row ready for Armageddon. Just saying.

Vampire Falls. Season three, episode seventeen –
"Signs of Life".

Not even Damon Van Schwartz and Amber Anderson riffing on stage lifts me from the pungent swamp of despair-excrement I'm neck deep in. *Despexcrement.* The crowd laughs at their Hollywood anecdotes and claps furiously when Damon Van Schwartz talks about how much he loves his dog (a Golden Retriever named Gandhi), but I'm impervious to the good cheer in Conference Hall A.

"Hi Amber, I know you're a fan of the show," says a man.

The audience turns to look at the man at the mic stand in the aisle, dressed as a punk version of Chester Burton, the archivist, from the multiverse episode.

"Sure am, honey," replies Amber, smiling at him.

"Would you mind telling us what your favourite scene is that you *didn't* appear in?"

"Gosh, you guys are knocking it out of the park with these questions today, I gotta say." Punk Chester Burton looks pleased with himself. "I know this is a favourite for you Fallers too. It's gotta be that scene in the asylum between Lila and possessed, or non-possessed, Orion."

Music pipes out of the speakers, sending goosebumps racing down my arms. Amber looks off to the side of the stage and smiles.

"See? I didn't even have to tell you guys the episode name. You nailed it."

I could hear any one of the instrumental versions of this song and tell you exactly what scene, episode and season it's from. The version playing now is from "Just For Today", and it triggers a pandemonium of emotions inside me. The audience claps gently over the music and I look at Charlie Chamberlain, wondering if he remembers the song too.

Because that episode, that actual scene, is where this whole thing started.

Week by week, month by month, Charlie Chamberlain fell face first for *Vampire Falls*, and I started falling hard for him. Our time together spilt out of my living room and he gravitated towards us at school, until we became a tight little cluster.

Vampire Falls was always on the agenda, but we'd loop and swoop around each other in conversations about anything and everything. Often it was just me and him doing the talking, and Roxy would observe as he teased me or when I made ridiculous observations that would have him in stitches. I told him everything, from my secret fantasy about Damon Van Schwartz showing up in the common room to whisk me away, to my fear that Roxy would one day realise I'm too weird for her and leave me.

He'd laugh and shake his head, saying I was ridiculous, but I'd be thrilled that he had any kind of opinion of me. I remember sharing a show theory with him, and as I explained why it's feasible Lila was in a coma since the first episode, he pulled a tiny leaf from my hair. I spent the rest of that day twirling that curl, my heart fluttering at the memory of his gentle fingers.

I loved those lunchtime moments where he'd clock me, and the tension would just melt from his face. I'd ask to see photos of his pug, Chuck, knowing he'd lean in closer, pressing his shoulder against mine. Roxy had teased him for being overgenerous with his deodorant, so he'd cut way back, revealing the vanilla and sweet orange aroma of an aftershave Sadie had given him for his sixteenth birthday. In the mornings, his coconut shampoo joined the mix and tingled its way from my nose to my fluttery stomach; he smelt like dessert.

There was an energy hustling between us when we were close, and it took my breath away.

Every night, as I played our interactions over in my head, analysing the type of smile I got when we said goodbye, I wondered how it would feel if he kissed me. Wonder became hope, until one day we were alone at my house.

We were watching the season three episode "Just For Today", which routinely appears in fan top five lists. Orion is possessed by a demon that's draining the life from him. While the gang prepare a spell to turn Orion back into a ghost (the only way to expel the demon), Lila sneaks off to see him chained up, but he's broken free and, under control of the demon, he grabs her. Lila fights against him (that girl is scrappy) until he pushes her against the wall and we realise, from the way he looks at her, that in that moment he's *her* Orion.

A single tear rolls down his cheek, his hands and eyes exploring her shoulders and her face, checking he hasn't hurt her. Strings start up, the instrumental theme twinkling gently between them, pulling the viewers into their pain as Orion tells her he can't fight much longer, that he's getting lost inside the demon's darkness.

Lila looks up at him, shaking her head as her own tears fall. Orion runs his fingers through her hair, then cups her face in his hands and leans in, pressing his lips against hers, squeezing their eyes closed as they take in the moment, take in each other before she loses him. Maybe for good (spoiler: it's not for good).

It was a moment Fallers had been waiting for since Lila and Orion danced together at the Vampire Ball in season one. I'd seen it dozens of times, so I looked at Charlie to see what he thought.

He was looking right at me.

He blinked slowly and the side of his mouth curved up in a smile, like he was preparing to be happy about something.

I froze as he leant into me in slow motion and super speed all at once, then kissed me, his body pressed up against mine in the familiarity we'd built up over years of friendship.

I held my breath and put my hand on the back of his neck, a spot I'd become obsessed with, and melted into him. Suddenly, a loud clang broke us apart, and he clutched his chest, laughing because he'd knocked the remote off the sofa into an empty snack bowl. He straightened up and looked at me, like he was memorising every one of my freckles, then broke into a wide smile.

"I've been thinking if I didn't kiss you soon, I'd explode," he said, drawing a little circle on my knee with his finger. "Then there was a bang and I thought we'd *both* exploded."

I laughed, he laughed. It was us and it was cute, and I'll never forget that moment. I think about our kiss daily and it makes my heart race and break at the same time.

Goosebumps still prickle my skin and I narrow my eyes at Charlie Chamberlain who is fixated on Amber Anderson, not a ghost of that same memory twitching on his face.

". . . and that's the opening ceremony, guys. Although . . ." says Damon Van Schwartz, that crooked smile of his teasing the audience into a frenzy. "I heard a rumour there's some kind of surprise, Felix. Is that right?"

"That is correct, sir," says Felix, without missing a beat. "We know you're all *suckers* for surprises."

Roxy looks at me, her eyebrow raised. I sit up from my slumped position. Felix now has my attention.

"All right. First off, Damon Van Schwartz is giving us the ultimate treat by playing with his band tonight. I can't think of a better start to the weekend, can you?"

Roxy and I whip round to each other and grab hands.

"BRING ME THE GHOST ARE *PLAYING*!?"

We squeal in tandem, and Damon Van Schwartz's band name ripples across the audience, punctuated by whoops and clapping. This news makes my heart beat as fast as the drum solo on the track "Master of Los Angeles" from their third album.

Felix looks out at the audience, a huge grin on his face. He's been running *Vampire Falls* conventions for over five years now. He's a Faller, just like the rest of us.

"But that's not all, right, Damon?"

"Right, Felix." Damon Van Schwartz turns to us, his face serious. "You guys have the opportunity to take part in a competition at this very convention. And the prize is *big*, guys."

Damon Van Schwartz pauses for the audience chatter; he knows who he's dealing with.

Roxy looks at me, her eyebrows high. I shrug.

"I hate competitions," I say. "I never win anything."

"That's the spirit, babe," Roxy says, ruffling my hair.

"Are you guys ready to roll?" says Damon Van Schwartz, looking at the big screen behind them.

"They are," says Felix, beaming at him.

"OK," nods Damon Van Schwartz, clapping his hands together. "Do we have a treat for you Fallers! Hold on to your butts for this never-before-seen footage from *Vampire Falls*, filmed especially for you guys."

Roxy and I whip round to look at each other; in our entire

convention experience, from my mum chaperoning us, to us being the mature grown-up types we (OK, one of us) now are, this has never happened.

"He looks like Viggo when he's about to reunite Juliana with her childhood hell-mongrel," says Roxy, beaming at me.

"Totally," I say, nodding in agreement, the look on his face exactly the same (yes, I know they're the same person but he's usually *so* Damon Van Schwartz).

Excited chatter flutters over the crowd, everyone wondering what we're about to see until the *Vampire Falls* theme blasts from the speakers and the opening graphics flash up on the big screen. Conference Hall A is silent, as every pair of eyes behind every latex mask stares at the screen. Lila Murphy's montage rolls to the music, followed by Orion Fenimore's clips. I know these clips better than I know the photos inside my mum's family album.

But that's it. There's no Viggo Rassmussen waltzing with a skeleton, and no Juliana the Demon Huntress throwing a knife into the single eye of a Fraaxalon demon. The usual *Vampire Falls* title graphic emblazons the screen, but with three extra words underneath in the same font.

A Convention Special.

My little heart leaps and I squee at Roxy, who's basically my mirror right now. We turn back to the screen at the sound of Orion's voice.

"Lila, get back here. You shouldn't go in there alone."

I hold my breath. This is *new* dialogue. New dialogue especially for *us*!

"Walk through a wall or something then."

Classic Lila.

"You know I can't walk through walls. It makes me itch."

Orion's a ghost, for most of the series, anyway.

"You're incorporeal. You can't possibly itch."

OK, I'll shut up now.

"Well, you'll find out whether ghosts itch if you go in there alone. Maksaka Skinners love blond chicks."

"Good job there are no chicks here then."

Laugher tinkles around Conference Hall A. Lila's in her signature scuffed Dr Martens, high-waist torn jeans and has a blue check (or *flannel*, as they say on the show) shirt tied at her tiny waist. She twirls her blond waves into a bun then secures it with the tiny hatpin Juliana gave her in the episode "Quiet Now". I love her hair in a bun; she has the most immaculate hairline in the world.

"There it is."

Lila points at a chest tucked under a white metal bed frame. My heart is beating so hard I can hardly hear what they're saying.

"No sign of the Maksakas."

Lila pulls the chest from its hiding place. Orion sticks his hands out like he's trying to stop traffic.

"Don't open it!"

"Well, you can't open it." She looks at her watch. *"It's not sundown yet so no touchy-touchy for you."*

"You always rub that in my face."

"Can't rub anything in your face until sundown."

"Ha ha."

(Orion's incorporeal but in season two a warlock owed

him a favour and made him corporeal from sunset to sunrise. OK, I *promise* I'll stop now.)

"*Fine, just open it. But be careful.*"

"*I was planning on not being careful actually.*"

More laughter from us. Classic Lila and Orion banter.

Lila pulls the splintered chest towards her, its open padlock dangling from a cast iron link on the top. Everyone around me is frozen as she reaches inside and pulls out a torn scroll, wrapped with a leather cord. She glances at Orion, who nods at her, and she unties it.

"*What's it say?*"

Lila's eyebrows pinch together as she scans the scroll. She looks up at Orion, her eyes wide with shock. Roxy looks round at me, but I can't look away; there's something *important* written on that scroll.

"*Lila? Come on, you're killing me here. I mean, if I wasn't already dead.*"

No laughter this time. The audience is invested as Lila swallows a lump then reads from the scroll.

"*It says . . . it says . . . attendees at the* Vampire Falls *convention in London, England are invited to enter the first ever Fall Games. Three contestants will be chosen to battle it out for the ultimate Faller prize.*"

Roxy and I are holding hands and nearly breaking each other's fingers, but it's fine; bones can be fixed.

"*What prize, Lila?*"

Lila suddenly breaks the fourth wall and looks out at us. I gasp, as her perma-frown melts from her face and she breaks into a wide smile.

"The prize is courtesy of my boy Damon's production company, Karma Kaleidoscope. Love you, Damon."

She blows a kiss out towards the camera and Damon Van Schwartz, on stage in London, reciprocates. Lila (or Megan? I'm so overexcited and giddy right now, I have no idea) does a heart sign with her hands then smiles at us again.

"The winner of the Fall Games, along with a friend, will be my personal guest at next year's San Diego Comic Con."

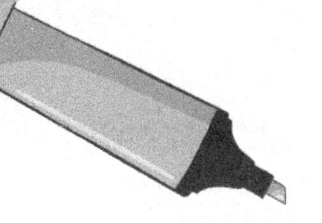

CHAPTER TEN

ORION FENIMORE
Breathe, Lila! Just breathe!
LILA MURPHY
You breathe! I can't feel my damn face!

Vampire Falls. Season two, episode fifteen –
"We've Been Expecting You"

I can't possibly tell you what just happened but I'm standing on my chair and a steward is yelling at me from the aisle, and I can't hear what she's saying because the entire hall is screaming. *Screaming.*

I have a singular, one-track, blinkered thought flashing in neon inside my head, and that thought is that I must win that trip to Comic Con. Nay, not must, I *will* win that trip for me and Roxy if it's the last thing I do.

"*Not only that*," says Megan Nicole Jefferies, amid some deranged ssshh-ing but mostly still screams, "*but the runner-up gets to have coffee with the nicest guy I've ever had the pleasure of working with . . .*" More pausing. OMG my heart. "*That legend right there, Mr Damon Van Schwartz!*"

Apart from taking certain people who have done the Heimlich on him out to dinner, Damon Van Schwartz *never* does one-to-ones. I turn round to scream with the rest of the audience. A few are on their chairs. One woman has pulled her T-shirt up over her head like footballers do, so her Rassmussen family crest tattoo on her chest is on display in all its glory. Good for her, I say.

Hands grab at my legs, and I try to kick Roxy away until I realise she's lifting me onto her shoulders. Fake McKinley helps steady me, and I raise my hands to the ceiling of Conference Room A in thanks to Varelia, the Goddess of Good Fortune. The crowd chants WE LOVE DAMON and I scream the words even though my throat is on fire. Happy fire. Damon Van Schwartz is smiling, wiping tears of happiness from his cheeks. Only he would do something like this for his fans; only he gets what it means.

"Guys, guys. I know we're . . ." We can just about hear Felix's voice above the noise. "I know we're excited, but it's *gravely* important we set up for later. After we've changed the hall around there'll be a small window to put your name into the *actual* Cauldron of Metallica prop from the season four finale, to enter the competition. Then names will be drawn tomorrow. I think that's it for now, right, Damon?"

Damon Van Schwartz nods and then pats his chest, right where his big loving heart is. He looks out at us with his Sharpie Nano Blue eyes, wet with tears, and I love him so much I just want to crawl inside him and love him from the snuggly confines of his ribcage. Roxy lowers me onto the chair and helps me hop down. I smile at her but she's giving me *a look.*

"What?" I ask, my voice croaky.

"You just screamed *I want to crawl inside you*."

"Did I?" I say, shrugging. "Heat of the moment. I'm sure nobody noticed."

Roxy raises her eyebrows and gestures to the rows in front of us, and behind, where everyone is looking at me like I've maybe crossed the line from superfan into stalkerdom.

"I'll rein it in," I say, crossing my heart.

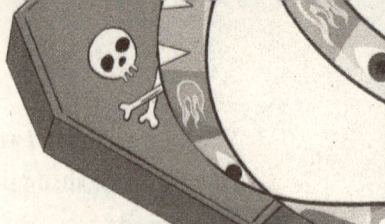

CHAPTER ELEVEN

BUD LEROY

*We can't just leave it here, guts and
entrails hanging out all over the place.*

LILA MURPHY

It's fine; nobody will know what happened.

BUD LEROY

But still . . . intestines and spleen should never be seen.

Vampire Falls. Season one, episode nine –
"Not On Our Watch"

We've spent the last what feels like few hours hanging around in the bar waiting for them to let us back into Conference Hall A. The combo of beers, nervous competition energy and my tiny bladder means this is our fourth trip to the toilet.

I grab Roxy's hand and we head back to the bosom of our fandom. Not everyone's dressed in masquerade; there are loads of *Vampire Falls* T-shirts, plus a few bootleg *Midnight in Portland* ones, which doesn't bother me because this is our convention and people can wear what they want. Like Derek, who Roxy reminded me about earlier. He wanders past in a turtle-neck jumper, gold sequinned hot pants, stockings and Crocs. We each give him a high-five.

We have selfies with Cantatrix and Venefica, congratulating them on the insanely detailed work that's gone into their witch costumes, from the flaking skin and rotten teeth, down to the way they're floating along (both on hover boards under the floor-length cloaks). This is part of the experience and I'll share these photos on Insta, but I'm also assimilating as these people are potential competition for my trip with Megan Nicole Jefferies. My trip with Roxy, I mean.

"Another drink?" asks Roxy, nodding at the bar.

I glance at the double doors but they're still obstructed by two stewards, so I nod and she heads to the bar. I wander around, partaking in a spot of people-watching.

I glance back at the doors again, which are still covered by the stewards, then slam into what feels like a gorilla and stumble backwards.

"Sorry!" I say, looking up at the guy dressed as McKinley the Pessimistic Werewolf from earlier.

His wolf head moves left to right, until I stand on my tiptoes and wave in his eye line.

"Oh," he says, doing a sort of I-didn't-see-you-because-of-my-mask gesture, "hey. Sorry."

"It's OK," I say, pointing at his werewolf mask then adjusting my own eye mask in solidarity. "Convention hazard. They should assign handlers."

"Yeah, handlers. Right," he says, nodding his furry head, then laughs a little. "I love your outfit."

"Thanks, I'm kind of sweltering under all the layers but

it's worth it," I say, smoothing my dress down. "You must be roasting in yours? Do you want some water?"

He shakes his head.

"I'm cool. I mean, I'm not *cool* cool, I just mean I'm OK. Thanks though."

A group of Cyanfide demons next to us crane their necks and point, and I look round Fake McKinley to see Damon Van Schwartz walking through the lobby. Walking with Charlie Chamberlain, who's half-heartedly wearing a black eye mask on his forehead. My cheeks warm as Damon Van Schwartz laughs and claps him on the back. Debbie is close behind, chatting with Sadie who looks adorable in a purple sparkly dress and matching mask.

Fake McKinley has to physically turn his whole body to see what I'm looking at.

"So, you were pretty, um … psyched about the competition in there. That's a great prize."

"Right? So exciting," I say absently, still watching Charlie Chamberlain.

Debbie suddenly trots ahead and swipes a door open, ushering everyone through. Is that some sort of secret place for VIPs?

Before Charlie Chamberlain follows them, he stops and looks around the bar. Everyone is watching him, wondering what magical things are laid out for him behind those doors and wishing they'd had his catlike reactions so they could have saved their own TV star. He lingers in the doorway and then, just to rub it in, looks right at me.

I hope he's good at non-verbal because I am so consumed

with jealousy right now, I shoot off all the swears via my eyeballs and folded arms. A smile plays on his lips, then he lets the door close behind him.

A cold bottle is suddenly thrust in my chest and I gasp at Roxy, who's simultaneously grabbing me and marching me from Fake McKinley. Practically in an arm lock as if I'm some kind of felon, I'd like to add. I look back at Fake McKinley who gives me a little wave. I have no idea what I've done to deserve this treatment, officer, but I wave back.

"The doors are open, Eliza!" she hisses. "What's wrong with you?!"

Oh, that's what I've done. I deserve every twisted joint. People are surging through the doors of Conference Hall A, but I didn't notice because I was busy glaring my hatred at damn Charlie Chamberlain. We bundle through the crowd and spill into the flashing lights and thumping bass, then pause and turn to each other. I can't hear Roxy properly, but I think she's saying the same words as me.

What the fuck?

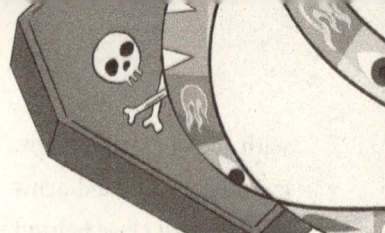

CHAPTER TWELVE

VIGGO RASSMUSSEN

You must prepare yourself for the absolute worst, Lila.

LILA MURPHY

Have you ever considered motivational speaking?

Vampire Falls. Season one, episode four – "Bury Me"

Some of us (me) consider ourselves somewhat expert in the art of convention queuing. Some people (me) might use the word *gifted*. There is much to consider when one joins a queue. Which queue, for a start. Assess who is waiting in your queue options. Bored-looking, handsome type, holding lots of bags? He's holding the space for his girlfriend and possibly even her friends, so your queue size will likely increase. Middle-aged, pony-tailed man holding folder and wearing backpack with pin-badge covered straps? Seasoned pro: *efficient*. Get behind him.

What we are witnessing, however, is not a queue, and goes against all my convention training. Swathes of bodies push towards the stage, and with the music blaring and lights flashing it looks like a mosh-pit at a concert, but with low fantasy superfans clambering over each other instead of metal heads. Four sweaty and frizzy stewards try to maintain some kind of order, plus one more on stage next to a large cauldron with two red handles made from intertwined snakes.

It's the Cauldron of Metallica, the first step towards Comic Con – and my destiny.

"Let's do this, babe!" Roxy shouts over the music.

I nod, and we clink our bottles together and rush across the dance floor, to the edge of the furore. Another steward at a small table implores, "PLEASE RETURN THE PENS" above the music. They hand us a sort of parchment with instructions to write our name, phone number and convention badge number. We fill them out, then Roxy grabs my hand and we head into the eye of the storm.

"Why is it so insane?" I call from behind Roxy to nobody in particular, elbowing a tall tuxedo-wearing vampire who's trying to use my head to gain traction.

"There's only three minutes left to enter!" someone from low down responds.

A white-haired woman who looks a lot like my nanna, is crawling on the ground next to me, trying to get through people's legs. Nice tactics. Her glasses dangle from a chain around her neck.

"Three minutes?" I repeat, peering round Roxy then looking back down at the old woman. "It's not supposed to start for another half an hour?"

"Yes! Three fucking minutes! The organisers have pulled their usual last-minute shit." she shouts. OK, Nanna enjoyed the odd swear but never the F-word. "Keep your eyes on the prize, curly."

Good point. The steward next to the cauldron looks at his

watch then holds two fingers up in the air. I squeeze Roxy's hand and she pushes forwards. There's a yelp from behind me and I look round just as the old woman sinks her teeth into the ankle of Tuxedo Vampire.

"You crazy old lady!" he screams.

"You stepped on my finger!" she shouts back. "I have arthritis!"

I swallow. It's like *The Hunger Games* in here.

We keep pushing forward but the crowd is at least ten deep, and I can tell from Roxy's tense shoulders we might not make it. There's another shout and the pressure from the crowd behind me lessens. I look round and Tuxedo Vampire is on his back, on top of the old lady. Fake McKinley leans over them trying to help her up. I frown at the three of them; it's possibly the strangest thing I've seen at one of these conventions and, let me tell you, you see a lot of stuff.

Fake McKinley manages to roll Tuxedo Vampire off the old lady, but they're getting jostled so much she can't get up. He hunches over and shields her from everyone. She spots me watching.

"Curly! Curly!" she calls, her voice shaky.

She's holding something up in her hand. I glance at the steward on stage. He's holding one finger up. One minute to go. The crowd pushes harder and Roxy and I move closer with it. People clamber onto the stage, cheering and jumping around after they drop their name in the cauldron. I swallow and look back at the woman. She looks smaller now.

"Curly!" she calls again.

I let go of Roxy's hand and push my way through the

bodies back to the old lady. I reach out to her, and Fake McKinley nods at me. I put my arm around her shoulders and he takes her wrist, but she shakes us off, holding up a piece of paper.

"You came back for me," she says, her eyes watery.

"Come on, let me help you," I say, glancing over my shoulder.

"It's too late for me," she says. "You're young; you still have a chance."

"I won't leave you," I say, trying to pull her up, but she feels so small, so fragile.

She shakes her head and pushes the paper into my chest.

"Take this. Please," she says. "You're my only hope."

I look down: it's her entry form. Her name – Dorothy Churchman – written on it in beautiful curvy writing.

I glance at Fake McKinley, who's watching me (I think) through the mesh on his mask. He's managed to get Dorothy into a sort of sitting position and she's put her glasses on.

"Eliza!" Roxy frantically waves me forwards, her eyes darting around in panic. "Eliza, what the fuck?!"

I take a breath and look back at Dorothy, her eyes, now giant behind her glasses, pleading with me. My fingers tighten around her entry form and I nod, my resolve as strong as my crowd-dodging thighs.

"OK," I say, then kiss Dorothy on top of her soft white hair. I nod at them both. "Mind your hip, Dorothy!"

I stand and assess the crowd. There are less people around now, some have given up and are floating towards the bar, and others are making a final push to the stage.

"Twenty-nine, twenty-eight . . ."

The countdown starts without warning. Roxy is standing a few people ahead of me, a mix of anger and confusion on her still beautiful face. There's no way we're getting to that cauldron through this lot. My mouth is dry and my heart clangs in my chest. I take one last look at Dorothy, who nods at me, her eyes full of hope, and I know I have to find another way up onto that stage.

"Twenty-three, twenty-two . . ."

There's nobody behind us now; everyone is at the front, scrambling over each other. I race over to Roxy and, ignoring her protests, rip her entry from her hand and run back towards Dorothy and Fake McKinley, where the Tuxedo Vampire is still sitting, slightly bewildered on the floor.

"Eighteen, seventeen, sixteen . . ."

I step up on his shoulder and jump onto the table where people were filling in their forms, ignoring the steward who looks like his head might implode. I still have my beer in my hand, so I finish it off and put it down gently on the table (it's glass and there are people around; I'm not a sociopath) then leap onto the big round table next to it, still hearing Roxy screaming my name.

"Fourteen, thirteen . . ."

There's a row of stacked chairs along the wall, lined up all the way to the stage. I back up as far as I can on the round table, smooth down my dress and take a breath.

"This is for you, Dorothy," I whisper.

I run across the white tablecloth and leap from the edge, my hands out ready. I hit the top of the chairs and grab at the plastic, but I can't get my grip and I fall, feeling the stack of chairs wobble ominously as I cling to them, falling backwards.

"Ten, nine . . ."

"No!" I cry out, Dorothy's big, wrinkly eyes clear in my head.

I'm going backwards. I'm going backwards and the stack of chairs will land on top of me and crush me, but probably not as badly as Roxy will because I expect she's livid with me right now.

It's over. It's all over.

"Eight, seven . . ."

I look towards the stage, trying to pull myself up, when I feel someone suddenly take my weight and push me up from my feet. I gasp and climb up until I'm standing on the top chair, and look round, my heart overwhelmed with hope.

"Go!" shouts a voice. Someone dressed as Masquerade Ball Orion waves his arm towards the stage, jumping up and down a little. "You can still make it!"

I nod, then turn and leap along the stack of chairs until I get to the last one – but there's a gap in front of me.

I'm not going to make it.

"Give me your hand!" another voice calls from the edge of the stage.

I look up, but the lights are blinding and the sound of people counting down is disorientating, so I can't see who's standing across from me. Plus, I probably shouldn't have just chugged that beer.

"Give me your hand!" they shout again.

It's a girl's voice, I think, and I reach towards her

outstretched hand. I clasp my fingers around hers and she grabs me firmly. I jump across the gap and land safely in front of her. She lifts up her jewel-encrusted mask, the rubies co-ordinating with the floor-length gown she's absolutely rocking, and she smiles down at me. I look into her green, feline eyes, and realise, with horror, who she is.

"You're welcome," says Vivian Erikksen, Queen of the Awfuls, looking me up and down.

"Six, five . . ."

She reaches into her cleavage and retrieves a folded piece of paper. I mean, who *does* that? Vivian, apparently. She turns towards the cauldron and flicks her long hair over her shoulder, getting me right in the eye in the process.

"Four, three . . ."

She strides across the stage and drops her entry into the cauldron, and I gape at her as she takes a little curtsey before jumping off the stage and actually crowd-surfing away. I mean . . .

"MOVE YOUR ARSE, CURLY!"

Dorothy's voice snaps me back to the present and I spot her in the audience with Roxy and Fake McKinley, all three of them waving their arms like windmills.

"Two . . ."

I blink and stumble across the stage, falling a few feet from the cauldron, but dropping the three entries in as I tumble to the ground.

"ONE!"

The crowd erupts and I roll my head to the side, smiling back at Roxy, Dorothy and Fake McKinley who are jumping up and down (if their hips allow) and clapping. A fourth person stands next to Roxy, and I smile at Masquerade Ball Orion then mouth *thank you* to him, because it seems like something a hero would say to an innocent bystander in a film. He mouths back *you're welcome,* then smiles back at me.

My stomach lurches. That's not the smile of an innocent bystander. It's the smile of my arch nemesis (or one of them. I feel like they're multiplying every hour I'm here). I lift my head, just as he reaches up and pulls his mask off. Roxy's eyebrows fly up when she realises Masquerade Ball Orion is actually Charlie Chamberlain.

Roxy looks back at me, clapping even harder, and I drop my head back to the ground, totally exhausted and now a little confused.

Did Charlie Chamberlain just help me get up those chairs?

CHAPTER THIRTEEN

VIGGO RASSMUSSEN

First, there's blood. Then you have music.

Vampire Falls. Season seven, episode three – "Say It Again"

After downing a couple of glasses of water and eating Fake McKinley's protein bar, my heart has stopped racing from the surge of adrenaline that got me across those chairs and onto the stage. I'm not thinking about the other people who may or may not have helped me or whether they're playing mind games. I'm not thinking about that *at all*.

Bring Me the Ghost are on fire. Damon Van Schwartz on vocals was born to front a band, as well as to play Viggo Rassmussen. And do all his humanitarian bollocks, of course. Halfway through "Smile/Cry", which is the percussion-heavy song that made me resurrect my drumming career, I got overexcited and bit my tongue, so now we're having a little sit down. We're at a table with a couple of Malcorr demons who've been shouting muffled accusations at each other and now face away, one with its arms folded and the other scrolling on their phone. Love is hard, even for Malcorr demons.

Damon Van Schwartz closes his eyes and whispers the

opening lines of "Person of Mine", from their second album, also from the season two episode, "Not Now". The crowd screams and everyone loops arms, swaying to what is basically Viggo and Juliana's theme song. I search the crowd and spot Charlie Chamberlain, Vivian pressed up against his side, shouting something in his ear. He nods, smiling at whatever she's said. I turn to Roxy.

"Do you think he knew she was coming?"

"Obviously," says Roxy, not even asking who I'm talking about.

"Why obviously?" I say, looking Vivian up and down.

Her dress is amazing; sort of Morticia Addams shaped but in bright, blood red. Her bum looks incredible. And her boobs. It should be illegal to have both a good bum and good boobs.

"Because they're friends," shrugs Roxy.

"Why are they friends though?" I say, curling my lip as Vivian starts dancing like one of the pros on *Strictly*.

"People probably wonder the same about us, babe."

"Funny."

Roxy leans forward and ruffles my (very sweaty) hair.

"And I'd tell them, Eliza Gellar, it's because you're so adorable, and not at all obsessive."

"Obsessive? *Me?* How am *I* obsessive?" Roxy finishes her drink and raises an eyebrow. I turn in my seat and get as close to her face as I can, in case she didn't hear me, not because I'm obsessive. "Tell me right now! What do you mean, *obsessive*!?"

Roxy shakes her head and laughs (*what* is she laughing at?!) then stands and pulls me out of my seat.

"Time to dance, my low-maintenance friend."

"Fine, but I'm not enjoying myself until you tell me what you mean by *obsessive*."

Roxy grabs my hand and spins me round, which obviously makes me wildly enjoy myself but halfway through my spin I spot someone who isn't. The guy in the McKinley costume is watching everyone from the side of the dance floor, alone again. I elbow Roxy and she looks round.

"He looks so lost," she says, as he runs a finger along the inside neck of his mask. "I mean, as lost as a werewolf can look."

"Right? I haven't seen him with anyone; I think he might be here on his own." He jumps out of the way of a couple of vampires twirling each other round. I look up at Roxy. "Shall I?"

Roxy nods.

"You shall," she says, nodding. "I'm getting drinks. See you in a minute."

I walk over and have to stand on my tiptoes and wave in front of his snout before he registers me.

"Sorry," he says, shaking his head and pointing at his mask. "I'm smiling at you under here. Hey."

"Hey," I respond and gesture at the costume, "are you sure you don't want some water?"

His snout bounces up and down, so I turn and catch Roxy's eye, mouthing for her to get him a water. She nods, and I turn back. He's watching the band, nodding his head to the music.

"They're good right?" I say.

He looks down at me. I wish he'd take that mask off. The glassy eyes remind me of taxidermy. Not that I've been around much taxidermy, but I listened to a podcast once.

"Sorry?" he says, leaning closer and putting his hand up to his ear. His wolf ear.

"The band," I say, louder this time. "Aren't they great?"

"So good," he says, nodding. "I actually saw them last year but didn't know who they were. Just thought they were a cool band."

"Where?" I ask.

"In LA."

"LA?" I repeat.

"Sorry?"

"You've been to LA?" I shout over the music.

He looks at me through those marble-like eyes, but someone shoves past and I fall into his wolf chest.

"You OK?" he says, putting his hands out to steady me.

"Yeah, I'm OK," I reply, checking I haven't had a wardrobe malfunction.

"Everyone looks amazing," he says, his snout following someone dressed as a masquerade-ball version of Juliana as they walk past us. "You all really go for the costume stuff, right?"

"You tell me, McKinley," I say, pointing at his suit.

"McKinley?" he says, looking down, then nodding. "Oh, right. McKinley, yeah. I actually . . ."

He carries on talking but I can barely hear him over the music and through his mask. I step closer and cock my head, trying to follow what he's saying.

"Sorry?" I say.

"I said, I'm sort of new to watching the show so don't know all the characters properly yet..."

"Oh, right."

"Yeah, and I wanted to go for something easy, so it was either this werewolf costume or the guy in the robe thing... what's his name..."

Unsurprisingly, *robe things* make quite a few appearances in *Vampire Falls* so I'm not sure who he's talking about.

"I can't hear you," I say, shaking my head as he goes on.

"I said, it was either this guy or that other dude, Cox the Observer."

"Who?" I say, turning my ear to him.

"Cox the Observer," he repeats, louder.

"Oh," I shout, realising he's talking about one of my favourite characters, "I love Cox!"

Yeah. Yeah, I shouted that just as the song finished and there was a couple of seconds of silence, but long enough to shout that out nice and clear. Everyone in the vicinity is staring, including Fake McKinley.

"I didn't mean it like..." I implore to them all, my voice drowned out by the start of the next song.

They give me a quick look up and down then turn back to the stage. Roxy pushes through the dance floor and joins us.

"Oh my god, did you just—" I blurt.

"Hear you shout *I love Cox*?" she cuts in, handing me a beer. "Yes, babe."

Fake McKinley hasn't deserted us, so he hasn't taken my

declaration the wrong way. Roxy hands him a bottle of water.

"Thank you," he says, looking at it in his paw. He tries the lid, but between the gloves and his obscured vision he can't manage it. "Sorry, can you hold it for me a minute."

"Sure," says Roxy, taking the water back as he reaches up and starts pulling his mask off.

All the shouting has made my throat dry, so I push the lime into the top of the bottle ready for a cool swig, as I watch Fake McKinley pull his head off. I mean, not his *actual* head, because his head is . . . wow.

He's like something off a dating show for the top tier of beautiful types.

As I gape at him (correction: Roxy and I *both* gape at him) my beer erupts over my hand so I do the only thing a sane person would do and shove the bottle neck into my mouth. Foam rises up my nostrils and I start coughing, the sour taste flooding my throat.

Roxy claps me on my back, my eyes bulging out of the sockets.

"Are you OK?" asks Fake McKinley, looking down at me with deep, dark brown eyes. Umber, I'd say in fact. Possibly even *burnt* umber. "Can I get you something?"

"*Love Island* . . ." I splutter.

He straightens up and scratches his beard. His thick hair glistens with sweat and there are tiny, sweaty curls against his neck and forehead, like one of those cherub paintings you see – but those cherubs are always blond, and his hair is jet black. He's handsome. *Incredibly* handsome. He's like a tall, handsome, slightly sweaty, cherub-man.

"What did she say?" he asks, peering at Roxy.

"Nothing," she says, rubbing my back. "We'll be back in a minute."

She steers me towards the toilets, leaving him looking very puzzled.

"I was *not* expecting that," I wheeze.

"Neither was I, babe," she says. "Good call taking pity on the insanely handsome dude."

"Yeah, go me," I croak, clearing my throat. I look up at her. "Did I say *Love Island*?"

"It was more of a *gurgle*. But I think he was probably distracted by the beer dribbling out of your nose."

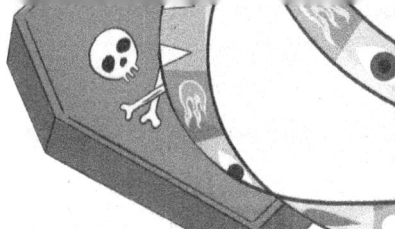

CHAPTER FOURTEEN

VIGGO RASSMUSSEN

Stop, Juliana! You're bleeding!

JULIANA THE DEMON HUNTRESS

Not enough.

Vampire Falls. Season six, episode nine –
"All Together Now"

"Why are you glowering at me?" asks Roxy, chomping on a sausage.

She doesn't look up from her obscenely large breakfast. Two whole plates; one full English, one continental.

"I'm not *glowering.*"

I am glowering. Maybe. Honestly? I'm not sure what glowering actually means. We were some of the last ones to get pushed out of the hall. Someone dressed as a Suckling Crone had lost her shoe, so we were crawling around under the tables looking for it, but the bar staff got very uppity and insisted it was time to leave. The joke was on them though because Roxy and I carried on drinking in our room. Then I woke up clutching a dry pot noodle and had a sweet and sour taste in my mouth, so actually the joke is on me.

Anyway, what I'm trying to say is that I'm feeling a little

jaded, as is the norm the morning after first convention night. I can't eat anything for fear of it coming right back up, but Roxy is chowing down, fresh as a daisy. It's annoying. Or glowering. I don't know. Words are hard.

I look around the restaurant at our fellow attendees stocking up on calories for the day, some in *Vampire Falls* hoodies, some in full cosplay mode, ready for today's photo ops. I spot Venefica and Cantatrix quietly eating breakfast together. This would not happen in real life due to their mutual status as mortal enemies being from warring enchantress factions, but I'm pretty sure these guys are in a relationship. Cute. Despite my head pounding, the familiarity of having these people around makes me feel warm.

"If you say so, babe," says Roxy, smiling at something on her phone. She looks up at me and types at the same time. "Have you found your Bristol linguistics group on Insta yet? I've worked out who's cool and who to avoid on my course already."

"No," I say, worry double-churning my already churned stomach. "So, we're expected to make friends with new people before we've even arrived? How am I supposed to do that? I don't come across well electronically."

"I just used the hashtags I sent you and found a few people," she says, not disagreeing with my statement about not coming across well. Charming. "No pressure or . . ."

A smatter of applause bubbles through the restaurant and Roxy stops. We crane our necks to see who's come in. It's regular for a change in atmosphere when a guest appears among the mortals, but an actor having breakfast with the civilians is unprecedented.

Then I see who it is.

Charlie Chamberlain follows the waiting staff to a table, his arm around Sadie. His right eyebrow is slightly raised, which means he didn't sleep well. I don't know what's keeping him awake at night; it's not like *his* favourite weekend's been ruined. He's wearing a *Vampire Falls* T-shirt that I gave him for his birthday three years ago. Sacrilege. Sadie is wearing a matching one, so they actually look adorable, which is annoying. They sit down at a table set for three people: him, Sadie and ...

"Oh yeah, Vivian's here," Roxy cheerfully reminds me. "She looks great this morning, right?"

"Average," I say, frowning as the server pulls a chair out for her. "Why didn't he do that for me? He practically pushed me into my seat. Outrageous."

"Probably thought you were going to faint. You look like dog shit."

"I love you too." Roxy blows me a kiss and I look back at Charlie Chamberlain and co. "Why do you think she's here? She's not a Faller."

"Maybe Charlie needed help with Sadie."

"She's not exactly Mary Poppins," I say, watching her apply lipstick using the reflection in her knife.

"She would make a *hot* Mary Poppins," says Roxy, biting her lip.

"Ew," I say, taking a mouse-sized bite from my croissant. "Gag."

A couple of people with vampire fangs go up to Charlie

Chamberlain's table and clap him on the back. He stands up to talk to them, like he's just won a golf tournament or something.

"When is everyone going to drop the hero worship. So, Charlie Chamberlain knows the Heimlich manoeuvre. OK: big deal."

"DVS nearly choked to death, babe."

"We can't say for sure he would have choked *to death*. Don't you get all dramatic as well."

"Sorry, you're right. Charlie should have left him, just to see what happened," she says, sipping her coffee.

"Well, everyone's making such a big deal," I say, watching Charlie Chamberlain sit down then stand back up when an old couple go over to him. "They're obsessed."

"Yeah," says Roxy. "*Obsessed.*"

I look back at her. She has her elbows on the table, staring at me with her hands clasped together, like a therapist. Or a supervillain.

"What?"

"Nothing, my love," she says. "Nothing at all."

I pull the Jawfain onesie hood over my head then pick at my deflated croissant. I reach for my glass, which is empty (why are hotel breakfast glasses like thimbles? Don't they know people are dehydrated?), so start to get up when I realise Roxy is still staring at me.

"What now?"

"Nothing," she says, then leans forward and flicks one of the ears on my hood. "You look cute in this."

"I'm always cute," I say, fluttering my eyelashes.

Roxy lifts an eyebrow.

"Wearing it down to breakfast every morning?"

I nod. "As long as I don't barf on it."

"Hmm."

"*Uh.* What does *hmm* mean? I'm extremely, extremely fragile, Roxy. Please, just decide what you want to say, say it, then stop saying it."

She sits back in her chair and folds her arms.

"Just think it's interesting that you chose to wear that vile T-shirt yesterday, when you could easily have worn this, your favourite onesie," she says, gesturing at my attire like it's an exhibit in a court case. I blink at her. "Why was that, do you think?"

I shrug. "Forgot I had it, I guess."

"Hmm." I could fake a post-drinking dash to the loo, but then she'd know I'm admitting to something. Which I'm not. Also, I wish Iris was here to divert this sudden attention to my motivations. "Some people might think you'd rather wear a misogynistic T-shirt just to make the friend who caused the latte drenching incident feel worse, rather than changing into something you felt perfectly comfortable in, thus making her feel less bad. *Some people* might think you get so blinded by a grudge you can't see the bigger picture."

"*Thus?*"

"Yes, *thus.* Is that all you have to say?"

"No."

"No what, babe?"

"No, your honour," I say, squirming.

Roxy watches me lick my finger and pick up croissant

crumbs as I look all around the restaurant; everywhere but at her. Her napkin suddenly lands in my lap, and I look up.

"You are the most stubborn person I have ever met," she says, smiling and shaking her head.

I spot Fake McKinley walking round the waffle station, peering at the toppings on offer before he heads through the restaurant.

"Hey." I wave him over, before Roxy can cross-examine me any further.

He smiles and wanders over, weaving between the tables in his werewolf costume, minus head.

"Hey, guys," he says, stopping at our table, his face bright. "How was your breakfast?"

"She couldn't eat," says Roxy.

Fake McKinley looks at my pathetic leftovers and raises his eyebrows.

"Too much fun last night?" he says. I glare at Roxy. "You should try and eat; it'll make you feel better."

"You obviously did," I say, looking up at him. "Is that pain au chocolate or pecan twist crumbs in your beard?"

He smiles and rubs his chin but misses the crumbs.

"Both. What can I say? I'm a Taurus; we love our food," he says. "Did I get them?"

"Nowhere near," I say, pointing. "It's *there*."

"That it?" he says, rubbing the opposite spot.

"I can't cope," I say, pulling myself up. "Let me."

"Oh . . . OK . . ."

He frowns but holds still so I can pick out the crumbs. I brush down the front of his costume as well, and lock eyes with Charlie Chamberlain just over the horizon of Fake McKinley's broad shoulder. Charlie Chamberlain shifts in his seat quickly and his knife clatters to the floor. Ugh. Will I have to look at him every morning?

I clear my throat and sit back down.

"When is it then?" I say.

"When's what?" says Fake McKinley glancing over his shoulder.

"Your birthday. You said you're a Taurus, so it must be . . ." His eyes widen and I glance at Roxy who's smiling. "Oh my god. Is *today* your birthday?"

"Yes, but . . ."

"How old are you?" I ask.

He takes a deep breath and shrugs.

"Twenty-one."

"Happy birthday, man," says Roxy.

"Thank you." He nods and starts backing away. "I'll see you around?"

"Definitely," I say, watching him go.

I turn to Roxy who's already looking at me.

"You're going to make him a birthday crown, aren't you?"

"Obviously," I say, watching him wander out of the restaurant. "It's his birthday and he's here all alone, Roxy."

"And also, very hot."

"Yes, but the breakfast in his beard has totally ruined it for me," I say, waving her comment away.

We both look round as Dorothy comes scurrying between the tables.

"Hey, Dorothy. How's your hip?"

"No time for small talk about my damn hip, Curly."

Wow.

"You OK?" asks Roxy.

"Haven't you seen the notices?" We look back at her blankly and shake our heads. Dorothy tssks and points over her shoulder. "Move your bony arses and get in that hall."

Roxy and I frown at each other, and Dorothy rolls her eyes.

"They're about to draw the players from the cauldron," she says. "The competitors in the Fall Games."

CHAPTER FIFTEEN

LILA MURPHY

Good luck in your quest thing.

JULIANA THE DEMON HUNTRESS

I don't need luck. I have this very sharp sword.

Vampire Falls. Season one, episode eleven –
"Family Ties and Family Cries"

The hall is clear from last night, though the smell of stale beer and bad decisions lingers above the rows of banquet chairs. You would never know that those above the legal (and not legal) drinking age are hungover; everyone is sitting up straight, talking slightly louder than necessary, movements jerky with nervous energy.

We are *on edge*, people.

"I can't see Felix," Roxy says, for the seventh time, looking at her watch then frowning at the stage as if Felix is a bus. "Where is he, babe? Where *is he*?"

I don't reply. I don't blame you for thinking I'd be pacing up and down the aisle, clothes-lining any stewards who dare to cross me, but I'm not. I remain in my seat, my posture reminiscent of a southern belle, because I am cool. I am uncharacteristically, ethereally, cucumber-like, baby.

Because I know, *I just know*, that something life-changing is about to happen to me. I know it like Juliana knew the only way to stop her sister, Renata, from using the Casket of Diurnacles to eradicate Portland of demons, and possibly humans, was to overpower her with a sword forged of the first huntress's armour then hold Renata beneath the surface in the Lake of Rogressa, which would reverse time so Viggo could conceal the Casket, therefore saving the world, but not their relationship. That was beyond strained, and we all knew it. Also, sorry for spoilers.

The curtain at the edge of the stage ripples, resulting in *very* loud shushing from all around me, including Roxy who sprays my face a little. Felix appears and Roxy grabs my hand as he walks over to the mic. Someone wearing the hotel uniform follows him, pushing the cauldron on a large trolley. Felix clears his throat.

"Good morning, fair Fallers. Please listen up, as there's a lot *at stake*. I'm drawing three names. Those people should come up to the stage to claim their position and receive further information about the competition." Whispers tear through the audience; we were all expecting more than three participants. "If I draw a name and they are not in this hall right now, they forfeit their position, and another name will be drawn. Stewards, please close the doors."

The audience turns to the back of the hall where four stewards nod at Felix then shut the doors one by one. One of them has a chain hanging around his neck, jangling it with every movement like he's a prison warden. The suggestion that we could be locked in here just adds to the tension, despite being wildly illegal in terms of fire evacuation procedures.

Everyone turns back to the stage. We're a flock of sparrows, I tell you. Conference Hall A is silent, which makes Felix's gulp down the mic even more audible.

"Dimitri, who works here at the hotel, has agreed to act as an independent witness. So, if he's ready?"

Felix looks at Dimitri who's staring at us all in the manner of someone who's just walked on stage in front of a bunch of desperate superfans: a little scared, a little bemused, and possibly a little stoned.

"I guess . . ." says Dimitri, shrugging.

Felix turns to us, his face serious.

"Let the Fall Games draw commence."

CHAPTER SIXTEEN

VIGGO RASSMUSSEN

Destiny is simply for those who have run out of luck.

Vampire Falls. Season four, episode nineteen –
"Make Me"

Have you ever been in a hotel conference room with approximately eight hundred people holding their breath? It's a surreal experience, especially compared to the usual cacophony of individual conversations and convention soundtrack.

I look at my hand. My fingertips have turned white where Roxy has squeezed the life out of them, but the pain is good because the rest of my body feels numb. I just need to sit perfectly still on my banquet chair that smells faintly of Jägermeister, remain calm, and all will be well. I know it.

Felix rolls up his sleeve like he's about to deliver a newborn calf, and leans over the cauldron. Some audience members can't contain themselves and there are a couple of actual yelps as Felix pulls out the first piece of parchment. He unfolds it, shows it to Dimitri, who shrugs (I know Felix needed someone independent but show a little razzmatazz, Dimitri) and goes back to his mic stand.

"The first name is . . ."

He looks up at us, his eyes scanning the chairs. Even from this distance, I can see a sparkle in his eye. He's already happy for whoever it is.

". . . Rashawn Thompson!"

We don't need to look round to find Rashawn, because everyone turns towards the eardrum bursting scream at the back of the hall. A guy with blond, shoulder-length dreadlocks jumps up and down, as people around him smile and clap (almost genuinely) for him.

"Come up and join us, Rashawn! Congratulations!"

He lets one last scream fill the air, then stops jumping around. He beams at everyone, smoothing down his *Hemoglovin'* T-shirt as he makes his way to the stage. A steward directs him to one of three chairs lined up at the side. The winners' chairs.

The next one is mine. *I just know it.*

Felix lifts his hand again, miming the sleeve-rolling action, and the audience goes quiet.

I close my eyes.

"And the next name from the cauldron . . ."

I think Roxy might have fractured my pinkie, but it's fine.

"is . . ."

I pledge my allegiance to you, Immortal Fortiana, and that of my future born, and theirs, and theirs, in perpetuity.

"Dimitri, can you just check that . . . thanks . . ."

I await your generous gifts. I am not an impatient person, Immortal Fortiana, but if Felix could hurry up and spit it out, that would be great.

"... the name is ..."

Manifestation secretes from my every orifice, Immortal Fortiana.

"Eliza Gellar!"

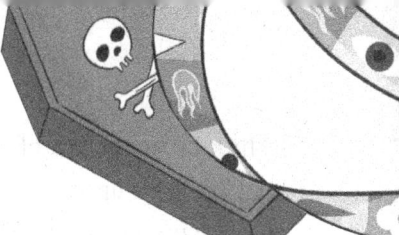

CHAPTER SEVENTEEN

JULIANA THE DEMON HUNTRESS

Whitlock Abrahams. I thought you were dead.

WHITLOCK ABRAHAMS

You did?

JULIANA THE DEMON HUNTRESS

*Accept my apologies. What I meant
to say was, I hoped you were dead.*

Vampire Falls. Season two, episode four –
"Return and Renew"

You know in those fantasy films where there's an explosion in the middle of a battle, and the main character goes kind of unconscious then wakes up with that whistling noise in his ear, then tunes back into the actual audio of the carnage going on around them?

Yeah, that's me right now.

I'm seated but with one arm waving around above my head, Roxy clutching my wrist. Whilst I'm apparently still processing what's just happened, she is standing on her chair shouting obscenities, euphorically, which is not something I've ever witnessed before.

Felix repeats my name, inviting me up to the stage.

I blink up at the sea of eyes looking at me, then oblige as Roxy pulls me up onto my jelly legs. She steers me to the end of our row, and I feel like I float towards the stage and up the steps where the steward meets me, hands me a big envelope, and shows me to the chair next to Rashawn.

Rashawn grins at me, holding up his hand which I manage to high-five.

"Can you *believe* this?" he says.

I shake my head. I mean, I knew it was going to happen, but I definitely feel like I'm hovering above my body right now. I'm no mathematician but I have a one in three chance of taking Roxy to Comic Con. Like, those odds are doable. I think?

"On to our third and final contestant. If I could have some quiet, please."

I take a deep breath, concentrating on the air filling my lungs, then feel it slowly leave my body as a I look out at the audience. I didn't realise how comfortable I'd be with a sea of eyes glaring back at me, but I'm totally fine with it. I've put the viewing hours in to be sat up here, I've spent a fortune on the merch (my mum still puts my *Vampire Falls* duvet cover on when I'm surfing the crimson wave), and I've trawled forums just to find out when Cox the Observer is making another appearance in the show.

Roxy is sitting straight up in her chair, nodding and clapping her hands together every time I look at her, like I've just done a trombone solo in the school talent show. Love that girl. I sweep the rest of the crowd and spot Fake McKinley, whose ears bob up and down as he nods at me.

I jump back in my seat a little when I make eye contact with Dorothy, who's holding up two knitting needles in her gnarled little fists like, quite frankly, weapons. Maybe she's the only person who wanted this more than I did.

"The third and final person to participate in the Fall Games, is . . ."

I lean back and cross my ankles together, smiling back at Roxy. I wonder what it is that—

"Vivian Erikksen!"

"WHAT THE INTERROBANGING FUCK?!"

Yeah. That was me.

Rashawn looks at me, shuffling as far to the other side of his chair as possible then sort of folds his whole body up. I swallow, then try a coy *was that me* giggle but even I know it comes out more deranged serial killer than cute pixie. I look out at Roxy for support and she's standing up, watching the third contestant sashay to the stage, high-fiving people like a pro wrestler.

My fingers dig into my seat as my heart races faster than a Lunar Dragon during a blood moon. Roxy catches my eye and shrugs. She knows that as deliriously happy as I am to be in with a chance of getting us to Comic Con, losing to Vivian Erriksen would be the worst thing on this particular plain of existence, therefore making life for those around me basically intolerable.

Vivian waves at the audience as she makes her way to the third and final seat, one hand on her hip and the other on the back of the chair.

"Thanks, bitches," she says to Felix and Dimitri.

"You are *welcome*," says Dimitri, looking at Vivian like she's a quarter pounder with cheese.

Vivian waves at the audience again, twirling her chair round then straddling it backwards.

I gape at her then look out at the audience. Roxy mimes turning a dial down, her signal for me to not lose my shit.

It's a little late for that.

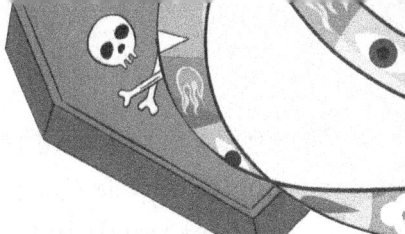

CHAPTER EIGHTEEN

LILA MURPHY

I'm not leaving my bedroom today.
Not after that. It's too embarrassing.

BUD LEROY

You can't hide in your room every time you make
an ass of yourself, Lila. You'll never leave the house.

Vampire Falls. Season one, episode six – "Did You See?"

My beef with Vivian isn't just because of the gold medal in gymnastics thing, or because she makes me feel like a hovel-dwelling goblin whenever I'm in her vicinity, or even because she calls everyone *bitches*. It's also because she's part of the reason I lost one of my best friends.

When Charlie Chamberlain left after our kiss, I spent most of the evening texting Roxy as she demanded every single detail. If she was worried our little group dynamic would change, she didn't show it but instead teased me with kissing GIFs and names for our firstborn. Because she didn't need to play it cool the next morning, her head whipped round at school looking for him, probably so she could make fun of him too, but we didn't see him that morning, not until English, just before lunch.

Roxy and I bustled into the classroom with seconds to spare, so Charlie Chamberlain was already sitting at his usual desk near the back. Once we were settled, Mrs Egleston explained about the literature project for that term, which we'd be working on with a partner. Roxy high-fived me, but then Mrs Egleston said she wanted boy-girl groups, and if we didn't choose our partners, she'd do it for us.

Everyone groaned but my heart fluttered wildly, especially when she started with the back row. Charlie was the third person she called on, and I hadn't made eye contact with him since we arrived, so I looked at him over my shoulder and smiled, waiting for him to say my name. He looked around the room, his eyes almost moving through me, like we were strangers, and then he picked his partner. He didn't say my name. I don't think I need to tell you whose name he said.

Roxy gasped and grabbed my hand, but I pulled away, trying to fold myself up as small as I felt. He ignored both of us for the rest of the week – like the kiss, our friendship, *Vampire Falls*, all of it, had never happened.

I'd never thought about the word heartbreak until that day. I've never been ashamed of my love for *Vampire Falls* but being passionate about anything other than contouring or chasing a leather sphere around made me an easy target, so I never trusted anybody. I let him into my favourite space, and he crushed it. He broke my heart, he broke me, and he broke us.

Now Vivian's here too, potentially about to break my ultimate dream. Roxy places a plastic cup in front of me and takes the envelope I've been clutching since the steward gave it to me. I pick up the cup and take a long sip, the cool liquid snapping me out of a delirious haze.

"What is this?" I ask.

"Iced latte." Roxy takes a sip from her own cup, then opens the envelope. "*Decaf.*"

Probably a good idea.

"Thank you," I say, slumping back into my wooden seat.

"You OK?" she says, looking up at me from the sheets of paper in her hand.

"Yes," I say, shaking my head. "I mean, I should be *ecstatic*, right? I *was* ecstatic for about thirty-eight seconds." I look round just as Vivian struts through the foyer, Charlie Chamberlain and Sadie at her side. She catches my eye and winks at me. I turn to Roxy. "Of all the people, Roxy. *All the people.*"

"I know, babe. She's . . ." Roxy tilts her head, watching Vivian walk towards the lifts, "intimidating."

Vivian bends over to adjust her trouser leg and Roxy's eyes kind of mist over. I clear my throat.

"Sorry." Roxy gives herself a shake. "It'll be *fine*. This isn't about looks or personality."

"Hey!" I say, crossing my arms.

"You know what I mean," she says, dismissing my shattered feelings with a wave of her hand.

"Like I haven't been through enough," I humph.

"This is about *Vampire Falls*, babe, and who wants the prize more. You are the biggest fan in this hotel." She frowns at the notes in her hand, nodding as she turns a page over. It has the *Vampire Falls* logo at the top, a table and lots of text. "It's all here but, shock horror, times are subject to change.

It's a quiz later, with points for first, second and third place, cosplay tonight with guest judges, and then a mystery heat tomorrow. We just need to strategise, and you'll nail it. I have zero doubt."

Her faith in me wipes the slate of that comment about looks and personality. A bit. I uncross my arms and lean forward, watching Vivian glide effortlessly through the hotel and life in general. I turn back to Roxy, who is watching me with an eyebrow raised.

"Please share," she says with a sigh, shuffling the paperwork together and sliding it back into the envelope. "What's wrong?"

"Did you see how she sat down on that chair on stage?" I say, rolling my eyes.

"I did."

"I mean, was it necessary? Who sits on chairs like that?"

"Sexy people," says Roxy, smiling a little.

"But why? Chairs are designed to be sat on in a specific way – *comme ci*," I say, with a flourish.

"I get scared when you think you can speak French, babe."

"Like she didn't have the attention of the entire hall already, she has to sit on a chair like that. Am I missing something?" I say. Roxy looks like she's preparing for sudden movements. "I'm trying it."

"Why," she says, more of a statement than a question.

"Get into the head of the enemy." I stand up and turn the chair round. "Maybe I've been missing out. Maybe I'll love it."

I force my leg over the chair, catching my boot on the seat, but I don't let that stop me.

"It doesn't really work if it's not . . . babe, stop. What's gotten *into* you this weekend?" Roxy stands and puts her hands up, looking over her shoulder. "You're wearing a skirt, Eliza. It doesn't work with that kind of chair. Nobody wants to see *that*."

I ignore Roxy and, though I absolutely hate saying this, I actually see the appeal. Apart from the underpants and tight gusset flashing, I'm extremely comfortable.

"I get it; the backrest is a like a front-rest for your arms. Not bad," I say, aware that I'm still exposing myself through the open back of the chair. "Maybe if I put my legs . . . through . . . this . . . bit."

I manage to get a foot through each section. I smile up at Roxy, triumphant.

"Happy?" says Roxy, shaking her head. I nod. I can tick sitting on a chair backwards off my bucket list. "Let's go then. I don't want to wait ages for autographs, and it starts in ten minutes."

"OK."

I go to get up, pressing my hands on the seat and the back of the chair, which is now the front of the chair.

"What's wrong?" asks Roxy, in the tone of someone who knows *exactly* what's wrong.

I swallow, and look up at her.

"I'm stuck, Roxy," I say. "I'm stuck in the chair."

CHAPTER NINETEEN

VIGGO RASSMUSSEN

*You must focus your gift, Lila. Concentrate
or it will consume you. (Lila hands him
a small piece of paper) What is this?*

LILA MURPHY

It's the receipt for my gift.

VIGGO RASSMUSSEN

*I can barely make out your terrible penmanship , but
it's a piece of paper with "screw you, Viggo" written on it.*

LILA MURPHY

Same thing.

Vampire Falls. Season five, episode two –
"Two Heads Are Better Than None"

Roxy closes her eyes for a few seconds. She's counting to ten.
She smooths her hair back then puts her hands on her hips.

"What did we say about sticking our body parts in small
spaces, babe?"

"Two times that's happened! Bringing it up now isn't
helping," I say.

Roxy tries pushing my legs, then blows her hair out of
her face.

"Try shuffling your arse back," she says.

"Don't say it like that," I say.

"Say what like what?"

"*Arse*. It sounds like you're thinking *fat* arse."

"Your arse is great," she says, rolling her eyes. "Just do it, please."

I frown and wiggle my *arse*, but the chair just rocks side to side. Roxy pushes on my knees, but nothing budges, and I've managed to sweat through my tights, increasing the friction between my legs and the chair. She moves behind me and tries pulling me up, but I'm a hundred per cent wedged.

"You OK?" asks the worst possible voice at the worst possible moment.

I reluctantly look up at Charlie Chamberlain, who's looking at me like he's watching a documentary about talking dogs. He and Vivian (why? *Why*, universe?) have joined the fun, coffees in hand. I try to casually cross my legs, but of course this is not possible, neither casually nor in any other manner, so I fold my arms instead, resting my cheek on my hand.

"Fine. You OK?" I ask, *casually*.

"Who did this to you?" says Charlie Chamberlain, smirking. "Wait. Haven't you got stuck in a chair before?"

"No, it was a pool triangle stuck round her neck and under her arm, remember?" clarifies Roxy. "Then a vending machine."

"I don't think anyone's interested in your catalogue of my mishaps, Roxy," I say, glaring at her.

Sadie steps up and puts a hand on my arm, surveying the situation.

"Are you OK?" she asks. I nod, and she leans in. "Do you

need to pee?"

I realise I *so* need to pee, and nod again, and she gives me a little cuddle around the chair. I look up at my audience, which now includes a few convention guests who are helpfully filming the situation for posterity. One of my butt cheeks has gone to sleep now. Thanks for abandoning me, left butt cheek. I'm glad someone can relax at a time like this.

"Have you tried rubbing butter all over her," giggles Vivian, "then giving her a good push until . . ."

She makes a popping sound with her perfect cupid's bow lips. Roxy looks at me, her eyebrow raised.

"What?" I ask, my stomach dropping.

"Worth a try? You're really wedged in."

"*What's* worth a try?"

Roxy swallows.

"The butter thing?" she says, looking to Vivian and Charlie Chamberlain for confirmation.

"Oooh, yes please," says Vivian, clapping her manicured hands together. "I'll go ask for some."

"Nobody is rubbing butter on me!"

Vivian's shoulders sag in mock disappointment but a wide smile is still on her face as she rejoins the taskforce. Charlie Chamberlain steps up and peers at me. Is this how those old Victorian sideshows felt? It's not great.

"Have you tried pulling her?" he says. Roxy folds her arms and raises an eyebrow. "Pushing her?"

"No, Charlie, I have not tried either of those straightforward methodologies. Thank goodness you're here."

"Are you . . ." We all look round at Fake McKinley who's

also joined the fun; he frowns at the group then looks at my legs, "stuck in there?"

"How'd you guess?" I say, rolling my eyes.

"Everyone's talking about it back there. And it's on TikTok."

I look at Roxy, who takes a deep breath and turns to everyone.

"OK, can anyone actually help?" A few murmurs from the group but people mostly shake their heads. "Piss off then. I'm pretty sure the Dax St. James photo session is about to start."

A few gasps then people turn and rush out the door, including Sadie and her supervisors. If you want to clear a room at a convention, tell people they're about to miss their photo op. Roxy looks at her phone, then frowns, biting her lip when she makes eye contact with me.

"I'm so sorry, babe, but I need to answer this," she says, backing away.

"*What?*" I blink at her. "Roxanne Fu, you are not leaving me alone like this?!"

"I'll be right back, I swear," she says, backing away. "And you're not alone, Fake McKinley's with you."

"*Roxy?*"

She holds up her finger and turns away, ducking her head as she answers the call and merges with the autograph crowd in the foyer. I blink at the lack of Roxy in this particularly classic Eliza fuck-up, then turn to my assigned guardian who looks down at me, his arms folded.

"So," he says, "this is unfortunate."

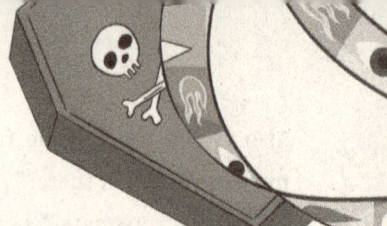

CHAPTER TWENTY

LILA MURPHY

But why the 'pessimistic' werewolf, though?

VIGGO RASSMUSSEN

Wouldn't you be? If you were a werewolf?

Vampire Falls. Season two, episode sixteen –
"Come Back Moon"

"That's a word for it."

"This stuff happens to you a lot, right?" he asks, sitting down, a book tucked under his arm.

"Only when Charlie Chamberlain is around to witness it, apparently."

"The hero guy?"

"Yeah," I sigh.

"Damon sure likes him." I frown at the casual address. Is it just me who full-names Damon Van Schwartz? "I mean, he's kind of looked after him this weekend, right? Since he did CPR or whatever."

I roll my eyes.

"Can we talk about something else?"

"You brought him up, but sure," he says.

"I didn't bring him up." Fake McKinley raises his eyebrows

at me, and I slump forwards on the chair. "Fine, I brought him up, but only because he and his red-headed sidekick are ruining my life, so I have him in my peripherals to anticipate his next move. It's bad enough that he swans around at school like he's the king of swans, or whatever, but now he's here swanning around. At my sanctuary."

"You really like all this that much?" he asks, running a finger around the neck of his costume.

"This?"

"The convention. The show?"

"I don't just like it, I love it. *Usually*." My soul normally swells with affection when I talk about *Vampire Falls*, but it just feels limp, like a deflated balloon, punctured by a sharp fingernail. "But yeah, it's my heart. You must get that?"

"I guess," he says.

"Sorry, this is obviously your first convention," I say, remembering he's new to the show. "Are you loving it?"

"It's a lot to take in. There are *so* many people and you're all, like, really, *really* big fans."

"Guilty. But that's kind of the idea."

"I know. I know, it's just..." he watches a couple of succubus (succubi?) squeal at their latest autographs over flat whites. "It's kind of intense."

"It can be, for a first-timer, but we were all newbies once. You just have to let yourself lean into it. There's no judgement here. This entire group, wherever they're from, whatever they're going through, is connected by a shared love. It's more than a fandom; it's a family. We look out for each other." I look at my watch. "Most of the time. I can't believe Roxy left me for a phone call."

"Maybe it was an emergency?" he offers.

"More of an emergency than *this*?" I say. He looks around, biting his lip as he watches everyone rush through the foyer. "You don't have to sit with me if you want to go."

"I'm fine," he says. "I think I've had my crowded room quota for the day."

He puts the paperback on the table and leans back. I pull the book towards me. I'd recognise the cover upside down and back to front, stuck in any type of household furniture.

"I love the *Lock Keeper* trilogy," I say, looking at the cracked cover. "I read it every summer. What do you think of it?"

"I'm actually enjoying it," he says, nodding. "The characterisation is excellent."

"Gloria Hannigan's the best," I say, running my finger over the scratched letters of her name. "She was actually a writer on the show for the first few seasons, but she's a full-time author now. She's Irish and moved back there from Hollywood."

"How do you know all this stuff?" he asks.

"I'm a *Vampire Falls* fan: I make it my business to know," I say, raising an eyebrow. He smiles at me. "I follow her on Instagram. She runs this writing fiction course once a year, and her best students get to do a residential at the Penrose Hackett Library in Ireland. It's where she got the inspiration for the Draíleabh Athenaeum in season two. It looks incredible."

"Sounds really cool, Eliza," he says.

He smiles tightly and clears his throat, then there's the tiniest moment of awkward silence across the table until I remember it's his birthday.

"Oh yeah. This is for you," I say, almost dislodging some thoracic vertebrae by reaching down for my backpack. I rummage inside. "Sorry, it's not my best work, but it's the law that you have to wear a crown on your birthday."

He takes the mostly crushed crown I made using manicure scissors, a hotel room notepad and a ton of gold sparkly eyeshadow (do NOT tell Roxy).

"Thank you," he says, nodding. "That's really sweet."

He smiles at me, but his eyes seem emptier than I've seen them before. His hands shake as he fiddles with the crown and there's a sheen across his forehead. He's either suffering from heat exhaustion, or there's something else going on.

"Are you OK? Do you need a drink of water or something?" He nods, and I go to stand and remember my predicament. "Oh, um . . ."

"Don't worry, it's fine."

"I can shout for them to bring one over?" I suggest. He shakes his head, his smile wavering and his eyes darting around the room. "Are you sure you're OK?"

He looks at me. Tears glisten in his brown eyes, and I blink at him, a huge lump forming in my own throat. If I knew him better and I wasn't currently trapped in a chair, I'd be wrapping him in a huge hug right now. He takes a deep breath, grimacing as if the air is peppered with broken glass.

"I've been kind of in the middle of . . . an anxiety attack for a couple hours now," he says, his vocal cords strangling his words so they come out tight and muddled. He shakes his head. "Reading sometimes helps but . . . I . . . I'm sorry, it's . . ."

He grimaces as the cappuccino machine hisses loudly.

"Hey, it's OK, let me . . ." I say, pushing myself back from the table. "Come with me; I know a place."

I take a deep breath, grab the underside of my chair with both hands, then pull myself up until I'm standing. Or semi-standing. Wearing a backwards chair. I shuffle from my spot, offering *sorrys* and *excuse mes* as I stumble through the coffee shop.

"Are you there?" I call over my shoulder. "Are you following me?"

"Um, yes."

I ignore the very strange looks as I amble across the foyer and down a long corridor. The convention noise starts to hush, and we reach a pop-up banner that reads *Press Pause*. We walk into a medium-sized room with roof lights and bifold doors letting actual outside light and air in. People slumped on beanbags do a little double-take at my chair situation but look back at their books or phones.

"Where are we?" whispers Fake McKinley.

"Chill-out area. For when convention life gets too much. Roxy has been here many, many times."

He nods and walks over to the doors that open onto the hotel grounds, and his chest fills with air. I give him a minute then follow him, careful not to trip on any beanbags.

"OK?" I ask, my back and thighs protesting against my weird body position.

"I think it's passing," he says, nodding. "Happens sometimes. Sorry."

"You're fine," I say, trying not to think how fucking weird

we look right now: someone with a chair stuck around their thighs talking to a headless werewolf. Anyway.

He takes a deep breath and puts his hand on his chest as he smiles weakly at me.

"Sorry," he says again, his skin pale.

"Don't apologise," I say. "We don't even need to talk. You're cool."

"Thank you." He runs a hand through his hair and tries a laugh, but it comes out empty. "I'm knackered now."

He slumps against the door, making it wobble ominously. He needs to get off his feet but all the seats are occupied and I'm not sure he'd get up from a beanbag. I look for somewhere else he can sit before he collapses.

Duh, Eliza.

"Sit down," I offer, turning away from him and sitting back on my chair.

"Huh?"

"There's room, isn't there?" I say, craning my neck. "My bum isn't that big. Despite what *some people* might imply."

He frowns at the chair like I'm tricking him into mounting a wild stallion. He raises his eyebrows at me.

"It's honestly fine," I say, shuffling forward a little. He lowers himself onto the seat so we're sitting back-to-back. I turn away so I'm not right in his face. "See?"

I feel his back muscles start to relax, and I think he's nodding. He doesn't say anything for a few beats, then he lets out a long sigh.

"It's actually kind of nice," he says, looking over his shoulder at me. "Weird, but nice."

"Maybe they'll put that on my gravestone," I say.

"They should," he says. We turn to look at each other, and I'm relieved to see the colour returning in his cheeks. "Thank you for this."

"Any time," I say, totally meaning the sentiment but maybe not the literal set-up.

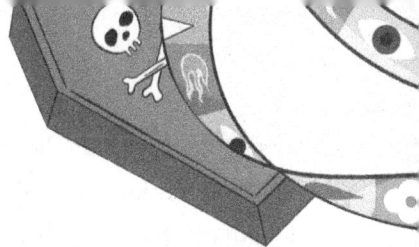

CHAPTER TWENTY-ONE

BUD LEROY

It'll be OK, Lila.

LILA MURPHY

Juliana is gone, McKinley is about to turn,
and Viggo still thinks he's being stalked by Illias.
In what way is any of that OK?

BUD LEROY

I said OK. I didn't say anyone's idea of a perfect situation.

Vampire Falls. Season four, episode seventeen –
"Alone On My Own"

I won't go into detail about how Roxy found me once Fake McKinley gathered himself, but if you guessed along the lines of me being wedged in the lift doors, you'd be on the right track. She helped me hobble from the lift to our room and, after applying layers of hair wax stick along my inner and outer thighs, Roxy managed to pull me free. If we weren't close before, it would have been an incredible bonding experience.

The first heat of the competition is about to start, and Roxy is nearly pulling my arm from the socket as we tear towards Conference Hall A. Despite my almost broken arm, I am thankful she is on top of this competition stuff because, frankly, I've been a little befuddled since I stepped foot in this place. Yes, befuddled.

We flash our badges at the stewards as we bundle through the doors and I run right into the back of someone flicking her hair over her shoulder, catching me in the face. It smells like a sea breeze rolling off crystal blue waves on a perfect summer's day, which is annoying.

"Better get your team up there." I blink at Vivian, who nods at the stage where they've set up tables for the *Vampire Falls* quiz. Three tables of *four*. "You've got your little team together, right?"

Shit. Team? I turn to Roxy who blinks at me.

"Yes," I respond, confidently, but it's all lies.

"OK then," Vivian says, backing away from us. "Just getting a lemon tea for my voice. Want everyone to hear all my correct answers. See you centre stage, bitches."

She sashays through the doors and Roxy grabs my arms and spins me round.

"Did you pick up the envelope earlier? In the coffee shop?" says Roxy.

"No," I say, my eyes widening.

"Shit, Eliza! I only glanced at it; I thought this was a solo quiz," she says, blinking wildly as she looks around. "Why didn't you pick it up?"

"I'm sorry, I was having a slight crisis at the time, Roxanne."

"I can't *literally* pick up after you wherever your trail of destruction leads, babe." She releases a puff of exasperation then rubs her forehead. "Whatever. We need to find you a team. Like, now."

Roxy and I look frantically around Conference Hall A but anyone who makes eye contact either laughs (because of the chair thing) or glares (because they're jealous I'm a contestant). Sadie sees us from the front row where she's sitting with her brother, because, you know, they have front row passes. She jumps up and scurries towards us, looking very cool in an oversized *Vampire Falls* hoodie, red leggings and leopard-print boots, her cheeks flushed with convention excitement. She throws her arms around my waist and squeezes me, and for a moment I forget about the quiz. I mean, I still have one eye on the clock, I'm not a total softie.

"Damon Van Schwartz gave me a signed cast photo!" she squeals.

"Did he?" I say, only partly envious and mostly thrilled for her.

"And he introduced us to all the other actors in the blue room."

"Green room," Charlie corrects her, as he joins us from his gold-plated front row throne.

I look at Charlie Chamberlain and shake my head. Correcting an eleven-year-old child? Is there no end to his reign of terror?

"You want to call it a blue room, you call it a blue room, Sadie. Don't listen to this charlatan," I say.

Roxy raises her eyebrows and nods at Charlie.

"So, I guess we're in competition then?" she says to him.

I frown at Roxy, not understanding what she means until I look back at them and Charlie Chamberlain averts his eyes.

Of course: they're on Vivian's team. Sadie's ponytail swings back and forth as her head swivels between me and Charlie. I wonder if her brother ever told her why Roxy and I suddenly stopped hanging at her house. After blanking me for over a week he actually called me a few times, but I didn't answer. One of his garbled apologies was cut off by Sadie's squeaky voice, and my heart cracked at that little soundbite from our old friendship, but I was too far gone to break completely.

Charlie shrugs and takes Sadie's hand, a defensive move if ever I saw one.

"Charlie? Sadie? Ready?"

We all look round as Vivian appears from the side of the stage with a porcelain cup and saucer in her hand. She puts them on the table then settles onto a (backwards) chair next to a slight, mousey-haired boy. I turn to Charlie Chamberlain who glances at me, blood rushing to his cheeks.

"She asked us earlier," offers Sadie, wringing her hands together, her eyes taking on Disney Princess roundness.

Roxy puts her arm round Sadie, not taking her eyes off Charlie Chamberlain.

"Don't worry, sweetie. It's cool." Roxy smiles at Sadie, whose shoulders relax in relief. Roxy leaves her side and walks past Charlie Chamberlain, the smile sliding from her face as she leans into him. "Just so you know, Charlie, *not* cool. You know what this means to Eliza. Not cool at all."

"Why not?" he replies, trying a nonchalant shrug which just comes off juddery and confrontational. "She should have asked me if she wanted me."

Roxy frowns at him.

"Wanted *us*," he says. "Wanted *us* to be in her team. Vivian asked first."

Blood rushes to my face as I watch the Disney villain taking selfies on stage, and before my brain can register what's happening, I've stomped up the steps to her table.

"Why are you even here, Vivian? Why did you enter the competition? You're not even a fan but you're getting the best of everything because you're here with Pride of Britain back there." I put my hands on the table, like Billy Big Balls in some Canary Wharf board meeting. "Go compete for you own dream prize at the Bitch Cheerleaders From Hell convention."

"Um," says mousey boy, swallowing and leaning back a little. "This is way too intense for me, Vivian."

"Oh, you signed up for intense when you joined her team, whoever you are, random cult member."

I hear someone clear their throat and I look round. Roxy is mouthing something, looking from me to the small boy on Vivian's team but I can't lipread because of the rage.

"What?" I hiss at her. "What are you saying?"

Roxy shakes her head, then Charlie Chamberlain pipes up.

"Roxy's trying to subtly tell you that he's not a random cult member, he's the guy whose helmet you barfed into the other night."

I gape at the small boy, wondering how drunk someone would have to be to think this person looks even *remotely* like Kit Connor. Then I realise I don't need to wonder, because *I was* that drunk.

"*Toby?*" I say, then look at Roxy. "*That's* Toby?"

"Yes, babe. That's your Kit Connor."

"Er, my name is actually Toby. I'm here with my mum."

We all turn to look at the woman Toby's pointing at in the middle row. She looks up from her paperback and waves. We wave back.

"Well," I say, bemused at the thought of wanting this fragile-looking person to take me home the other night. "Good for you, Toby."

"I'll take it from here, Toby. Don't worry about her."

"Yes, Vivian," he chirps.

Vivian stands up and, not in the least bit intimidated by my Alan Sugar bit, mirrors my position across the small table like she's Billy Bigger Balls, and looks right into my eyes.

"To answer your questions, I like to win, bitches, and I *will* win." I snort and push myself away from the table. "And one more thing."

"What?" I say.

"I *am* a fan," she says, folding her arms. "A big fan."

I hate to admit this, but I turn away and actually gulp. Roxy waves me back down as Charlie Chamberlain and Sadie slope past. Sadie looks up at me like a lost baby duck, so I give her the biggest smile I can manage before I reach Roxy.

"We have like two minutes," she says, grabbing my shoulders and shaking me. "We need to find someone. We need to find *two* people or it's game over."

"What's the point?"

"Do not *what's the point* me, babe. I know you can win this;

I know you can beat her. You know that too, right? Don't let her flame-coloured hair trick you into thinking you don't want this the most."

I look over my shoulder at Vivian, who's examining her nails, not a speck of self-doubt anywhere on her. I'm certain about two things in life. One is that The Stranger from season five, episode nineteen is actually Bud Leroy's future self, and the other is that I'm the biggest *Vampire Falls* fan in this hotel, possibly this country. I turn back to Roxy.

"OK, I'm back in the room. But I still need two teammates, like, now." I look around. I recognise a few faces from over the years, but nobody I know well enough to . . . "Hold on."

I stride down the aisle and stop at the end of row F, where two people have just sat down together.

"Dorothy, uh . . . Fake McKinley," I say. Dorothy peers at me through her thick glasses, and Fake McKinley turns, his snout slightly wonky on the end. He must be feeling better. "Would you do me the honour of joining my team?"

"What's that, Curly?" Dorothy says, holding her hand to her ear.

"Sorry?" A muffled voice comes from inside the mask before he removes it and wipes his forehead. "What did you say?"

I swallow, then look at Roxy who nods at me. They might not be the team I'd assemble if I had more time, but right now they're all I have. I look into Dorothy's crinkly eyes, full of confusion and possible medication-induced dilation, and Fake McKinley who still looks drained from earlier. I get down on my knee, placing my fist across my heart, then bow my head.

"*I come to you in this time of desperation. Please, say you'll fight with me and the Vampire Clan of Sanguis and we can enter this battle with honour and hope.*" I look up at them, crossing my fingers over my heart. "*Will you join me?*"

Dorothy blinks at me, her wrinkly face not registering Viggo Rassmussen's plea to Vermillion Vasquebois from the season five finale, and I try to pull myself up, my heart shattering that I won't even get a shot at the trip.

Suddenly, I feel a gentle hand on my shoulder and I look up.

"*It's been three hundred years, Vermillion, and I haven't left you to battle alone once. I won't start now.*" Dorothy nods, then tries to cross her arthritic fingers over her own heart. "But there's no way I'm getting up those steps, Curly. Not with my hip."

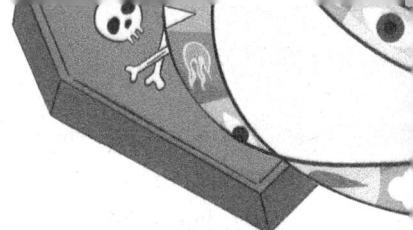

CHAPTER TWENTY-TWO

COX THE OBSERVER

You must search your soul, Lila Murphy.
The world's fate lies in your hands.

BUD LEROY

(whispers) Cox, dude. She doesn't do well under pressure.

Vampire Falls. Season six, episode ten – "Music, Maestro"

We're twenty-three minutes past the alleged start time of the quiz. If my literal happiness and life's fulfilment weren't hanging in the balance right now, I'd write a passive aggressive tweet about how not starting at the planned time is like breaking a promise – a *promise*, I tell you. My nerves are in shreds.

My Trip to San Diego Comic Con and Megan Nicole Jefferies. ROUND ONE.

I study the other two teams. Rashawn is wearing dungarees adorned with *Vampire Falls* and *other* TV show badges which means that his loyalty, and therefore knowledge, is divided and diluted across several fandoms. Good for me. His teammates are not wearing any *Vampire Falls* merch, but then neither is Roxy, and who's to say there isn't a tattoo of Owfain the Odious hidden beneath their clothing.

I'm more concerned about Vivian's team. If she's telling the truth and *is* a big fan, then her knowledge, along with Sadie's burgeoning superfan status and Charlie Chamberlain as a lapsed fan, will be a threat. I'm not sure about Toby's knowledge, although he has the pale hue of someone who spends a lot of time indoors.

"Welcome to the first and only Fall Games," says Felix, finally. "Just one person will win the prize of a lifetime, an all-expenses-paid trip for two to San Diego Comic Con as Megan Nicole Jefferies' personal guest."

I clear my throat and immediately feel Roxy's hand circle my sweaty fingers. I glance at her and she nods at me, her face stern and serene at the same time. She squeezes my hand and I try to absorb her energy up my arm. I lean forward and look at my other teammates.

Meh.

Dorothy has her knitting in her lap like she's waiting for a bus, and Fake McKinley, whose real name we should probably find out, looks like he's going to barf.

"Please welcome our quiz master, Dax St. James, onto the stage!"

Dax St. James saunters on, waving to the audience, his chest swelling with the knowledge that every person in that room loves Whitlock Abrahams, a favourite recuring character on the show and in our hearts. He steps up to the mic, feedback screeching from the speakers when he knocks the stand with his leg. He thrusts his arms out wide, almost getting Felix in the eye with the plastic bottle he's clutching.

"Hello, Manchester!"

Everyone laughs.

What a kidder he is, mixing up his cities.

"I said, hello, Manchester!"

Less laughter this time, but he launches into a hilarious story about his journey here. Roxy turns to me, her eyebrows high, and mouths, *he's drunk*. I nod, also noticing his slurring of *Manchester* and that he doesn't realise he's a little down south of there. In London. He takes a swig from the bottle he's holding.

The audience responds to his anecdote, politely laughing in all the right places. I focus on getting my head even further into the world of *Vampire Falls*, ready for the battle to commence.

"... and I was, like, that's not even my carry-on!"

"Let's begin, shall we?" says Felix, a stretched smile betraying his chit-chatty voice.

Even from over here, I can see Felix is worried that he's appointed a mildly drunk fan favourite as quiz master.

As long as he can read the questions, doesn't matter to me.

CHAPTER
TWENTY-THREE

JULIANA THE DEMON HUNTRESS

For Bydona's sake, Viggo, look at yourself!
You can barely stand.

VIGGO RASSMUSSEN

I have fought in worse conditions than this, Juliana.
Don't worry about me.

JULIANA THE DEMON HUNTRESS

I'm not worried about you. The smell of your singed
hair is going to give away our location.

Vampire Falls. Season one, episode six – "Did You See?"

So, Dax St. James is so drunk he can't read the questions properly. Also, one of my teammates, not mentioning any names (Dorothy), has fallen asleep.

"OK, hike up your underpants for question fourteen," Dax says, waving his arms and sending some of the question cards flying to the floor. I rub my face in my hands and take a cleansing breath. "How many times has Julian died?"

"Juliana!" hiss a handful of voices from the audience.

He nods and takes a swig from the never-ending bottle.

"Juliana. Yes: Ju-li-aaaa-NA," he says, his mouth so close

to the mic we can hear every breath between each syllable.

I remove my hands from my face and look out at the audience, where mostly empty seats stare straight back at me. This thing is taking twice as long as it should and all the corrections mean the normal tension and excitement of a quiz has evaporated.

Vivian finishes conferring with her team, then leans into the little mic on her table.

"Twice," she says, confidently.

"Twice is right, gorgeous," he says, the third pet name he's given her.

Vivian folds her arms, glaring as he looks her up and down. Felix goes to his side (again) and tries to pull the question cards from his hand (again) then whispers something when Dax doesn't let go (again).

"Next question, for the frizz queen." That's me, if you hadn't guessed. He stares at the card, closing one eye before he looks up again. "What is Lila's address? Where does she live?"

I lean into the mic, looking right at Vivian.

"It's 1406 Elmwood Drive."

"Correct, Team Frizz," he slurs.

Vivian looks back at me, gently clapping her hands and smiling but I turn away, resistant to her psychological manipulation.

"OK, Farm Boy next. How many humans does Viggo have to drain each week? Remember, it's one male and two female."

Rashawn groans and gently bangs his head against the table. I don't blame him; this is painful. Felix is at Dax's side again, and I can hear words like *contract* and *embarrassment*, but Dax just shoves Felix away and carries on.

"Sorry, my bad, dudes. Let's try another. The actor what . . . who played Viggo's father also appeared . . . played Eidolon." He looks up and shakes his head. "I did not know that."

Someone shouts *finish the question,* and he looks back at the card.

"So, what was the name of the episode. With Eidolon."

One of Rashawn's teammates leans over, pushing up her sleeve to reveal a House of Huntress tattoo. Told you. Rashawn nods and leans into the mic, frowning at Dax.

"The episode was 'Lies and Fruit Flies'."

"Correct-amundo," Dax says, nodding.

Felix is at his side as fast as a newly sired vampire. The audience goes into overdrive, people standing and shaking their heads as, quite obviously, the answer is incorrect-amundo.

"I'm sorry but that is the wrong answer," says Felix. "The correct answer is 'Age of Killing'."

Rashawn glares at Tattoo Girl who looks like she wants to climb up one of the curtains. That's their third wrong answer. Sucks for Rashawn.

Felix and Dax are now in a sort of tussle over the cards. Felix looks up at the audience, trying to pretend Dax isn't draping himself over his shoulders.

"That brings us to the end of the quiz, and we have a tie." He looks at me and Vivian. I glance at her and she's staring back at me, an eyebrow arched above a green cat-like eye. "Eliza, Vivian, would you mind joining us up here please."

"You can do this, babe," whispers Roxy, nodding at me. "Just keep calm. There isn't a question you can't answer, I swear."

I give her a little smile and walk to the middle of the stage with Vivian. I crane my neck to look into her eyes, otherwise I'm just staring at her chest. I look down; she's not even wearing heels.

"This is a quick-fire decider, so whoever correctly answers first wins, and will be awarded ten points towards the overall score. Rashawn has six points so whoever gets this wrong wins eight points. OK?"

"No," says Dax, rocking back and forth. He drops the now empty bottle and wipes his forehead. "I am very much not OK, dudes."

Understatement of the century, I think as I look at him. His skin looks grey, maybe even green, and he is incredibly sweaty.

"Go take a break then," says Felix, his smile tight.

"No, I must fulfil my ob . . . my ob . . ."

He stumbles around, grabbing at Felix's shoulder, Vivian watching him like he's an earthworm squirming on a scorching hot day. I turn and look over my shoulder at Roxy, whose expressions move through the following sequence: confusion, realisation, danger, horror, oh-my-god-Dax-St.-James-just-vomited-in-your-hair.

I freeze on the stage, the back of my neck prickling as I sense the mixture of bile and solids caught in my hair. I slowly turn around to find two horrified faces and one indifferent (pasty, sweaty) face staring back at me, just as the smell of Dax's guts hits my nostrils.

"I think I'm gonna barf," says Dax, wiping puke from his mouth.

He's so hammered, he doesn't realise he *has* just barfed.

A couple of stewards escort Dax off, leaving the three of us at the mic. Both Vivian and Felix now look at me like *I'm* a squirming earthworm on a scorching hot day, and, to be honest, it's totally warranted because that's how I feel right now.

"Do you want to go and . . ." Felix looks at my hair, his mouth pulling further downwards, "get cleaned up?"

I nod and turn away.

"So, I win then, right?"

I turn back to Vivian. What?

"*What?*"

"She forfeits the question, so I win the quiz," she says to Felix.

"He hasn't asked the question yet," I say.

Vivian pulls a folded-up piece of paper from her back pocket like she's the starter in a *Fast and Furious* movie. She waves it in front of my face: the competition rules.

"It says in here that if a contestant is incapable of continuing the competition, they forfeit." She looks me up and down. "I can't think of anyone more incapable looking right now."

"I just need to rinse my hair and then I can carry on," I say, looking at Felix.

He rubs the back of his neck. I swear he's ageing each time I see him. The convention game is not conducive to youthful skin.

"I'm afraid we don't have time." He looks over his shoulder

at a guy waving a clipboard around. "We started late and now everything is backed up. We're on a really tight schedule trying to fit all these extra elements in. I don't want anyone to miss out on autographs this year."

"Really?" I say.

He shrugs. "I'm sorry."

I know he's right. One year, I didn't get Josh Steele's autograph because things got heated between him and Logan Landon during a fight demo, and nobody was brave enough to step in (do you blame them? The size of those men, plus the rumour about Logan standing Josh's sister up. They obviously needed to process their issues, and on stage in front of a hall full of fans was the place to do it). Nobody got his autograph that year because he broke his pinkie.

Nobody at this convention is not getting what they want. Apart from Vivian. I take a deep breath, wincing as the smell of stale bourbon stabs at my nostrils, although it kind of makes me feel like a cowboy. Or even better, a cowgirl.

"Ask the final question," I say to Felix, my eyes on Vivian.

Yeehaw, *bitch*.

"What? No, she—"

"There's nothing in those rules about answering a tiebreaker with barf in your hair," I say, over Vivian. "Is there?"

She flips her hair over her shoulder and puts a hand on her hip.

"Fine," she says.

I smile and turn to look at my team, who all look back at me hopefully. Apart from Dorothy, whose eyes are closed, her head lolling back on her chair as a demon-like noise comes from her wide-open mouth.

Felix nods and quickly rearranges us so Vivian and I are facing each other, then he steps in front of the mic.

"OK. Quiet please." The tiny audience goes silent. "In season one, episode six, "Did You See?", what does Bud Leroy decide he wants to be when he's older?"

I blink at the floor, a thousand scenes clicking through my brain, my eyes darting back and forth as I take myself back to the maybe thirty-three times I've watched that episode, until there it is. Bud Leroy, cross-legged on Lila's bed, just after the opening credits, her head in his lap as they finish their Chinese food and talk about their future, and he tells her he wants to be a . . .

"Fortune-cookie writer!"

I scream the words out, just as Vivian shouts . . .

"Horticulture therapist."

The audience gasps, and we both look round at Felix, who looks between us until his eyes settle on me, filled with sorrow.

"The correct answer is horticulture therapist."

Vivian turns to her teammates and gives them a wink, which is somehow worse than if she was jumping around in my face. I feel like my knees are about to buckle as I stare at Felix, shaking my head.

"No . . . I . . ."

I gave the right answer, I *know* I did. But then I look at Roxy, who's looking back at me with such a pained expression, I know I must be wrong. Which means that Vivian is right.

And then I realise; I didn't think far enough into the episode. I answered too fast.

My brain fast-forwards through the rest of the episode, past the flesh-eating Cranzig Serpent and the Vampire Triplets, to the final scene where Bud reveals to Lila that he'd rather be a horticulture therapist, because after Dorian at the underground bookstore betrayed them, he trusted plants more than he trusted people, and then he says . . .

"*That's my official choice, Lila,*" I murmur, my insides crumbling, "*I'm done with the fortune cookie-writing game.*"

I could argue it. I could say it's a trick question because he says both things in the episode, so technically both answers are correct. Maybe. Would it stand up in a court of law, because Bud makes his decision clear at the end of the episode (and then starts plumping the leaves of Lila's spider plant)? In my nerd heart, I know it wouldn't. I can tell from Felix's sorry, puppy-dog eyes that his team of researchers checked and double-checked the answer against the script, because he knows exactly who he's dealing with. Superfans. Or at least, I thought I was.

If I can't get that right, then the who the hell am I?

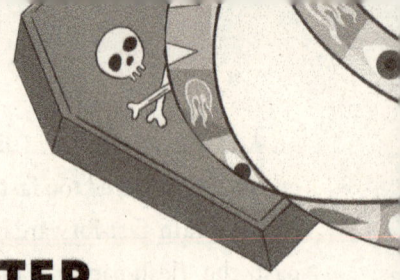

CHAPTER TWENTY-FOUR

ORION FENIMORE

What part of be quiet do you not understand?

LILA MURPHY

The part where you're telling me to be quiet.

Vampire Falls. Season one, episode nine –
"Not On Our Watch"

"Everyone's looking at me."

"Nobody's looking at you, babe," says Roxy. "They're looking at the Kaltenbrande demon and the dude with the claw marks across his cheek. How is the blood spurting like that?"

Do not be alarmed. There has not been a demon massacre at the hotel. We're looking round the special effects demos in one of the breakout rooms. You can have an actual artist from the show make you up to look like a vampire, demon or zombie – whatever's your poison. Guess who had a reaction to the glue last year and had to take an antihistamine then lay down with a flannel over her face for the entire last day? What was under the flannel looked way worse than the Verrucrust demon prosthetics, believe me.

"And me, because I'm a big fake fan loser person," I grumble.

Roxy ignores me and takes a photo of a zombie doing the peace sign. After the quiz, I raced up to our room to pack my bags and flee my failure, only to discover Roxy had anticipated this move and confiscated my key card. So here I am instead, dragging my hopeless, hollow shell around, a fraud among my peers. At least I've been able to shower.

"You're not a loser, and you still get points for second place, remember?" says Roxy, putting the envelope in her backpack. We retrieved it from the coffee shop, where they referred to me as Chair Girl. "Reception said we can use one of the empty conference rooms so you can practise for the next part of the competition. You can do your usual routine, but you should still go through it."

"What's the point? Big fake loser people don't win cosplay competitions."

"They don't if they don't practise." I pause and raise my eyebrows at her. Roxy rolls her eyes. "And you're not a loser. You're amazing, blah blah, I already said that."

"Charming," I grumble, shuffling along.

We watch a make-up artist pull a werewolf mask over the head of a woman who is absolutely thrilled at the prospect of seeing through the eyes of a lycanthrope. Roxy looks at me.

"Have you seen Fake McKinley since you snapped at him at the quiz?"

"I didn't *snap*." Roxy raises an eyebrow, and I sigh. "Fine. But he didn't answer a single question."

"Excuse me, but you hissed at him every time he tried to contribute," she says, then sticks out her bottom lip. "His poor, handsome, chiselled face was so sad, Eliza – so, so sad."

"Don't," I say, feeling bad for snapping. Roxy's used to it, but Fake McKinley isn't. "I should probably make sure he's OK."

"You should probably apologise to Toby as well then. I think he thought you were possessed."

"Toby will be OK; he has his mum and he's not on my team, anyway," I say, shrugging. "Fake McKinley is all alone, Roxy. He has nobody else here, but more importantly he's . . ."

I do a chef's kiss and Roxy nods in agreement.

". . . so *symmetrical*," I say, still moved by the symmetry. "His face is just *perfection*."

"Resurrecting your DVS fan club, are you?"

My stomach plummets right into the toes of my Docs as Charlie Chamberlain saunters up to us. Where did he come from? Does he hover in the shadows, like Death?

"Actually, we never closed it, for your information," I say, pleased with myself.

"She's talking about her new boyfriend," says Roxy, slinging an arm around me.

"Haha," I say.

"You have a boyfriend?" asks Vivian as she joins us, then she frowns at Charlie Chamberlain. "Ew. Why are you doing an annoying throat-clearing thing? It's gross."

"I'm not," he says, clearing his throat.

"Are we talking about that guy in the werewolf costume?" asks Vivian, her eyebrow arching. Roxy nods. "My, my.

He is quite the hottie, bitches."

"He's not my boyfriend," I clarify. "He's just a guy."

I catch Charlie Chamberlain's eye and he blinks triple time then looks away quickly.

"WHERE IS IT?!"

Surprised, I fall into Roxy, my hands up ready to fight the angry, if quite small, vampire who has just leapt from a stool on the other side of the room and headed straight for my jugular. At least, I think that's what's happening.

"Where's what?" I manage, looking around in case I'm part of a flash mob or something.

"The last chapter!" says the vampire, her voice desperate and menacing, and also kind of like . . .

"Sadie?" I say, frowning. "Is that you?"

"Duh."

Vampire Sadie folds her arms and taps a foot, her pre-tween stance in contrast with the pointy fangs and wrinkly forehead. She doesn't take her blood-red eyes from me as she shrugs her brother's hand from her shoulder.

"She's in a mood," he says.

"I'm not in a *mood*," she snaps, then waves her phone in his face. "I just have to know what happens. I *need* to know."

We take a step back in case her head starts spinning; we've never witnessed her rage before.

"Happens with what, Sadie?" says Roxy.

"In *Never Leave*," she turns to me, her vampire eyes wide, "does Viggo get to Orion in time? Does Lila lose her connection to the ghost of Desvoria? *What happens?*"

Roxy looks round at me, but I can't take my eyes off

Sadie who just said a bunch of words that wouldn't mean anything to anyone who hasn't read that particular *Vampire Falls* fan fiction. Or anyone who didn't write it.

"You're reading *Never Leave*?" I ask.

"Uh-huh, but no, because I can't see the final chapter," she says, waving her phone again.

It's been so long since I even thought about *Never Leave* that I forgot it was still out there.

"How did you find it?" I say.

"Charlie showed it to me," says Sadie.

I look at Charlie, who shrugs immediately and frowns.

"I didn't *show* it to her. I mean, I just explained what fan fiction is and she found it."

"No, you said you'd show me something cool," says Vampire Sadie, shaking her head, "and you found it on Wattpad and then we read the first three chapters together on your iPad, Charlie."

"Oh, *did you*, Charlie?" says Roxy.

Charlie Chamberlain clears his throat and looks everywhere apart from directly at me.

"I'm reading it too," says Vivian.

"What?" I say, gaping at her, my entire ecosystem turning on its head.

"It's really good," she says, raising an eyebrow. "When's the final part going up?"

"It's not," I say, folding my arms.

Sadie steps forward and looks up at me, her red eyes burning into my soul.

"Why not?" she gasps.

"I . . . I just stopped writing it," I say, wondering if I should beg for my life.

"Why?"

Damn these children and their incessant questioning.

"Because . . . I just did," I said.

"When?" demands Sadie.

I swallow, desperately trying not to look at Charlie Chamberlain.

"About a year ago, I guess."

"But *why*?" implores the tiny vampire.

Why indeed, Sadie, I think as my eyes flick to Charlie Chamberlain of their own accord, much like my memory has a tendency to do.

CHAPTER TWENTY-FIVE

LILA MURPHY

What are you thinking? What are you thinking right now?

ORION FENIMORE

I don't want you to go.

LILA MURPHY

So don't let me go

Vampire Falls. Season five, episode three – "Finally Here".

Not only did I introduce Charlie Chamberlain to *Vampire Falls*, I also pointed him down the fan fiction rabbit hole. I showed him some of my favourites then he found his own, which generally featured Lila and Juliana in various *let's-get-out-of-these-wet-clothes* type scenarios. Anyway.

It was probably over a year of us being friends before I showed him any of my own fan fiction. I'd been writing it since I first watched the show, so the early stuff was *bad*, especially when I insisted Roxy take turns writing it with me. Those chapters came across in an unintentional Jekyll and Hyde style, then Roxy retired from the fan fiction co-authoring game. But I continued to hone my craft.

My favourite (and my seventy-eight WattPad followers'

favourite) was a story where Orion's mentor, who has fallen in with a dark magic crowd, uses him as a trade for some necromancy sorcery. Orion is pulled into another dimension and the rest of the gang don't know where he is. This all happens while Vistoria Falls is under threat from a deadly race of witches called Death Witches (I know), Lila finds out she's actually related to Viggo, and whenever Bud Leroy drank a pumpkin-spiced latte, he was able to teleport. It was quite the page-turner.

As it turned out, Charlie Chamberlain was also a fan.

My sixteenth birthday was the day my feelings went from *I-think-maybe* to *oh-my-god-definitely*. I was looking for my school tie when the doorbell went. Assuming it would be adult business and because I was, of course, queen for the day, I carried on tearing my room apart until Mum shouted up the stairs.

"Eliza! Charlie Chamberlain is here."

I froze, mid-laundry-basket-emptying. Sometimes he and Roxy would call for me on the way to the bus but we'd usually text first, so I was surprised.

"Kaaaaay!" I yelled back.

I checked my hair in the mirror then as casually as I could (which was tough because the very mention of his name sent my adrenaline spiking at that point) trotted down the stairs and found him in the conservatory.

"Hey," I said. Casually.

He looked round at me and stood up like I'd just called him in for a job interview. He was tall then but hadn't filled out, so he seemed generally awkward in whatever space he was in.

"Happy hello day . . . happy birthday, I mean," he said, a gift bag dangling from his hand clunking him in the chest when he waved at me. "Hello."

"Thanks," I said, peering at him when he cleared his throat. "You OK, Chamberlain?"

"What?" he said, his eyes darting around the conservatory, then finally resting on me. He shook his head then let out a long breath. "Yes, all good. OK."

Rain pitter-pattered on the glass (it always rains on my birthday. My dad says the rain clouds match my soul. Love you, Dad) and Charlie Chamberlain watched the water trickle down the glass. He stared at it for a minute or so, until it was my turn to clear my throat. He blinked, the spell cast by the rain broken suddenly. Even though we weren't standing close, the energy was there between us, but it felt unsteady, like it hadn't worked out what kind of force it wanted to be yet.

"Is that for me?" I said, pointing at the bag.

He looked at me, his brown eyes wide, then ran a hand through his thick hair, leaving it standing up in adorable, haphazard tufts.

"It's silly," he said, the tops of his ears pink. "Childish."

"My two favourite things. Gimme."

I sat on the sofa, yanking his blazer sleeve in a shameless excuse to touch him. He flopped down next to me, and I could feel the tension coming off him in waves. I closed my eyes and held my hands out, his sweet, fresh scent teasing my senses as I felt the bag dumped in my palms. I opened my eyes to find him inched as far from me as possible.

"You're being so weird today," I said, reaching inside and pulling out a square scrap book.

Two lone letters were scrawled across the front in the same font as the *Vampire Falls* graphics.

F.F.

Faller Forever

I traced the letters with my finger and glanced at him. He looked like he was about to have a stroke.

"Cool," I said, opening the scrap book, my heart stopping when I saw the first page. "Oh my god."

It was a drawing of Juliana the Demon Huntress, but not like I'd seen her before. It was still *so her* that I immediately recognised who she was, a sword over her head, mid-swing, drawn with such detail that the image almost looked like it was moving across the page. Her outline was done in delicate black lines, and her colours were bold and smudged out of the lines, giving her movement. Her eyes burned with fury, and strength sung out of every shaded muscle. It seemed such a familiar scene, but I couldn't place it from the series.

I looked at him again and his eyes quickly moved from my face to the page.

"This is *so* good. Did you *do* this?" I asked. He nodded, squirming next to me. "Oh my god, Charlie."

I stared at him, stunned by his hidden talent and his adorable embarrassment about it, then looked back down at the page. There was something written on a piece of paper pasted beneath the image, and I frowned as I read it, recognising his writing.

My breath caught in my throat.

"Oh my god, Charlie. I . . ." I tried, shaking my head as I flicked from the words to the detail of the image.

"I got it from Wattpad – it's from . . ."

"*Never Leave*," I said, blinking tears away so I could absorb every detail.

"Is that cool? I mean, when I read it, I saw it in my head, and I just wanted you to see what a good writer you are." He rubbed the back of his hair, oblivious to how every move he made and every word he said was pulling me further into him. "How talented you are."

"How talented *I* am? You're insane," I said, turning the page and gasping at the absolute joy of his next drawing. "Oh my god – Jawfain! Look at him with Viggo!"

"That's Sadie's favourite. She helped me with the cutting and sticking," he said, trying to shrug the attention away from himself.

"Charlie," I whispered, swallowing a lump as I ran a finger over Viggo's blue eyes, blown away by how Charlie had captured the exact hue and sparkle.

"You like it?"

I nodded, reading my words under the drawing of Viggo in his rocking chair with Jawfain perched on his shoulder.

"It's . . . it's amazing," I said, shaking my head.

We'd got closer as I turned each page, our legs and arms touching. For weeks after, I replayed us sitting together, the rain tapping gently, his thigh against mine and the tiny sparks it generated. I remember the sensation of his body next to mine like it's happening right now.

"All you," he said. "Your words."

I looked round at him, not afraid to let him see how emotional his gift had made me.

"This is . . . thank you. It's you though, not me. You've brought it to life." I stared at him. "Charlie this is the most—"

"Time to go, Eliza!" called Mum, with impeccable timing. We looked up and I don't think he could have looked as disappointed as I felt, but it was close. "You're going to miss the bus!"

"Kaaaay!" I called.

The moment I got home that day, I ran upstairs and spent a good hour looking at that scrapbook, gently turning the pages and tracing my finger over the lines and colours he'd drawn for me. It was the most incredible present anyone had ever given me. After that, I'd often find folded bits of paper tucked in my bag or coat pocket. I'd unfold them, my heart racing, as I was presented with the latest of Charlie Chamberlain's drawings to go along with *Never Leave*.

Until one day, that day, it just stopped.

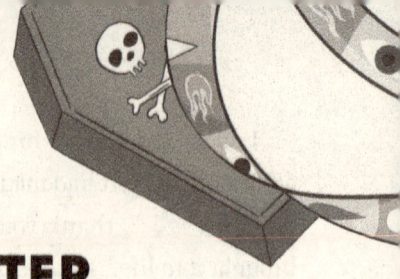

CHAPTER
TWENTY-SIX

JULIANA THE DEMON HUNTRESS

The urge to throw my favourite knife at you is overwhelming.
When I return, I suggest you are gone.

VIGGO RASSMUSSEN

(to Bud Leroy) She desires me still.

BUD LEROY

Vampires. Got to love your confidence.

Vampire Falls. Season two, episode five – "Shadows Behind"

We left Sadie getting re-glued after she resorted to tears to manipulate me into writing the final chapter of *Never Leave* just for her. Honestly, it nearly worked, but the thought of revisiting that time of my life gives my soul period pains.

A steward ushers us through the door to the photographs. I crane my neck, looking past the giant silver umbrella, and see Orlando Wilde. Despite his character now being an eternal reminder of my total failure as a fan, he's a steady presence on the show and at conventions, full of heart and always has an open smile. The fandom was devastated when Bud Leroy died in season five (possessed by a Dominion Hellion), and we screamed with joy when they resurrected him in season six.

I pause for a moment, basking in the queuey goodness, and breathe in the stale, conditioned air: its familiarity cleanses my soul of Charlie Chamberlain. We hurry to the end of the queue that's zigzagging its way back and forth across the large room like we're in airport security, but instead of jetting off on holiday I'm jetting off into the bosom of my fellow fans also queueing for photo ops.

Toby bounces past us from the front, smiling ear to ear.

"Hey, Toby," says Roxy.

"Hey! I just had my first photo," he says, beaming at Roxy. "Orlando Wilde said he dug my sneakers."

"Good for you, Toby," I say.

His smile falters as he looks at me, then heads to the door, passing others filing into the room. Someone else joins the end of the queue, and trying to get Toby to forgive me for barfing in his helmet becomes the least of my problems.

I sigh but force myself to wave at Sadie, who is still in vampire mode, making sure to direct my wave at her, and only her. Roxy puts her hands on my shoulders.

"Just ignore, babe," she whispers. "Let's focus on the queueing. You know about queuing; you're good at queuing."

Not when Charlie Chamberlain is trying to ruin this core convention experience for me, as well as everything else. I'm literally seeing him and Vivian at every turn.

"Move ALONG please," bellows a steward wearing cat-eye glasses, right in my ear. I glare at her and trundle forwards.

"Hey, one of the guys on my course told me that her cousin went to Bristol," says Roxy, looking around the room.

"How interesting, Roxy, and what's that got to do with

anything?" I say, my entire body tensing at the mention of Bristol, aka our future.

"Well, if you let me finish, Snappy McSnapface, it's relevant because on your first day you have to queue up in this massive common room and they make you buy all these, like, *Wi-Fi permits* and *compulsory licences*, but it's all fake and they're shaking you down for charity." She frowns at me. "Why are you being shitty whenever I mention Bristol?"

"Moi?" I blurt.

"OK, why are you being shitty *and* French?"

"I'm not. I'm just . . ." I say, swallowing a dry lump, "concentrating on the queue."

"Fine. I hope we're both in Wills Hall," she says, her eyes sparkling. "Did you see the photo I sent you? The Old Quad covered in snow?"

I shake my head, irritated that Roxy's bringing up Bristol when I should be basking in the anticipation of standing side by side with my favourite actors for a good three seconds each. We shuffle forward in the long queue that snakes back and forth, and the line we're next to moves in the opposite direction, bringing my rivals closer. I risk a look at them, just as Charlie Chamberlain reaches over his shoulders and pulls his hoodie off. I grab Roxy's arm and point. My throat has clammed up for unknown reasons.

"Did Charlie Chamberlain get vampire abs prosthetics done?" I say.

Roxy forgets about the snow-covered bollocks and sucks in a breath.

"Shit the bed!" she says, her eyebrows flying up. "Look at

those v-lines!"

I am somehow unable to *stop* looking at the v-lines, or the quite substantial section of torso Charlie Chamberlain has unknowingly revealed to a room full of Fallers. He quickly pulls his T-shirt down, his cheeks pink when he looks up to see if anyone's noticed.

Not me, I did *not* notice that. And anyway, rock hard abs do not maketh the man.

"That boy's been working out," says Roxy, doing that weird finger flick thing. "Gainz."

"What does that mean?" I ask.

"Gainz with a zed. It's gym-speak, bro."

"Is that what it is? He puts that on Insta, but I just thought he couldn't spell."

"You still follow his Insta?" asks Roxy, raising her eyebrow.

"No," I say, not sure why I lied and making a mental note to unfollow him.

The queue moves again until we're face to face with the King of Gainz himself. I realise with horror that Orlando Wilde has requested a toilet break, so we'll have to wait in this unpleasant arrangement for a bit longer. The steward escorts him out, and I try to work out if he needs a number one or number two from the way he's walking. Orlando Wilde, I mean, not the steward. I can't speculate about his bowel movements right now.

"Hi, Eliza," says Sadie, her vampire fangs skimming her wide smile.

"Hi, Sadie," I say, relieved she seems to be over the *Never Leave* drama. "Orlando's going to love your make-up."

"Do you think?" she says, touching her vampire features. "I'm singing 'Silence if it's Ending' at the karaoke party. The one Bud and Lila sing. I'm singing it with Charlie."

"That's cool, Sadie," says Roxy. "We can't wait to hear Charlie sing."

Charlie rolls his eyes and Vivian flips her hair over her shoulder (she does that a lot, right? Pick a side of your shoulders and just commit to it) and smiles at me. But not a nice smile. A viper smile, like if they had perfect, Invisalign teeth.

"So . . ." she starts, "the quiz was an eye-opener, don't we think?"

Roxy stands firm next to me and jumps in before I can respond.

"The question was unfair, Vivian. Not cool. Half the audience thought so."

"But the other half didn't, Roxanne."

Vivian looks at me, her insanely long eyelashes almost hypnotising me into agreeing with her.

"It wasn't a straightforward question," I say, immune to those eyelashes.

"Well, I thought it was. But we already knew that because I got it right," she says, raising her eyebrows. "Anyone who's watched the show properly would know the answer."

"I have watched the show properly, thank you," I say through clenched teeth.

Vivian smirks and glances at Charlie Chamberlain who is looking right at me, his arms folded and shaking his head.

"What?" I say, although I do prefer him quiet. "You can't tell me you thought that question was fair?"

"Would you even listen if I did?" he says.

"Not if you're not on my side," I say, putting my hands on my hips.

"Exactly," he says, shaking his head.

"What does *that* mean?" I say, incredulous.

He opens his mouth to answer just as Orlando Wilde returns, and the queue moves again. Charlie Chamberlain and co head off, but he looks over his shoulder then turns away and shakes his head.

"Why is *he* shaking his head?" I say, shaking my own head because if anyone should be shaking heads around here, it's me. "What does *that* mean?"

"I'm sure he just—" starts Roxy.

"Can you please move your girlfriend along," says Cat-eye Glasses, fixing Roxy with a look.

"She's not my girlfriend, but OK," Roxy says, nodding.

"No, doesn't quite work, does it? You," says the steward, nodding at Roxy. She looks down her nose at me, starting with my messy ponytail right down to my scuffed DMs, "and her."

Roxy checks whether I heard what Cat-eye Glasses said. Oh, I heard. I heard that loud and clear, my friend.

"What does THAT mean?" I gasp.

OK, I might be more sensitive than usual right now, but she has to know that hurt, right? The steward scurries off towards a gap of more than 50 cm and I turn to Roxy, too deflated to speak.

"I know, babe, she's just drunk on power," she says, giving me a consolatory smile. "I'd be lucky to have you."

"Well. *I* think so. I'm adorable." Roxy raises her eyebrows. "I mean, I *can* be adorable."

"If you say so," Roxy says, patting my cheek as the queue starts moving again.

We stop again and I don't even need to look round. I can sense them in the queue next to us, feeding on my misery.

"Oh, hi again. We're in a little pattern," says Vivian, clapping her hands. "This is hilarious."

"Is it?" I say. I look at Charlie Chamberlain, who's fiddling with the strap of his watch. "What did you mean by that?"

"I literally said nothing?" he says, blinking at me, the picture of innocence.

"Before, about the quiz you said, *would you even listen if I did?* What did you mean?"

"It doesn't matter," he says, doing a sort of one-shouldered shrug, like I'm not even worth both of his broad, stupid shoulders.

"No, tell me," I say.

I put my hands on my hips and look up at him until he finally rolls his eyes.

"I just meant that sometimes you're so intent on making your mind up about someone that you've already decided what they think before you've given them a chance."

I blink at him, then look up at Roxy who's grimacing. I can't tell if it's an *outraged* grimace or a *what-he-said* grimace.

"No, I don't," I say, my nostrils flaring.

"Yes, you do. You've decided what my answer is, so you won't listen properly when I actually tell you. It's what you always do when you think you're being confronted."

"No, I don't," I try again.

I don't, guys. I really don't. Charlie Chamberlain can't give an accurate assessment of my character, not any more.

"Tension much?"

Vivian looks from me to Charlie to her vamp nail polish. My cheeks feel like they're melting off, leaving two hollow craters in my face, then I feel a gentle hand around mine. I look down at Sadie, who's looking up at me with almost heart-shaped eyes. It's quite the contrast with the blood-red contacts.

"I didn't think it was a fair question, Eliza," she says, squeezing my fingers.

"Thanks, Sadie," I say, squeezing hers back.

"Are you going to ask what I think?" says Charlie Chamberlain.

"About what?" I ask.

"About the quiz," he says, his cheeks turning red.

"I don't care what you think," I say.

Charlie Chamberlain scans my face. I don't think we've held eye contact for this long in over a year and my mouth goes dry as he blinks at me.

"Forty-two," he says, his voice soft.

"What?" I say, frowning at him.

"Forty-two," he repeats. "Or forty-three now. That's the most words you've said to me in a year."

I swallow a dry lump, and open my mouth to say something, anything, but my lip is wobbling.

"Move ALONG," shouts the Cat-eye Glasses.

I've never been so grateful for an unnecessarily loud instruction. I look straight ahead and move forward, not giving Charlie a single glance, even though I can feel his stupid long-lashed eyes boring into the side of my face.

"You OK?" Roxy asks, standing behind me. "That was full on, even for you two."

I nod, and she puts an arm across my chest. Raspberry and apple blossom wafts over my face and I feel safe nestled in front of her, even though I can hear Vivian and Charlie laughing together about something. Probably me.

"You two are cute as hell together," says a voice.

We both look round, and I'm thrilled to see my favourite pensioner. Going by her bright red lipstick and the matching kiss mark on his cheek, Dorothy's just had her photo with Orlando Wilde.

"Thanks, Dorothy," Roxy says, squeezing me. "We're not together though; she's way out of my league."

Dorothy takes her glasses off and points a gnarled finger at us.

"Nobody's out of your league, girls. Nobody. You understand?"

"We understand, Dorothy," I say.

Dorothy nods and shuffles towards the door, calling over her shoulder as we watch her go.

"I would never have shagged William Shatner if I thought that way."

A few people do a double take, processing what they've just heard, but I'm starting to tune into Dorothy's vibe. Roxy loosens her arm and I look round at her.

"What does that mean?" Roxy says, shaking her head and smiling.

"Right?"

I smile back at her, and my soul settles back into the queue as we get closer to Orlando Wilde, back into the convention, back into being among these fans with the person I'm the biggest fan of. But there's something stopping me from slipping fully into it, like I can't click back into place because there's a jagged Charlie Chamberlain-shaped splinter sticking out of my soul.

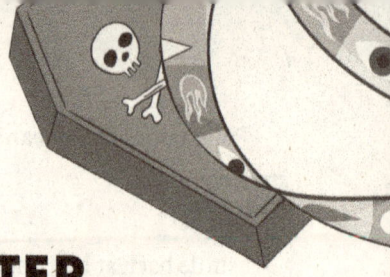

CHAPTER TWENTY-SEVEN

THE KINNUIX (DESTINY DEMON)

Come, my babies. Let us see what
mischief we can spin after nightfall.

Vampire Falls. Season three, episode six –
"This Is What We Become"

Ordinarily, cosplay competition night is my favourite night of the convention weekend. The buzz around the hotel is infectious. People race around with those brass hotel trolleys (which, fyi, are incredibly difficult to steer when you and your very drunk bestie try to ride one back to your room), wigs and weapons akimbo, and a chorus of doors slamming as people race from room to room getting their mates to zip them up or sew them in. I love it.

I *usually* love it. I don't love it today, because today my life literally depends on the success of my costume. I know I'm misusing the word literally there, but you get me. There have been years where I've not bothered entering, kind of feeling like the whole competition element takes the fun out of it. The fun is in the making of the costume, in thinking how the character thinks.

But my favourite part is the unmistakable way people approach you, their phone in hand, hoping you'll pose for a selfie. Disclaimer, folks: I love cosplaying as Juliana so much that I'm always happy to show off my costume in a photo. That and getting asked for selfies kind of makes me feel like I'm Sarah Michelle Gellar or Lucy Lawless. Say it with me: LEGENDS.

Anyway, I digress. I am not feeling the love for it right now. Right now, I feel bile at the back of my throat, because we're not just talking cosplay here. We're not even talking cosplay competition.

"It's cosplay with something extra, babe," Roxy says, clarifying what we're heading into. She's standing at the desk, rifling through the enormous toolbox of make-up. "The competition guidelines say that your team is allowed to help you. Like, it's encouraged."

"Help me how?" I say, trying not to flinch every time Roxy homes in with the liquid liner. She's not as gentle as Iris. "You're doing my make-up; I don't see how the others can help."

I can't hold it any longer and do a triple blink. She tidies a smudge with a cotton bud. She's so patient with me. I could not be this patient with me.

"Correct. Make-up: check. But I've spoken to Team Awesome and—"

"Team Awesome? You mean Fake McKinley who's a total newbie and Dorothy who falls asleep the moment she sits down. That's Team Awesome?"

"Yes, Team Awesome – check your WhatsApp – and

you're underestimating them. We talked it through while you were having your disco nap, and we have a plan." Sometimes I need to have a little afternoon nap, OK? Convention days are long, and I get overtired. Like a toddler. "All you need to do is *bring it*." She puts her hands on my shoulders and looks into my eyes. "Can you do that, Eliza Gellar? Can you *bring it*?"

"Bring what?"

"That's the fighting talk I want to hear, babe," she says, checking my eyes are even. She lifts my chin and sucks in her cheeks, nodding at me to do the same, then applies bronzer. A *lot* of bronzer. "Just treat it like any other cosplay comp, and you'll be fine."

"But it's not like any other cosplay comp, my—"

"Life depends on it. Yes, I know. Just trying to take the pressure off." She snaps the bronzer lid shut and her eyes zigzag across my face. She nods. "Perfect. Spin for me."

I stand up, my bare legs unsticking from the faux leather chair, take my dressing gown off and manage a clumsy spin round. I'm wearing Juliana's first appearance look: black boots, knee and elbow guards, jagged thigh-length skirt embroidered with her family crest, and a pewter breastplate held in place with leather shoulder straps. They toned her outfit down when she became a series regular, but she'd just arrived from the Megna dimension, so she was in full warrior mode.

Roxy looks me up and down, then gives me a little side smile.

"Smoking, babe," she says, and I almost believe her. "Let me put this on you."

She pulls a red velvet cape from a hanger on the curtain rail, shaking it out then twirling it round me with a swish, in the way you have to when you handle a cape. It tickles the backs of my knees as Roxy secures the shoulder attachments. The skirt is *short,* but the cape basically covers all the pale bits.

It also makes me feel like a total badass.

"There she is." Roxy smiles down at me like a proud mum at a pageant. A pageant with swords. "Just need to do your tattoo and we're good to go."

Roxy's dressed as Marta Crowe, a demon-killing mercenary who doesn't play by the rules. She's in a black vest and cargo trousers, hair in a high pony, and the blackest, smokiest eyes in the history of eyeshadow. There's a realistic bloody gash across her cheek from the epic fight between Marta and Juliana in episode fourteen, season three, "Way Back Now".

Her eyebrows pinch together as she claws through the box, a mess of eyeshadows and lipsticks tumbling over the sides.

"What's wrong?"

"I can't find the tattoo pen . . ." she says, tipping everything onto the desk. "It's fine, I'll use liquid liner."

"Won't liquid liner smudge?"

"It'll totally smudge," she says, nodding. She frowns at her phone. "It's fine. I'll go knock on some doors. There has to be a tattoo pen in this building."

"Do we have time?" I ask, watching her pull her *Vampire Falls* onesie over her costume.

"We have loads of time; it's fine."

"You keep saying *it's fine.*"

She flashes me a smile. "Because it is."

I swallow, wringing my hands together.

"I don't have to have the tattoo," I lie. "Nobody will see it under the cape anyway."

"That was almost convincing, babe, but I know you: the tattoo is part of the costume." She grabs her key card then heads to the door, waving it in the air. *"I'll be back before the bloodletting."*

"And if you're not, I'll save you some O-negative," I respond, grateful she knows quoting *Vampire Falls* calms me down.

She sticks her phone in her pocket and heads out the door, leaving me alone. I look in the mirror, turning left to right. The costume fits me perfectly – put together by me, Mum and Roxy. We spent ages trawling Vinted for the right fabrics in the right colours, making sure every little detail from the embroidery to the dark red of the cape was right. The knee-high boots actually belonged to my mum when she was in her twenties. I couldn't believe it when she came down the loft ladder holding them in her hand, then Dad polished them until they were shiny enough.

A mutated, probably carnivorous, moth flaps its oversized wings inside my stomach. I check my phone. Roxy's been gone for nearly ten minutes. I take a sip of water through a straw, careful not to smudge her expertly applied lipstick. I pick up the lipstick tube; it's called *Cherry Vivian*. Ugh, I hope that's not a sign. I throw it back in the box with the eyeliners, brushes, foundation, highlighter and all the other magic paint Roxy used to get me looking like this. I've tried it myself a few times when I've done reels on Insta, but I never do as good a job as Iris or Roxy.

Roxy. I check my watch again. Eighteen minutes she's been gone now. I find an eyeliner and call her to say we'll just use that for the tattoo, but there's a busy signal. Maybe she's trying to call me? I wait a few seconds and try again.

"Shit!"

What the Baron of Hell is she doing at a time like this? Who is she speaking to?

Heat creeps up my neck and cheeks but in the mirror, I look as cool as a cucumber, due to the layers and layers of make-up. I check the time again. Twenty-one minutes now. I try her phone again.

"Fuck!"

I do a very angry hang up on the busy signal and go to the door, pull it open and step into the hallway, the pre-party soundtracks coming from behind doors as I look up and down. No sign of Roxy.

A handle clicks and I turn back as a head peeps into the hallway. Very sadly for me, it's not Roxy but is, of course, my arch-nemesis. Whatever. I don't have time for this crap.

"Have you seen Roxy?" I call, holding my door open.

Charlie Chamberlain leans out a little further, his hand on the doorframe.

"What?"

"I said, have you seen Roxy?"

"No," he says, stepping into the hallway. "Have you lost her?"

"Yes," I say, thinking why would I ask where she is if I hadn't lost her, doofus, but I remain reasonably polite in case he's holding her hostage in his room. "Has Sadie seen her?"

He shrugs, the light shoulder movement of someone

without a care, someone who has access to the most important person in the world at any time they want, not someone who's about to enter a cosplay competition completely tattoo-less.

"She's not here," he replies.

"Where is she?" I ask, about to berate him for losing his little sister.

"Vivian's room."

That genetically modified moth feels like it's getting ready for take-off. I shake my head and try Roxy again.

"*Fuck's sake*," I hiss into the phone, hanging up again.

"What's wrong?"

"She's not answering her phone and the cosplay's starting soon," I say, panic clawing at my chest.

"Can't you just meet her there?"

"No, she has to help me get ready."

Charlie Chamberlain looks me up and down, his eyes lingering on my boots. *Boots*, I said.

"You look ready already." He clears his throat. "You're already ready. I mean, you look like you're done."

"Well, I'm not."

He frowns for a minute then nods a little.

"She hasn't done your tattoo," he says.

I shake my head, just as the lift doors at the end of the corridor open and Roxy steps out, deep in conversation on her phone. My heart swells with relief but instead of walking back to our room, she takes a left and hurries through the door to the internal staircase.

"*Roxy*!?" I shout, hurrying towards her without thinking.

Charlie Chamberlain looks down the hall where Roxy's just disappeared, then turns back to me as there's an ominous bang and my door slams shut, trapping my cape and me in the hallway.

"Was that your door?" he asks, crossing his arms and leaning against his (open) doorway.

"Yes," I hiss, angry at the door, angry at Charlie Chamberlain, and angry at Roxy.

"Do you have your key card?"

I answer his question in the only appropriate way for this situation. With a scowl.

CHAPTER TWENTY-EIGHT

VIGGO RASSMUSSEN

The lady doth protest too much, methinks.

BUD LEROY

Doth? When did Viggy get a lisp? Why does he sound like Shakespeare? Why do you sound like Shakespeare?

JULIANA THE DEMON HUNTRESS

It is Shakespeare

Vampire Falls. Season two, episode eighteen – "My Person"

"Oh dear," he says, pushing himself away from his doorway and swaggering (swaggering?! At a time like this?) down the hall, spinning his key card between his thumb and forefinger. "Oh dear, oh dear. What a pickle you're in, Eliza. A pickle indeed."

"It's fine. I'll just wait for Roxy."

"Here?"

"Yes," I say, crossing my arms.

"With your cloak trapped in the door?"

"Yes. I actually love this hallway."

I lean back against the door to demonstrate just how cool I am about the situation. Charlie Chamberlain looks me up and down, a smirky looking smirk on his smirky face. God, he really knows how to boil my piss.

"What are you even doing in economy class, anyway?" I snap. "Didn't you get upgraded to the presidential suite or something?"

"Yeah, that didn't work out in the end," he says, his jaw clenching. He looks over his shoulder then back at me. "Do you want me to go and find Roxy?"

I swallow. I have no clue what she's playing at, but she must be on her way back here, surely? Even in this dire situation, I can't accept help from Charlie Chamberlain.

"No. I'm sure she'll be back in a minute," I say, folding my arms.

"What about your other friend?" he asks, his mouth tight.

"What friend?" I ask, frowning at him.

"Never mind. You want to wait in my room?" he says, gesturing over his shoulder.

"I can't move from this doorway, can I, genius?"

"I'm sorry, is that cloak fused to your skin, genius?"

"*Yes*." The side of his mouth twitches, and I look at the ceiling with a sigh. "No."

"So, take it off and come and wait."

"No, thank you," I say through gritted teeth.

"Sure?"

"Yes."

"Fine."

He strolls back down the hall into his room, letting the door shut loudly behind him. I try Roxy again and nearly throw my phone down the hallway, but even I know that's not a good move. I watch the door Roxy went through, waiting for her to come rushing through holding a tattoo pen triumphantly over her head, maybe even throwing in some parkour as she comes back to me, but she doesn't. The competition starts in less than twenty minutes, and I have zero chance of winning if I'm stuck here. I yank my cape, but it doesn't budge. I take a deep breath and close my eyes.

"Charlie?" I call.

The door clicks.

"Yes, Eliza?"

"Please can I wait in your room?"

"Why of course; what a good idea."

He heads towards me, not exactly smiling but not *not* smiling either, and there's something in his eyes that's way too sparkly given my circumstances. He stops in front of me, and I look up at him. I'd forgotten how tall he is, I'm so used to glaring at him from a distance. His scent hasn't changed much; that deodorant he wears but with a new scent sprayed into the mix so he smells like an upgraded version of the boy I was friends with. We face each other for a few seconds until he slowly lifts his hand and reaches for my face. My heart clangs against my breastplate and I press myself harder against the door.

"W-what are you doing?" I manage.

"Helping you get your cloak off?"

"Oh," I say, clearing my throat. "Cape."

"What now?"

"It's a cape, not a cloak, and I can do it."

174

I swallow and my hands fly up to my shoulders, my fingers fumbling at the fastenings. I look down, hoping he doesn't notice my hands shaking.

Why are my hands shaking?

I manage to undo both fastenings, then step forwards and the cape falls from my shoulders. I'm suddenly very aware of how much flesh this costume shows without it. I swallow. Again. Why all the swallowing, Eliza?

"Here," he says, handing me a hoodie.

"I'm fine."

"You're shaking."

"I'm just . . . excited."

"Right."

He's still holding out the hoodie, so I take it and put it round my shoulders, not giving him the satisfaction of using the sleeves, even though I'm actually freezing. I bite the inside of my cheek.

"Thanks," I say.

He raises an eyebrow and turns away, so I start following him to his room, then stop suddenly.

"What about my cape?"

"What about it?" he says, walking into his room.

"I can't just leave it," I say, looking at it like it's Jawfain caught in an Arachno Demon's web (spoiler: he was fine).

"Roxy'll get it when she's back. I can tell her what happened," he says. I check my phone again; I barely have time to pee before the competition starts. OK, biting big chunks out of my cheek right now. "Eliza?"

"What?" I snap, hurrying into his room.

175

"You can still do the cosplay without the cloak . . . cape."

He closes the door behind us. We're standing at the end of his bed, and I can tell it's his because he's a neat freak and it's all smooth and tucked in like the Undead Princess of Vaquella is coming to visit. Two bottles of aftershave sit on the side, one all greys and smoky glass, plus the novelty one Sadie got him. She instructed him only to wear it for special occasions, because she'd spent a month's pocket money on it. I can't believe he still has it. It's cute he's brought it. Wait. Not cute. I have no opinion of that vanilla and sweet orange-smelling football-shaped aftershave.

"But I need it," I say, my voice wobbling a little.

Something flashes across his face, that look of terror boys get when they think you're going to cry. I try Roxy again, and when the busy cross pops up on my phone tears prick at my eyes, so he better get over it. I bite my lip and frown at my phone, unable to look at him, the last person I want to fall apart in front of. Being in his room, enveloped in his routine and his smell, is making everything worse; lost and further away from Roxy.

"But she doesn't always wear a cloak, right? Didn't they only add the cloak in season two anyway? So, there was a whole season where she looked like this." He pauses for a moment, and I look up at him. He smiles and scratches his head, leaving a tuft of hair sticking up on the side. "Like what you're wearing, I mean."

"You remember that?" I ask.

His eyebrows pop up. "Remember what?"

"When her costume changed."

"Duh. Probably every pubescent boy noticed what she was wearing in all her scenes."

I rush back three years to when he, Roxy and I were watching the episode "Yours or Mine?" from season four. Juliana pulled Viggo from the Reapers Chasm, straddled him (naturally), then ripped a piece of fabric from her skirt and tied it around his bleeding arm. Roxy and I paused at the end of the scene to get snacks, but Charlie Chamberlain couldn't move, stuck with a cushion over his lap.

"I forgot she was your first crush," I say, smiling at the memory.

"Kind of." He looks down at me, then shoves his hands in his pockets. "Anyway. Like I said, she doesn't always have the cloak. The cape, sorry."

"*This* version of the costume she does." I'm pulled back into the room, clock ticking, and the competition start even closer. I go to claw my hands though my hair, but my fingertips don't get past the hairspray and mousse. "And I don't have my tattoo."

"OK. You need to get over the cape, but we can do something about the tattoo." He shuffles past me and leans over Sadie's bed, grabbing a pencil case. "Hoodie off and turn around."

"What? No, I . . ."

"Do you want the tattoo?" he says, riffling through the pencil case.

"Yes, but . . ."

"I can do it," he says, pulling out a black pen. I shake my head. "You want to do it? I forgot you're double-jointed and have extendable arms."

I glance at my phone again. We have fourteen minutes and Roxy still isn't here. Charlie Chamberlain may be my only option.

"Won't it smudge?" I ask.

He shakes his head and waves the pen. "It's permanent; I woke up with an eye patch on me when Sadie was mad once. Had to go to football practice with it."

I can't help smiling as he throws the pencil case down.

"Let me find a picture then," I say, looking at my phone.

"Don't need it. I've doodled her tattoo a thousand times. Just turn around."

"What if you mess it up?"

"I literally drew it last week, so I think we're OK."

"What for?"

"An internship thing."

"A drawing internship thing?"

"Yes, a drawing internship thing," he says, rolling his eyes.

"You still do all that?" I say, swallowing. "The drawing?"

He nods. "What about you?"

"What about me, what?" I ask.

"You still following Roxy to uni? Bristol, isn't it?"

"Why'd you say that?" I ask, stiffening.

"That was the plan, wasn't it?" he says. I can't tell if he's making fun of me, so I don't say anything. "Wow. Your skin has literally just frosted over. Subject change."

"Or just quiet time is also fine."

"OK," he says, shrugging as he pulls the lid off the pen. "Turn round then."

I turn away then look up at the ceiling, waiting for

something to happen.

"Are you doing it then?" I say.

He clears his throat.

"Take the . . . can you take the hoodie off?" he says.

I pull the hoodie from around my shoulders. He steps up behind me, but does it so quietly the only reason I know he's closer is because I feel his breath on my neck. He clears his throat again and makes me jump a little. My adrenaline must be through the roof because of the competition and the costume and being late and the door and . . .

"Eliza?"

This time I clear my throat.

"Mm-yeah?"

Mm-yeah? What the hell dictionary did I pull that one from?

"Try and keep still," he says.

"I am."

"You're shaking."

"It's cold in here."

"It's like a thousand degrees."

OK, it's not actually cold and it *does* feel a thousand degrees, but that's because he's so close heat is radiating from his body onto my bare shoulders. I have no idea why I'm shaking. Suddenly and slowly, all at once, his fingers rest against my left shoulder. I flinch and he steps back.

"What now?" he says.

I turn round and look up. His face is exactly as I pictured it would be. His mouth in a firm line and his eyebrows slightly raised. This is the closest we've stood in years, and I can see the tiny freckle under his left eye.

"That's the wrong side," I say.

He rolls his eyes and turns me back round, resting his hand on my left shoulder again.

"I'm just steadying myself. I don't want to mess it up. Permanent marker, remember? Just . . . keep . . . still . . ."

His breath brushes against my skin with each word, and for some reason all I can think of is the epic cluster of spots I had across my shoulders for Shark Week last month. *Why* am I thinking about that? *Why* do I care what my skin looks like close-up to Charlie Chamberlain.

Why am I still shaking?

The tip of the pen presses into my right shoulder and I gasp as it connects with a pressure point that's linked to an eclipse of moths waiting to take off (not mutant ones this time, just regular brown ones, the same colour as Charlie Chamberlain's eyes . . . sorry, what?). I bite my lip as the pen traces across my skin, and close my eyes, picturing the outline of Juliana's tattoo.

"OK?"

"Yeah." But it comes out as a murmur, so I try again. "Yeah."

"Are you breathing?"

I let out a long, slow breath, not even realising that . . . My eyes pop open. Did I just let out a breath I didn't even know I was holding? *What the fuck is happening?!*

"I'm fine," I say, firmly. Because I *am* fine and being alone with Charlie Chamberlain joining the erogenous dots on my back is not making me feel anything other than *fine*.

"Are you nearly done?"

"Mm-yeah," he says, and I can tell he's smiling. I daren't move in case he smudges so I try to clear my mind of honey-brown moths and long, deep sighs. "Just . . . finishing . . . the . . . outline."

I swallow and glance at my phone. We don't have much time, but I don't want to rush him. The pen moves quicker, zigzagging against my skin as he fills the outline in.

"How's it looking?"

"Good," he says, and I imagine him frowning. "Nearly done."

He removes his hand from my shoulder, but it may as well still be there from the throbbing hot patch it's left. Is this some kind of allergic reaction? Have I not been around Charlie Chamberlain for so long that my body is now responding to his touch like it's succubus venom?

Suddenly, without any warning whatsoever, he gently blows on my shoulder, and though my brain knows he's simply making sure the pen is dry, other parts of my body take it as a mating ritual. I turn my head a fraction and look in the mirror. He's close behind me, his head dipped so I can see the nape of his neck curving into his shoulders as he frowns at his work. My cheeks must be like beacons under all this contouring, and I appreciate Roxy's talent even though I'm seething at her.

He moves his hand towards my right shoulder and I brace myself, ready to feel his fingers on my skin again, but instead he flaps his hand above the tattoo before giving it one last blow. I close my eyes, and a volt of electricity rushes through me as his fingertip gently traces the tattoo. Everything stills in this intensely intimate movement, and the electricity tingles up through my skin when Orion and Lila's theme plays faintly from one of the other bedrooms.

Suddenly, Charlie Chamberlain smacks his hands together and I jump, blinking myself back down to earth from wherever I just was.

I mean, what the hell was that?

"You're good to go," he says, checking his watch. "What do you think?"

I turn and shuffle close to the mirror. I let out a little gasp at the detail of the tattoo, every cross and curve the same as Juliana's. Smiling, I look at him in the mirror and his eyes flick from my face to my shoulder.

"It's amazing," I say. "Thank you."

"Welcome." He looks at me for a few seconds and I'm suddenly hit with a rush of nostalgia for this boy I knew so well. He fiddles with the pen then pops it back in the case. "You better go. *Death waits for no man.*"

"*But it does wait for woman,*" I respond, impressed that he remembers Viggo's line.

"For real though, you need to go."

I nod and walk past him, shivering as our arms brush each other. He follows me and opens the door and I step out, pausing to look at my cape.

"What's up?"

I shake my head. "I need my cape."

He looks around then grabs his hoodie from the bed and throws it to me.

"Wear that; you'll be fine."

I put it round my shoulders, not telling him I didn't just mean I couldn't walk down like this. Obviously, no, the idea of walking through the hotel lobby wearing this tiny outfit isn't thrilling but I can't do the competition without the cape. I just feel incomplete, like a fraud, because anyone who knows (which is *everyone* here) will see I haven't got it right.

"Just get down there, Eliza. You'll be fine once you get going. Just think, it's like filming one of your reels for Insta."

I look up at him.

"You look at my Insta?"

His eyes widen a little and he scratches the back of his head, then shrugs.

"Your reels sometimes come up if you search for *Juliana full costume*," he says with a little side smile.

"Perve," I joke.

"It's to appreciate her sword play and nothing else." I check my phone. No time and no calls from Roxy. "You can do it, Eliza – you'll nail it. You look awesome on those reels, for real. I mean, really, you do."

I shrug. "It's all just special effects though."

"You *are* the special effects," he says, his face serious.

We blink at each other, uncertain whether he's actually just said those words.

"What?" I say, stepping back towards him.

He shakes his head.

"I . . . I just mean you can do it. You've done it a ton of times, with and without the cloak. Or cape. You'll be fine. You better go."

I nod. I feel like I've just stepped out of a dream and my body wants back into the floaty vibes and the high-voltage touching, but it's too confused to find its way there again. He smiles at me for a moment, a smile from another life, then turns away and lets the door close so I'm standing alone in the hallway.

That was interesting. *Very* interesting.

CHAPTER TWENTY-NINE

ILLIAS (HEAD VAMPIRE)

*I warn you, girl. You do as he says, and I will become
more powerful than you could possibly imagine.*

LILA MURPHY

*I have a terrible imagination. (long pause)
Let's see what happens.*

Vampire Falls. Season one, episode twelve –
"Masquerade Brawl"

I've always felt indifferent about Abercrombie and Fitch,
but right now I couldn't be more grateful for their extensive
hoodie line. I rush through the lobby, Charlie Chamberlain's
grey hoodie pulled around me like a dressing gown, so
my costume isn't on display for the entire convention.
I can't deal with the parallel universe I was in just now.
I'll deal with it tomorrow. Maybe.

People mill around the foyer, whooping when their friends
emerge from the lifts in lovingly created costumes. Usually,
I'd be in heaven chatting to people dressed as Lila or
Nightmare Vampire Number Three. I love it. I love, love,
love it, but right now, if I interact with anyone I will hurl.

I turn down the corridor to the back entrance of the

main hall, into the stage area. Two stewards are on the door and I nod as I walk past them, but one puts their hand up.

"Lanyard?"

I instinctively reach for it but it's not around my neck. It must be back in the room. With my room key. And my cape. I let out a little whimper.

"I . . ."

"Sorry, ladies." We all look round as Vivian sidles up to us, waving her (damn) lanyard around for the stewards. "Almost didn't make it. Was getting my costume just . . ."

She does a chef's kiss with one hand, and a hair flip with the other. She looks like an advanced version of Vivian, like she's downloaded an update that automatically gets sent to supermodel-type people. She's wearing a Dalmatian-print onesie over her costume, and I'm surprised (and relieved) she's got trainers on so only towers above me in the standard, mortal kind of way. She looks down at me, smiling.

"Who are you?" she says, tugging one of the toggles on the hoodie. "Kip the Bartender?"

"Who are you?" I say, snatching my toggle. "Cruella de Vil?"

"Is that supposed to be an insult?" She rolls her eyes. "Please."

She looks me up and down until I step out of her way, then walks through the doorway. I try to follow, but the steward puts her hand up again.

"You're not getting through without a badge."

I swallow and look at my phone. I have four minutes to race back, get my badge, if I can even get into my room, and get back again. My lip wobbles and I back away from them, not even sure where I can go to lick my wounds.

"I'm sorry," says the steward, shrugging.

"*Sorry doesn't raise the dead, lads.*"

I spin round as Roxy rushes towards us, winning back my love with a perfectly timed quote. She's laden with bags and a pair of straighteners thrown around her neck, waving both our lanyards at the stewards then pushing me through the door.

"I'm so sorry, babe," she pants, squeezing my hand.

I look back at her as she ushers me towards the changing rooms, equal parts anger and relief squeezing up to my eyeballs.

"Do not cry and ruin my masterpiece." She reads a sign taped on a door with duct tape. "This is us, get in."

She swings me through the door, and I can't say I'm a huge fan of all this pushing and shoving and I would very much like my serene Roxy right now, but I think she might be in a pre-competition trance, like those pageant mums, or *moms*. She drops the bags, then pulls something long and red out of one of them.

"My cape!" I cry, my voice cracking as she shakes it out like a matador then fits it on my shoulders. "You got it. Thank you."

She looks down at me as she fiddles with the fastenings.

"Kind of, yes."

"What?"

"We do not have time, Eliza Gellar!" she says, squeezing my shoulders. "Have you seen the others?"

"Others?"

"Team Awesome! Have you seen them?" I shake my head as she sticks an earbud in her ear, like a frenzied wedding planner. "Good, that probably means they're in position already."

"In position?"

She ignores me and pulls my sword holders out of a bag then starts wrestling me into them like a toddler into a backpack.

"Roxy, stop!" I say. We managed some time in the conference room that afternoon so I could practise my routine. An alarmed-looking man in a suit and tie walked in while I was swinging my swords round. "Please, what are you talking about? Why are Team Awesome in position? What position?"

"Just trust me!" she snaps, which makes me not trust her, quite frankly. "Focus on your routine and character, OK? *OK*?!"

"OK," I whimper (totally *unfocused*, by the way).

"Good. Vivian is about to start, then it's you, then it's Rashawn. Do you want to watch her?"

I don't know what the right answer is.

"Yes," I try.

"That's my girl."

Roxy grabs my hand and we head out to the back of the stage area. The *Vampire Falls* soundtrack plays out front, which doesn't calm me down as much as it usually would, but it does remind me that I'm here, among my people, among my friends.

Vivian steps out of the shadows as if my very thoughts

summoned her from Hell. She's in full cosplay mode now, no cute dalmatian onesies here, and I gasp at her incredible height increase. Roxy puts an arm across me like she's a gang leader and we're about to have a rumble.

"Bitches," Vivian says, putting her hand on her waist and, you guessed it, flicking her hair over her shoulder. I don't know what shampoo she uses but I got a waft and she smells like Heaven.

If Heaven was in Hell.

I wait for Roxy to say something but she's speechless. Not good, not good at all. Vivian has brought her absolute A-game in the cosplay department. Actually, there should be a letter invented that comes before *A* and they should probably call it *Vivian*.

She's a waitress from the Full Moon Diner, in a short turquoise jumpsuit with bright pink buttons and piping around the breast pockets, a little pink sailor hat tilted to one side on her head (attached using real-life sorcery), bright pink knee-high socks, and a pair of pink roller skates, giving her the appearance and height of an actual superhero.

I point at the skates and turn to Roxy, who's forgotten how to close her mouth.

"Are skates allowed?" I ask. "Should *I* have skates?"

Roxy shakes her head. Vivian glides past us and I'm devastated to see that she's a natural on wheels.

"Good luck, bitches," she calls, then disappears behind the curtain.

"I don't think she's human," says Roxy, her mouth still open.

"Really?" I say, my palms turned upwards in the universal *why, God?* position. "Is that it?"

"Did you see her? I mean she's normally . . . but that's just . . ."

Roxy stares at the curtain, biting her lip. What the hell is going on here? I smack my hands together.

"What the hell is going on here?" I snap. Roxy blinks, then looks at me. "You're supposed to be pep-talking me, not wet daydreaming about the enemy."

Roxy shakes her head, then grabs the bag from her shoulder.

"Sorry, sorry, you're right. I just wasn't prepared for that level of Vivian. I don't think anyone is."

I half whimper, half shriek, and Roxy ushers me out of the Vivian perfume cloud, around the corner until we're at the edge of the stage. We both peek round the curtain. Conference Hall A is set up with round tables around the dance area then stretching back to the doors. Everyone, like, *all* the attendees are already sitting at the tables, most with drinks, ready to be entertained, including the table of special guest judges at the front.

"Right. Team Awesome are ready to get into position as soon as Vivian's done her bit." She holds a clipboard up and points at it. "This is you, babe. This is what you'll be doing, remember?"

I frown at the notes and diagrams on the clipboard. I swallow and take a step back, but Roxy has pre-empted me and grabs my hand.

"There is literally nothing on this page you haven't done

before, babe, and it was fine this afternoon. Suit-and-Tie Guy was surprised but impressed. I could tell."

"But I didn't feel pukey then."

"Nothing to be pukey about, babe. You do it on Insta all the time, and in stage combat," she says, fussing my hair. "Just hit all of your marks. Fake McKinley has taped crosses on the floor."

"Really?" I say, craning my neck and seeing small white crosses across the stage and runway. "Fake McKinley did that?"

"Yeah. He's a theatre nerd, apparently," she says, waving the clipboard. "Helped me work out the extra bits and he's going to do the second fight with you."

"Instead of you?" Roxy nods. "But my music is what we agreed?"

She gives me a don't-insult-me look.

"ACDC," she says.

"'Thunderstruck'?"

Roxy shrugs. "Of course."

It's the song Juliana chooses on the jukebox before slicing and dicing all the vampires in the Full Moon Diner in her very first episode. It was quite the character intro.

I peek out at the audience again. So many familiar faces, but they all look so judgey right now. A couple of them are literally dressed like judges. Demon judges, but still the same thing.

A Headset Guy ushers Vivian onto the stage and she rolls into the shadows, doing a quick spin when she hits her mark in the middle. She looks over her shoulder at us and winks. In an attempt to confuse the enemy, I smile back and give her a double thumbs up, but she smiles even wider and turns to face the curtains.

"What was that?" whispers Roxy.

"A smile and thumbs up might throw her off."

"You're not smiling, you're growling. And you're doing a double bird, not a thumbs up."

I look down. Look at that! It's like my phalanges know me better than I know myself.

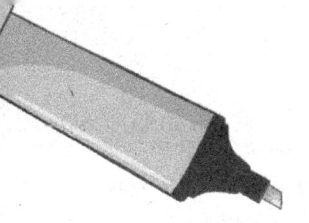
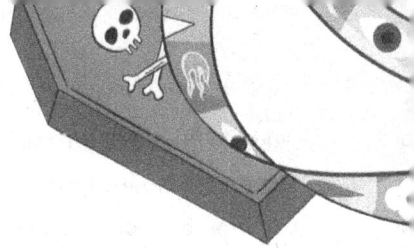

CHAPTER THIRTY

JULIANA THE DEMON HUNTRESS

Do not look directly into the eyes of the Brighidda, unless you wish to think of nothing else until the day you die.

Vampire Falls. Season three, episode twelve – "How Long Is Eternity?"

The lights go down, then coloured spotlights illuminate the sides of the stage. Roxy grabs my hand as the curtains open.

We jump when the guitar riff blares out of the speakers just above us, and Vivian is illuminated with a bright pink light, so she looks like she's glowing. She flicks her head round to the audience, her long hair flying around her like a cape, and throws her arms and hips out to each beat. Roxy and I look at each other, simultaneously realising the aptness of her song choice.

"'Wet Dream'," says Roxy, mesmerised.

Vivian sets off on her skates to the front left of the stage where she spins, starting on both legs then lifting one up and crouching down as she goes round and round.

The audience *roars.*

She stops abruptly, blows a kiss, then skates backwards, like a sort of moonwalk on wheels, waving at the guest judges. If I'm not mistaken, I hear a long whoop belonging to Dax St. James. I bite my lip as she skates to the runway, her hips and all her other best parts exaggerated by the skating motion.

"It's fine. It's fine," says Roxy, turning to me and shaking her head. "It's just hair and wheels. Hair and wheels. She doesn't have anything else."

I look back at Vivian as she picks up speed down the runway, does a split jump with her hand on the side of her head à la 1950s pin-up girl, then lands on one of the ramps and casually rolls past the front tables, high-fiving everyone as she goes.

"No," I whisper, swallowing a dry lump. "She has the audience."

Frankly, I'm equal parts terrified and excited to see what Vivian does next. She speeds down a ramp towards a table on the edge of the dance floor. Charlie Chamberlain and Toby hold up a giant mirror with lightbulbs around the frame. Everyone at the table, nay, *in the room,* goes wild when she skids to a stop and pulls out a (damn) lipstick from her cleavage and applies it perfectly. She leans forward and kisses her reflection, then everyone at the table hurries round to her as she spins again. They pull out hand-held fans, directing them so Vivian's hair dances around her head, taking on a life of its own.

The girl is a shampoo, luxury chocolate bar and tampon advert all rolled into one.

She skates to the next table and picks up a metal tray with a tall glass of strawberry milkshake on it. I stare, open-mouthed, as she rests the tray on the palm of her hand and her shoulder, then with the ease of an Olympic skater (which I think she might actually be), glides over to the . . .

"No," I whisper.

. . . judges table, where she stops right in front of Damon Van Schwartz, lifts the glass from the tray, and delivers him probably the best milkshake he'll ever have in his life. He beams at her, obliging when she encourages him to taste it. He sips it through the straw then nods and claps his hands, his behaviour encouraging but professional. Vivian high fives him, grabs the cherry from the top and pops it in her mouth as she skates off, expertly ignoring Dax St. James's wolf-whistles and *un*professional looks of pure lust. I look at Roxy.

"It's just," she says, swallowing and shaking her head, "hair and wheels."

I turn back to Vivian as the song starts to fade out and she's back in the middle of the stage where she started.

Needless to say, the crowd goes absolutely wild.

Also, needless to say, I. Am. Fucked.

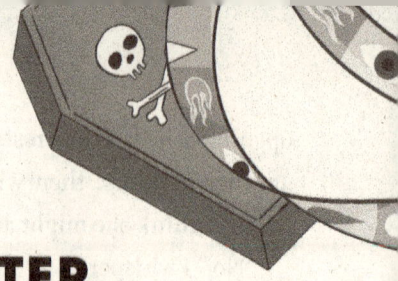

CHAPTER THIRTY-ONE

BUD LEROY

You can do this, Lila. You're always staking vampires.

LILA MURPHY

Never. I've never staked a vampire.

BUD LEROY

Never, always. Potato, potato.

Vampire Falls. Season one, episode six – "Did You See?"

Fucked, I tell you.

Thankfully, Vivian skated off the other side of the stage, so I didn't have to come to face to face with her, which was probably a good thing because I don't think it's a good idea to look directly into the eyes of a goddess.

"Babe!" snaps Roxy, slapping the clipboard on the side of her leg.

"Huh?" I say.

Roxy's trying to talk me through my set again, but I'm a little distracted. You know, by the VMA level performance just now.

"Are you taking this in?" She pulls the curtain back and watches the Headset People hauling stuff onto the stage.

"We have literal minutes until they're set up for you."

I shrug. It's all I can muster (I've always wondered about the usage of that word, and this feels like the right time). I watch everyone moving drums and ramps back and forth, but all I really see is Vivian. It's like she moved so fast around the stage she's left fragments of herself behind to remind people what they saw was real, and not a hot girl mirage.

I look down at my costume, created with such love and passion for a show that means everything to me, but now is just a symbol of my failure. I pull the headband from my hair.

"What the hell are you doing?" says Roxy, tearing it from my hand.

"What's the point?" I say, ducking out of her way as she tries to put it back on me. "I can't follow *that*!"

She looks at me for a moment, her shoulders sagging a little.

"RuPaul couldn't follow that, babe. I'm sorry. But it wasn't really what this is all about, was it? She just blinded people with her hair and incredible, incredible, *incredible* legs. I mean . . . balance."

"So that's it then?" I say.

Roxy shakes her head. "You have to try, babe. Come on."

"What's the point?" I repeat, falling into Roxy as one of the Headset People barges past me. "He didn't even see me and I'm standing right here. Wearing a *cape*. I'm just going to humiliate myself if I go out there."

I can tell from the placement of Roxy's eyebrows that she's torn between shoving me on stage to at least try and out-perform Vivian and scooping me up and running back to our room where she'd tuck me in bed and hand-feed me Haribo. She looks at a couple of guys shifting the last item on stage, as the song playing for the crowd comes to an end. She puts her hand on my shoulder and opens her mouth to speak.

"All set back here?"

We look round at Fake McKinley, who's not actually Fake McKinley for the first time since we've met him but is wearing a pair of black joggers and a black T-shirt. The T-shirt is tight, tight, tight, and he is *ripped* under his werewolf costume. Not that I'm in the frame of mind to appreciate that right now. OK, I totally take a few seconds to appreciate it.

Roxy gives him a look, and he ducks his head so he can see behind me then looks back at her, his palms up.

"Where are the swords and the sticks?" he asks.

I look down at my boots, guilt swelling in my stomach when I think about the input my parents had into creating them.

"She doesn't want to do it," Roxy says.

"Why the hell not?"

This is the most engaged I think I've seen Fake McKinley, like, ever. The muscles in his jaw are tight (not as tight as his T-shirt, though) and he's looking down at me with such intensity I think if he really concentrated, he could make laser beams come out of his eyes.

He puts his hand on my shoulder, turning me to face him. I suspect he considers crouching down to talk to me but decides against it.

"What's going on with you, Eliza?"

"I can't do it," I say, shaking my head. "I can't go on, not after that."

"After what?"

"Are you serious?" I say, gesturing at the Vivian fragments that are still spinning around on stage. "After Vivian."

"Why?"

"Did you see her?" I ask, chewing the inside of my cheek.

He nods and folds his arms. "She was sensational."

"Exactly."

"But that doesn't mean you won't be your own brand of sensational." I glance at Roxy, who nods, then I look back at him. "Sure, the crowd enjoyed what Vivian did. I did too. They enjoyed it because it was fun and carefree."

"And hot," I say, folding my arms over my breastplate.

"Very hot," confirms Fake McKinley. "But that is not what this is about, and she knows it."

He holds his finger up and nods at the Headset Guy who's pointing at his watch, then goes on.

"Roxy showed me your reels on Insta, Eliza. It's not fun, and it's not carefree, but it's full of heart. Passion. You do this because you love it, right?" I nod. "Do you think Vivian did that because she loves it, or because she looks incredible on a pair of hot pink roller skates?"

His voice is soft but firm, and I feel like we're the only three people on the planet right now. I look up at him.

"Probably the roller-skates thing?" I say.

He smiles, a relaxed gentle smile, and nods.

"You can learn to skate, but you can't learn passion. You either have it, or you don't. And *you* have it. Show them how much."

I blink at him, the hairs on my arms standing on end.

"We've talked this all through, and Roxy says you can do it. She says you love this so much, you probably do it in your dreams." I glance at Roxy, who has a little sparkle in her eye. "We've got everything you need – your song, your floor marks, the props. Even Dorothy is out there for you. We've all done our bit, Eliza. You go do your bit. You bring the passion. OK?"

I'm so pumped full of emotion right now I think I could somersault into a UFC ring and shoot flames from my bare hands. I nod at Fake McKinley who holds his hand out for a fist bump, but I hug him instead. He's *incredible* at hugs, and I soak up all his good vibes along with a calming zing of lemongrass I'm guessing from his shower gel. We break apart and I look over my shoulder, ready to go. Charlie Chamberlain's watching us from the other side of the stage, probably posted by Vivian as part of her tactical takedown, but I ignore him and turn to Roxy.

"Strap my swords on."

Roxy rushes to strap the sword holster across my body. Fake McKinley joins her and they confer, checking it's secured. I check I can reach my weapons and my cape is still hanging right.

Roxy moves round to my front, puts my headband back on, then puts her hands on my shoulders.

"Forgot to say," she says, kissing the top of my head, "you might get a little wet."

"What? How?" I look from her to Fake McKinley, who looks pleased, maybe even proud. "What?"

"Just wanted to warn you," says Roxy, tweaking my hair,

"but don't worry about it."

"Those two sentences don't go together?" I say, looking up for sprinklers.

"That's your cue," says Headset Guy, doing a sort of winding gesture with his finger then scurrying off behind a stand with lots of buttons.

Roxy and Fake McKinley step back, admiring their handiwork as though they've just got me ready to send down the aisle. I nod at them both, then bite my lip and walk to the centre of the stage. The closed curtains ripple in front of me, and I try not to think about the hundreds of eyes on the other side. I look over my shoulder at my friends. Roxy smiles and gives me a double thumbs up, and Fake McKinley makes a heart shape over his chest, then taps it with a closed fist and mouths one word.

Passion.

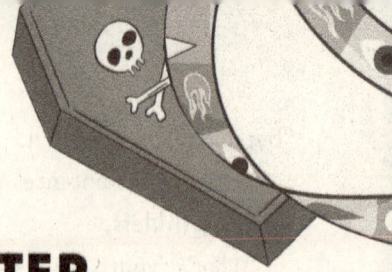

CHAPTER THIRTY-TWO

VIGGO RASSMUSSEN

It's right there, Lila. Right there.

LILA MURPHY

What is? Tell me what's there!

VIGGO RASSMUSSEN

You are.

Vampire Falls. Season two, episode ten –
"Death Cannon Kill"

My Trip to San Diego Comic Con and Megan Nicole Jefferies. ROUND TWO.

I close my eyes and imagine myself doing this in my sleep, or in a dream, like Fake McKinley said. The steps and cues scrawled across Roxy's clipboard are scrawled across the darkness in my mind and I see myself doing each movement like I have on my Insta reels so many times, but with higher stakes.

The quiet pulls me into its calm and I picture everyone turned to stone, unable to make a sound; they just have to sit and enjoy. I open my eyes and a Headset Gal steps from the shadows on the other side of the stage and nods at me.

I nod back. She nods at a Curtain Guy who heaves the rope he's clutching, and light slices through the curtains and the black space in front of me.

I look over my shoulder and give Team Awesome a smile.

"Let's fucking do this," I whisper to them, but more to myself.

I'm still hidden in the shadows and glance at Headset Gal who's holding up her hand. I look down at my boots, focusing on the right stance, feet apart, head down. Headset Gal stage whispers *five . . .*

four . . .

three . . .

two . . .

and one!

Lights flash above me, presenting me to Conference Hall A, and the music starts with a bang and no apologies, straight into that guitar. The crowd, who I still can't see, erupt when they recognise my costume, and the sound of their applause is like a firework under my backside. I fight the urge to partake with a spot of air guitar but pump my knee along with each crash of the cymbal, like I'm revving myself up to go.

I move forwards, keeping in time so I get to the first mark Fake McKinley has stuck down for me, then I slowly pull out my sword just as I come alongside the first drum, then hit the skin with the bottom of the handle in perfect timing with the song.

This is my call. This is my passion.

Thunder . . .

I glance up, and a few people in the audience have stood up from their seats, light squares waving around as they film me.

I keep moving forward, my sword trailing in my hand until I reach the next drum. I pull out my other sword and smack the drum with its handle in time to the music.

Thunder . . .

I move back and forth between the drums, looking out at the audience as I hit the drums with my swords. The song winds us up like a tightly coiled spring, until the lyrics scream out from the speakers. I cross my swords down in front of me, then thrust them outwards and spin around, executing the moves I've spent hours of my life studying on YouTube videos by Megan Nicole Jefferies' stuntwoman, Helen Yates, breaking down her favourite moves. I remember her saying the fight scenes were like a dance, so I focus on my steps and my hands, moving together in perfect sync.

I move down the stage until I reach the runway, where I see Roxy sloping towards me, dragging a sword along the floor. I holster one of my swords, then hold my breath, take a run-up, and somersault off the runway, landing in front of her.

Yes, I said somersault. You weren't expecting that were you?

Neither were they.

I flip the sword in my hand, trying not to let the audience's screams crack my game-face, and look at Roxy, dressed in black and ready for combat. Totally breaking character, she beams at me but makes the first strike like she has in our combat reels and like we practised this afternoon. We swing our swords through the air and the blades flash under the lights. The choreography takes us down to the dance floor so we're right in front of the audience, who watch me like I'm about to take flight.

I take a running leap and hop onto a chair, my foot right

between the guy's legs. He whoops as I jump over him onto the table, then I grab the beer he's holding and take a swig. The music is just audible above the screaming of the audience, and I run across the table, leaping over the guests (who naturally duck the fuck out of the way) to the next, and the next – Roxy running along next to me on the dance floor until I jump from the final table, swinging my sword through the air and hitting her (not really) in the stomach. She falls to the ground, a worthy opponent, defeated (still beaming).

I turn to the audience, throwing out some high fives but still not breaking character as I walk round to the other side of the runway, looking up at Fake McKinley who's skulking towards me, a sword in each hand. I've never fought with him before, but I can tell by the way he's holding his weapons this isn't the first time he's handled a sword. His face is stern; he's taking this seriously. Another worthy opponent.

I throw my sword onto the runway in front of him and he feigns surprise as he watches me run to the side, put my hand on the top and scissor kick onto the runway. I roll over, retrieving my sword, and jump up in front of him, slowly pulling sword number two from its holder, crossing them over as we circle each other.

Fake McKinley makes the first move, advancing quickly towards me but not so quick I don't know what he's about to do. He calls his moves before he does them, if he's going left or right, and which side he's swinging his sword. I focus on his words, knowing how much it hurts if you get hit, even though they're not real swords. He's graceful and light on his feet, but no match for Eliza the Demon Huntress as I take him out with an unexpected left-hander. He lays still until the spotlight blinks out then he jumps up and jogs back into the shadows, looking back at me and smiling ear to ear.

The crowd claps along with the song, so even though I can barely hear it, I can still follow the beat. I turn and give them a bow, then straighten up and head up the runway. My muscles are on fire, but I keep moving forward, my heart beating along to the song. The spotlight illuminates the end of the runway and gasps fill Conference Hall A when the audience realises what's happening next.

Drum solo, courtesy of moi.

Everyone jumps to their feet, screaming and clapping their hands together. I spin my swords round then throw them down. I'm drenched with sweat, so I detach my cape and drop it behind me, my hands up in the air, bringing on the screams from the audience. My thighs might not look like Vivian's, but can hers do this?

I run towards the drumkit, throwing in a cartwheel, a flip and a roundoff, then I leap through the air, landing on the drum stool with both feet. I clap my hands over my head, then bend over and pull two drumsticks from the insides of my boots. I drop down onto the stool, smack the sticks together, then beat them down on the skins – and that's when I realise why Roxy said I might get wet.

Water splashes up the moment the sticks hit the drums, sending droplets of water high in the air. They seem to hover longer than scientifically possible, dancing with the flashing lights and the sound from the crowd. The audience screams along with each splash and each crash. I spin the sticks in my hands, throwing my head down as I hit the skins, not caring that my hair is falling in my face and my make-up is probably running. Right now, I feel like I'm possessed by Juliana herself, fresh from the Megna dimension to claim her rightful place as drum goddess and all-round badass.

It's time to bring it home so I really go for it, hitting those skins like my life depends on it. I spot someone else clad in black moving slowly from the side, and a couple of Headset People hovering near the tables. I try to recall Roxy's clipboard, but I don't remember anything about a third person. I keep playing, nearly falling off the stool when a small torch suddenly bursts into flame in their hand as they creep across the end of the runway. One of the Headset People holds up a fire extinguisher and signals for me to carry on. I settle back into the drumming, just as the person carrying the flame stops a few feet ahead of me and turns to the runway. They hold the fire up to their mouth, suddenly expelling a mouthful of liquid through the flame and breathing an enormous cloud of fire across the runway in front of the drums.

The audience gasps. *I* gasp, and take this moment to look over at the guest judges who are all on their feet (apart from Dax St. James, who's staring at his phone), smacking their hands together, including Amber Anderson. We make eye contact, and she holds her hands over her head, clapping just for me, then blows me a kiss.

Finally, amazingly, the song comes to an end. The spotlight blinks off and I slump against the drum kit, looking off to the side where Roxy and Fake McKinley jump up and down, clapping their hands, *screaming*, actually screaming with the rest of the audience. I catch my breath and sit up, wiping the water and sweat, and maybe even tears, from my face. I shake my head; the noise is unbelievable. The fire-breather comes over to me and holds up a bottle of water. I take the lid off and gulp it down, nearly spurting it right back out when they pull off their balaclava.

"Dorothy?!"

Her hair's damp with sweat and there's a black smudge around her mouth, but she smiles at me, the sort of smile that hurts your cheeks but tickles your heart and you can feel it right through to your toes. I peel myself from the stool and crouch down at the side of the runway, the crowd still cheering us.

"Well done, Curly," she says. "That was metal as fuck."

CHAPTER
THIRTY-THREE

VENEFICA THE WITCH

You continue to underestimate us.

VIGGO RASSMUSSEN

You and your vile cat?

VENEFICA THE WITCH

Women, jackass.

Vampire Falls. Season four, episode seven –
"What Kills You Makes You Unpopular"

I don't think I'm capable of shock any more. She pulls her glasses from inside her black top then looks up at me.

"Are you OK?" I ask. She nods, as the *Vampire Falls* theme starts and the Headset People usher us away from the drums. "Where the hell did that come from?"

"Used to be in the circus."

"Of course you did," I say. Roxy and Fake McKinley join her, and she puts her arms around them. I look at them all. "Was that OK?"

"Fucking *OK*?" laughs Roxy. "How'd it feel?"

I throw a drumstick in the air and catch it after a couple of spins, then look at her and shrug.

"OK, I guess."

She shakes her head then throws her arms around me.

"So, so proud of you, babe. That was *intense.*" She pulls away and wipes her eyes. "We'll see you backstage in a bit. We need to get all this stuff down before Rashawn's on."

Fake McKinley shakes his head and smiles at me before they start dismantling the drum kit and I slope back down the runway, the sound of the audience and the drums and the music ringing through my ears. I head to the side of the stage, and something on the other side catches my eye.

Just behind the curtain, Vivian watches me walk across the stage, smiling as she claps her hands gently. I could worry about the streaks of mascara that probably make me look like a skunk (and I probably smell like one too) and my floppy hair falling out of place, but I don't. I just look right at her and smile back.

I hold my hand up and give her the metal horns sign, which makes her smile brighter. She nods and turns away, leaning into the person I can now see she's standing with. Charlie Chamberlain leans down to hear what she's saying, then nods, and they both shake their heads, laughing.

And there it goes.

There it all goes.

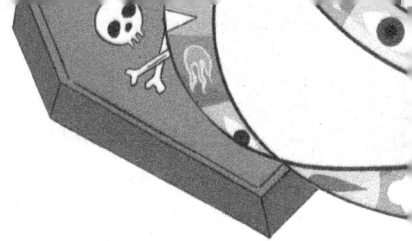

CHAPTER THIRTY-FOUR

ORION FENIMORE

You felt it the first time you saw me. Admit it.

LILA MURPHY

*If when you say it, you're referring to extreme
annoyance, then yes, you're right on the nose.*

Vampire Falls. Season one, episode nine - "Not On Our Watch"

Much, much alcohol has since been consumed due to all the
people in Conference Hall A insisting on buying me drinks, which
I have graciously accepted to counteract the adrenaline. Plus,
some vile pink milky shots Roxy appeared from the bar with.

Roxy had done such a good job on my hair and make-up
there was minimal smudging and frizzing despite all the
sweat and water. Oh yeah, and my general AWESOMENESS.
I kind of feel as close to a rock star as I'm ever likely to get,
so I'm making the most of the party and haven't left the dance
floor, apart from to go for the longest pee in history, because
of the adrenaline and the beers.

Roxy and I swing each other round, laughing and dancing
as the music thuds. She reattached my precious cape, and it
fans out behind me as we twirl.

"You look so good in a cape, babe!"

"I know!" I shriek into her ear. "Thank you for rescuing it."

"What?" she yells.

Suddenly needing her to know how deeply grateful I am for *everything*, I pull her to the side of the dance floor and yell again.

"I said, thank you for rescuing my cape. From the door. I wouldn't have gone on without it. I would have been naked. I mean, felt naked," I laugh.

We fall into each other laughing about me being naked because doing swordplay naked would be extremely dangerous, I imagine. She leans into me, catching her breath and shaking her head.

"I didn't."

"You didn't what?" I shout.

"Rescue the cape," she says.

"Huh?" I say. I'm so confused but still giggly about the naked cosplay.

Roxy shakes her head and sort of slumps into me.

"There were all these hotel people at our door, Eliza, and I was like, *what are these hotel people*? But Charlie was there, at the door, and I said, '*Charlie what are all these hotel people?*' and Charlie said he'd called the hotel people to open our door and escape your cape. Your stuck cape."

Roxy takes a swig of her beer and I frown at her.

"Charlie Chamberlain did?"

"Charlie did," she says, nodding.

She shimmies and takes another swig of her beer, but freezes, her eyes unblinking at something behind me. I mirror her, as she is my best friend and this is how one does things when you know each other well. Her mouth twists into incomprehensible shapes.

Incomprehensible to the non-best friend.

"*He's coming over.*"

"Charlie Chamberlain is?" I say, whipping round, not excited or tummy-fluttery in the slightest.

"Hotty McHotbod," Roxy stage whispers, then bursts out laughing.

"Hey, Team Awesome," says Fake McKinley, frowning at Roxy as she presses her finger against his arm, accompanied by a sizzling sound.

He's still in his lovely tight threads but now accessorised with his birthday crown. He smiles and fist bumps us both then holds out a bottle of water.

"Hi," I say, beaming at him, then turning my nose up at the H2O.

He rolls his eyes and takes my hand, placing the bottle into it.

"I need to whizz," announces Roxy before dancing off.

"OK?" Fake McKinley says, smiling down at me,

"Better than OK," I say, "I am *ebullient.*"

"I hope so, whatever that is," he says, laughing. "You did awesome."

"Thank you for helping Roxy put it together. And for getting me on," I say, sipping some water.

He waves my thanks away and folds his biceppy arms.

"No need. Roxy was all over it, and so were you. Just needed a little nudge."

"Well, you're both my heroes, anyway," I say, play-punching his massive shoulder muscle and actually hurting my poor knuckles. "I'm a lucky girl."

A new song starts, getting a big whoop from the dance floor, and Fake McKinley's face breaks into an even wider smile.

"You're about to get even luckier," he says, putting his hand out to mine as he steps backwards to the music. "This is my all-time favourite song! Come on!"

I let him take my hand but hold back still, enjoying him stepping from side to side as he sings his heart out to the song. I shake my head, laughing.

"So, you can dance as well as sword fight?"

"Hell yeah. My mum made me take dance lessons until I was sixteen. Said the girls would love it." He does a spin, then puts his hand to the side of his mouth and leans down to me. "And they do – thanks, Mum!"

He winks and we both laugh, then he holds out his other hand.

"I don't believe you took actual lessons," I say, shaking my head. "No way."

He stops moving around and steps in front of me, holding both his hands up in the universal *let's-tango-or-some-other-type-of-dance* position. I stare at them, then back away laughing.

"Come on," he says, grabbing the hand still clutching my water and pulling me up to him.

I tuck the water into my sword holster and stumble into him, my legs still a little wobbly from earlier, but his citrussy smell gives me a boost of energy. He smiles and attempts to lead me on our fun little side dance floor. I tread on his foot for the third time and he laughs, shaking his head.

"You, however, have clearly never had lessons," he says.

"True, but what I lack in technical training, I make up for in zeal," I say.

"Zeal?" he says, laughing as he tries to spin me.

"Yes, zeal!"

"Well, here's to zeal!" he says, managing to twirl me round then lean me back in a dip.

I giggle, letting him take my full weight as I enjoy the upside-down version of Conference Hall A, the lights flashing on the ground and everyone dancing from the ceiling. Someone appears from the dance floor and stops in front of us, and it takes me a minute to realise who it is looking down at me.

"Is that Charlie Chamberlain?" I say, still in full dip.

Charlie Chamberlain nods (I think; it's difficult to tell upside down). Fake McKinley pulls me up and I sort of fall into him as he steadies me.

"You are *terrible*," he jokes, high-fiving me then looking at Charlie Chamberlain. "She's terrible."

"Hey," I say, air-punching him because of my injured knuckles. "I'm not *that* bad."

"You backflip better than you pirouette," he says, then turns to Charlie Chamberlain. "Did you enjoy the show? Wasn't she incredible?"

"Yeah, I . . . uh," he says, glancing at Fake McKinley's crown. He opens his mouth to say something but shakes whatever it was away and looks at me. "You did great."

"She totally nailed it." Fake McKinley holds his fist out again and I oblige, but with an added explosion mime. He smiles at me, raising his eyebrows. "You nailed it."

Charlie Chamberlain nods, something like a smile flashing

on his lips before it vanishes and he looks down at his hand.

"Got this for you," he says, holding up another bottle of water and frowning at the one I already have (why is everyone making me drink *water*?).

"Thanks," I say, taking it from him.

Fake McKinley looks over the top of my head at the dance floor, his eyebrows drawing together.

"Guys, I think I just saw Dorothy squaring up to that Tuxedo Vampire who fell on top of her. I better go," says Fake McKinley. He heads onto the dance floor then suddenly turns, adjusts his crown, then throws his hands in the air and shouts, "Zeal appeal!"

I mirror him and shout it back.

"I don't even know what it means!" he says, shrugging.

I laugh, shaking my head as he ducks into the crowd towards Dorothy, who is indeed snarling at Tuxedo Vampire.

"What's that about?" Charlie Chamberlain asks.

"I think Dorothy has beef with that guy because he fell on her," I say, turning back to him.

"Not that," he says, stepping closer to me, sending a buzz of static up and down my body. "I meant . . ."

"Wooohooooo!"

We both look round as Roxy dances past us, her hands on the shoulders of someone dressed as Viggo, a long train of people behind her dancing in sequence around the dance floor.

"Haven't seen drunk Roxy in ages," Charlie Chamberlain says, gesturing at her.

How would you, after you abandoned us? I think to myself.

"What was that?" he says.

"What was what?"

"You said something about abandoning something?" he says, leaning in.

Shit. Damn me and my inability to keep my internal dialogue tucked up safely inside my head.

"Nothing," I say, taking a slurp of my beer which is actually *divine*.

We're standing nearly as close as we were in his bedroom earlier. He smiles, then looks round the dance floor. I watch him, his profile on perfect display for me. It's nice having free rein to peruse his features this close. Did I tell you Charlie Chamberlain's eyes are golden? Like, the colour of autumn, and if you look close enough you can see the reflection of leaves falling in them.

My own eyes wander around him, the flashing lights highlighting different parts of him for me. He's so tall, but he hunches his shoulders a little, used to talking to everyone lower down than he is. He takes a sip of his drink, and I perv at his bicep.

What? Sorry. I've never noticed Charlie Chamberlain's arms before. I mean, I know he has them, for I have seen them many times. Not sure where that . . . I swallow and glance round the dance floor like he's doing. It must be the booze and the skin-tingling closeness we had earlier. That's why I want to take another look at his . . .

"By the way," he says, interrupting my pervy thoughts (thank goodness), "you really were awesome earlier."

"Thanks," I say.

"Seriously. Best I've seen you do it."

"You've seen me *do it*?" I ask.

"Yes," he nods, then his eyes widen. "Seen you do that routine, I mean. On Insta."

"My cape though," I say.

"Your cape?"

I get my words in order and stand on my tiptoes so I can just about reach his ear.

"My cape," I say. "You saved my cape from the door."

"Oh," he says, nodding. He shrugs. "It was fine. I just called down to . . . they sent a couple of guys with a key card."

"Thank you," I say, and he shrugs again.

"You needed your cape."

I swallow, and look up at him, sure the flashing lights are hypnotising me into believing I want him to stand closer to me than he is.

"How drunk are you, Eliza?"

His eyes twinkle as he smiles at me.

"Medium to large," I respond, grinning at him.

"You're ridiculous," he says, shaking his head and laughing.

His eyes lock on mine, then he steps in a little closer, his aftershave scrambling my already quite scrambled thoughts. I stare into his eyes, feeling myself starting to fall into us.

"Did you get my—"

"Well, hey there, losers," says Roxy, interrupting him.

"Hey, Rox," says Charlie Chamberlain, stepping back from me. "Having fun?"

"Having the *best* fun," she says, then hands me a bottle. "Got you a drink, babe."

"It's not water, is it?" I say, gratefully taking the beer and clinking it against Roxy's. "Dudes around here all want to give—"

"I better check on Sadie," says Charlie Chamberlain, doing a little double wave as he backs away and turns towards the tables. My heart sinks as he disappears into the crowd, but I can't ponder as I'm now getting twirled within an inch of my life by Roxy.

"I want to twirl you for ever!" she says, smiling as my cape flows out behind me again. "You rock that thing so hard."

"Why, thank you. It's the latest in functional fashion," I say, forcing her to stop. I strike various poses so she can take photos. "It even has pockets . . ."

I shove my hands inside the pockets my nanna sewed into the bottom of the cape, frowning when my fingers brush against a piece of paper inside one of them. I pull it out and leave Roxy dancing on her own (not that she'd realise) to find some light.

A pink spotlight shines down in the corner so I head there, looking over my shoulder. Satisfied I've found the only solitary spot in Conference Hall A, I unfold the paper, a little breath escaping as I take in the page.

I look around again, then back at the line drawing of me in full Juliana cosplay, my cape billowing out behind me as I lean on my sword. I hold my breath and blink at Charlie Chamberlain's drawing and read the two words scribbled under it.

Good luck.

CHAPTER
THIRTY-FIVE

BUD LEROY

It's giving you the warm and fuzzies, isn't it?

JULIANA THE DEMON HUNTRESS

I feel neither this heat you speak of,
nor this strange texture.

Vampire Falls. Season five, episode twelve –
"Blood's Thicker Than Disorder"

I tell you what, if you're having trouble sleeping, I highly recommend spending a few hours panicking about a cosplay competition, followed by a performance channelled by sheer adrenaline, then getting hammered so your best friend has to carry you fireman's-lift style up to your room afterwards.

I slept like an Undead Corpser from the moment my head hit the pillow, after the hair-grip removal and micellar-soaked cotton pads and moisturiser, lest my skin not rejuvenate after the heavy make-up, thank you, Roxy.

The bedroom door closes behind Roxy with a soft thud as she returns from breakfast laden with coffee and every pastry she could stuff in her onesie pockets. I close my pen inside my notebook, still tucked up in bed, and beam at her.

"I had the *best* dream last night," I say, stretching my limbs out like a Penumbra Hellcat waking up from its death sleep.

"The Damon Van Schwartz appearing in the common room in full Viggo costume one?" she says, popping the coffee on the bedside table.

I nod and she gasps.

"What's wrong?" I say.

"Your notebook, babe!" She puts her hands to her cheeks. "I haven't seen you write in it in for ever."

"I'm not really *writing*," I say, rolling my eyes. "Just like, sparking, maybe."

"Sparking is good. Is it *Never Leave*?" I look at her, and she takes my non-response as the change of subject request I'd meant it as. "OK, I'll shut up, but it's good to see that creased little treasure of your warped imagination again, babe."

I roll my eyes again, but it does feel good just having it on my lap.

"How you feeling?" she asks.

A hangover looms, but my soul is the most buoyant it's felt since we arrived here.

"Goood," I say, wiping a crust of drool from my cheek. She sits on the edge of her bed and sips her coffee, smiling down at me. "Amazing. Knackered."

"I'm not surprised, babe." Her eyebrows lift and she nods her head a fraction. Classic Roxy seal of approval. "You were incredible."

"*We* were," I say. "No way I could have pulled any of that off without you."

"Awesome Team Awesome," she says.

"Awesome Team Awesome," I repeat. I cross my legs, thinking about the routine from last night. "Fake McKinley showed up with his sword skills. Wasn't expecting that."

"Right?" Roxy lifts an eyebrow and fans herself. "I asked if he would help because, well, I was desperate, and he agreed, no worries. I showed him my original plan which was just you with the swords. Cool, but probably wouldn't have stood up to Vivian's thing. We talked it through whenever we got a moment, but he made all the other suggestions. The drums, the water. Even Dorothy and the fire, I mean, what the fuck?"

"What the fuck indeed."

"It was all him," she says, sipping her coffee. "My song suggestion though."

"Obviously."

"Obviously," she repeats.

"Has he done something like this before do you think?" I ask, picking up my coffee.

"Said he did a lot of theatre at college," she says, "but we had so little time to plan we couldn't really get into it. He mentioned stage combat though, but then loads of people here have done stage combat."

"True."

I think about how naturally he moved around on the stage, and his little pep talk before I went on. There's no chance I would have gone on without his words pushing me. I pick up my phone.

"I wonder where he's from. I can't work out his accent," I say.

Roxy pulls up Insta, then rolls her eyes.

"We've never asked his actual name, have we? That's so bad," she says, shaking her head. "We'll hang with him more."

I nod and grab a pecan twist from the napkin on the side table, reminding myself to ask him what his real name is.

"Whoa."

"What?" I ask, looking up from my pecan twist. (OK, lies. The pecan twist is not there. I ate it up in one mouthful.)

"Nothing ... nothing ..." she says.

Not remotely convincing that she's looking at *nothing*, Roxy's eyes zigzag across the screen, her thumb moving around like she's in a texting competition. I open Insta and frown at the little red dots over the heart and the paper aeroplane thing; I never get any notifications or messages on Insta.

"*Vivian's* tagged me in a photo?" I say, a feeling of desperation suddenly giving me the urge to pee (my bladder is like the canary of my general wellbeing).

"No, I mean, yes, but not in the way I know your imagination and bladder is leaping to right now." See. "She's posted pics from last night."

Roxy holds up her phone, showing a photo of me from behind, sitting at the drums, lifting my drumsticks high above my head. I'm the focus of the photo, and the droplets of water hanging in the air plus the illuminated phones everyone's holding up makes me look like I'm headlining a concert.

I blink at the photo then look back at my own phone. They're great pictures. Amazing, *amazing* pictures. Each one is taken from backstage: me in position, waiting for the music to start; me slamming my sword down onto the drum; me frozen in the air as I jump off the stage.

"They're really . . . cool."

"Right?" says Roxy, putting her coffee down and bringing her legs up behind her on the bed.

I scroll down. Hundreds of people have liked the images, and some have even shared them to their stories. I scroll through the names, my heart fluttering a little, until I get to one sandwiched between a couple of cosplayers I follow.

charlie_lfc

Something inside me feels like its blooming as I press on the name and see a photo of me sitting on the drum stool. I'm looking over my shoulder and smiling at the judges, but it almost looks like I'm smiling at the camera. It's a closer one than the others, framed around me and the drums, but you can still see the lights of everyone's phones in the background, blurred and twinkling like drunken stars. I'm glistening with dampness, but, thankfully, my hair and make-up look amazing.

It's a contender for a new profile pic if ever I saw one.

"You OK, babe?"

"Yeah." I nod and look up from my phone. Roxy's smiling at me, watching me like she knows something. I hold up my phone. "Don't you think this is a cool photo of me? Loads of people have shared it."

"Loads of people like . . ." She takes my phone and looks down at it. "Charlie Chamberlain?"

I swallow.

"What?" she says, tilting her head.

"Nothing," I say.

"Vivian's posted loads of photos from the con," she says. "She must have done a little Insta admin session last night. She didn't seem as drunk as us."

"What do you mean?"

Roxy frowns at me, then nods.

"Sorry, I forgot you weren't there. I went back down after I'd tucked you in, Sleeping Beauty that you are."

"You left me here, *alone*?" I exclaim.

I don't care that I was alone, it's just pure FOMO.

"Perfectly secure, babe. You zonked out after I de-hair-gripped you, but I was still pumped, so went back down and found the others in the bar."

"What others?"

"Fake McKinley, Dorothy," she says, fiddling with her coffee cup. "A few others."

"*What . . .*" I cough, flakes of pecan pastry caught in my throat. I take a sip of coffee and try again. "*What others?*"

Roxy shrugs.

"Convention people, Eliza, OK?" She blinks at me, then rolls her eyes. "Charlie was there, and Sadie."

I fold my arms and turn my nose up. My coffee suddenly stinks of betrayal.

"You were hanging with Charlie Chamberlain?"

"Not *hanging*," she says. "He needed help with Sadie."

My cheeks feel very warm, but the mention of Sadie pulls me out of the grey cloud I was in danger of festering in.

"So . . . she loving her first convention?" I say.

"She did *not* stop talking the entire time I was down there,"

Roxy says, shaking her head and smiling. "I know about every exchange she's had with all the guests through each minute of the day."

"Aww, I'm so glad she's enjoying it," I say.

"Yeah, and she made me promise I'd sing with her at karaoke. I swore you in on a pinkie promise as well, by the way."

"Cute," I say, no intention of subjecting that child to my shrieking, but still.

"Guess what her favourite thing has been so far?"

I pull up my legs and eat another pastry. Pain au chocolate; jackpot.

"Um, probably sitting next to Amber Anderson on stage? I know she loves her." Roxy shakes her head. "What then?"

"It was watching you. Last night. She wouldn't shut up about it."

Tears materialise from nowhere and prick my eyes. My emotions must still be very high from my performance.

"Really?" I say.

"She's already texted her mum requesting drum lessons." Roxy smiles at me. "She says you're her hero."

I blink at Roxy then rest against the headboard, my heart swelling with validation I didn't even know I needed.

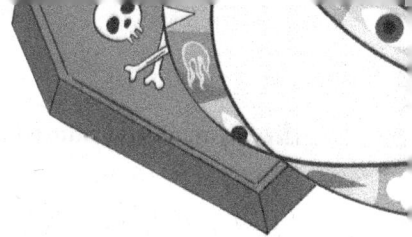

CHAPTER THIRTY-SIX

THE CURATOR

Remove anything from the Draíleabh
Athenaeum and I will smash my favourite
mirror and remove your fingers with the shards.

BUD LEROY

Wow. This librarian is strict.

Vampire Falls. Season two, episode four –
"Return and Renew"

An important (and usually expensive) part of the convention experience is exploring the merch stalls. It's ideal for perusing in between Q&As and autographs, or as a meeting point. *See you in the dealers' room* is like a convention pack howl.

You'll find tons of items perfect for Fallers in the dealers' room. Bored of your iPhone sleep alarm? Why not invest in an alarm clock with Viggo Rassmussen emblazoned on the face? Is your set of keys lacklustre and uninspiring? You need an overpriced Blood is Forever keyring!

I fish my *Vampire Falls* tote from inside my backpack in anticipation of buying shiny new things (Funko. Always a Funko) and spot Fake McKinley. I go up behind him and thwack my tote against his arm. He looks round and smiles when he sees us both.

"Hey, Billy Elliot," I say, Roxy bumping into me for the fourteenth time as she frowns at her phone. "What you doing?"

"Just hanging around," he says, looking at everyone in the lobby, "taking it in."

"Come to the dealers' room with us," I say, waving him along with us. "I've got a whole bag here waiting to be filled with product."

"Drug product?" says Fake McKinley, his eyes wide.

"Merch product!" I say, elbowing him. "We need to get you the convention handbook."

"There's a handbook?" he says.

"You're adorable," says Roxy, looking at Fake McKinley quickly before returning to her phone. "I need to make a quick call. See you in the dealers' room?"

See. Told you.

Roxy rushes off and we head into the large room. Fake McKinley starts floating to the middle aisle, but I grab his elbow and pull him back.

"What are you doing?" I ask, gaping at him.

"Err, looking around the drug dealer's little booth things, like you said?"

"Starting with the *left* middle aisle? What's wrong with you? Do you generally approach life in this haphazard manner, or are you a psychopath?" I say, pulling him to the start of the booths. "We start *here*, and work round *systematically* anticlockwise up and down each aisle."

He rolls his eyes but follows me to the first stall.

"Is all that in the handbook?"he says, looking down at me.

"Yes, actually, I believe it is," I say.

I pick up a handmade *Vampire Falls* bookmark and decide to buy it immediately. Fake McKinley hovers next to me, frowning at everything on the table. He picks up a Juliana coaster and shows it to me.

"I really like her character," he says.

"She's totally the best," I say, nodding.

"I thought the Lila character was your favourite? Isn't that why you're so . . ." He pulls the same hag face Roxy did the other day. Charming. ". . . for the competition? So you can meet her?"

"Yes, obviously," I say, ignoring the face, "but she's not my fave. Juliana all the way. She's the strongest character, and she knows herself so well. I love her."

We stop at a table covered in chunky metal jewellery, plus shields and swords, all replicas of characters' weapons. There's even a glorious House of Huntress family crest sitting on top of a wooden block at the back of the table.

"These are incredible," says Fake McKinley, picking up a goblet. "I could do with this for my protein shakes."

"Thanks, Brown Eyes," says Dorothy, suddenly peeking out from behind the crest.

"Oh, hey, Dorothy," says Fake McKinley smiling down at her. "Is this all yours?"

"I live for the metal." She nods, winking at him. "Enough bullshit though; your timing is perfect. Cover for me while I go powder my nose."

"What?" he says, watching Dorothy shuffle from behind the stall.

"Cashbox and card reader are back there. Curly, you help him."

She waves a hand and trundles to the door.

"So, Dorothy's a metalsmith as well as being a general badass?"

"I want to be her when I grow up, please," I say, raising my hand.

"*I* want to be her when I grow up, please," agrees Fake McKinley, also putting his hand up then looking round when someone stops in front of the booth.

"Hi, Toby," I say, enthusiastically.

Toby barely looks up at me from the Sword of Skallion replica he's holding.

"How much is this?" he asks Fake McKinley.

"The price is on that card," he says.

"I've always wanted a Sword of Skallion, but my mum wouldn't let me," Toby says, staring at it for a good thirty seconds. He looks over his shoulder then nods at us. "I'll take it."

"Good for you, Toby," I say.

He glances at me, unimpressed by my unintentionally patronising seal of approval. Toby pays for his shiny new toy and wanders off to another booth. Anticlockwise. We sit down while a couple of others look over Dorothy's merch.

"So, what *do* you want to be when you grow up?" he says. "Besides Dorothy."

"Not sure really. Was thinking of linguistics, but I'm not

sure now."

"At uni?" he says.

I nod. "What about you?" I say, trying to swallow the lump that always gets lodged in my throat when I think about post-summer. "What do you want to do?"

He leans back and lets out a long sigh.

"I'm trying to work that out right now, to be honest. I'm halfway through a course, which I *think* is useful and I *kind* of enjoy, but I've been offered another opportunity."

"And you're not sure whether to risk the opportunity or see out your course?"

"Exactly," he says. "I know what my limits are, and this is way, *way* out of my comfort zone but has the potential to be awesome. I don't want my limits to *actually* limit how I live my life. I feel like I should give myself a chance. I don't know if that makes sense."

"It does," I say, nodding, as it makes perfect sense; too much sense almost. "So what course are you doing at the moment?"

He opens his mouth to answer but the deathly call of a Siren interrupts him. My soul deflates as I look up at Vivian. I smile at Sadie then glance at Charlie Chamberlain who's looking right at me.

"Look who it is," says Vivian, smiling at us. She picks up an ornate mirror and checks her perfectly applied lipstick. "This is so cute."

I don't know if she's referring to the mirror or her reflection.

"Did you make all this?" asks Sadie, her eyes wide as she picks up a silver stake (suitable for killing vampire/wolf hybrids).

"No, Sadie, Dorothy made it all," I say. "We're just looking after it for her."

"Cool. I want to make swords when I'm older," says Sadie, her eyes sparkling as she looks at the rest of the weaponry.

"That seems to be the consensus," says McKinley, smiling at me.

Sadie blinks at Fake McKinley then turns to her brother.

"That's the man from breakfast, Charlie," she says.

We all look at Charlie Chamberlain, whose cheeks are flushing.

"What? I don't . . . I didn't . . ." he says, his ears flushing.

"Yeah, remember you said to find out who he was," Sadie says, nodding. "Subtly." Sadie looks at me and shrugs. "I don't know what *subtly* means."

Charlie Chamberlain shakes his head and smiles at Sadie but in a *not happy* way. "Come on," he says, putting a hand on her shoulder, "let's go."

Sadie says goodbye then rushes over to a stall and takes a red Jawfain hoodie from a rack. I turn to Fake McKinley who's watching me.

"What?" I ask, checking my nostrils. "Why is everyone staring at me today?"

"Your friend was *definitely* staring at you."

"He is *not* my friend," I say, folding my arms. Fake McKinley shakes his head and smiles. "What now?"

"Nothing," he says, smiling.

"I think perhaps this should be more of a silent business partnership," I say, straightening Dorothy's merch.

I read a text from Roxy. I sigh and sit back in the

uncomfortable chair.

"What's wrong?"

"Nothing," I say, "just Roxy's not done yet."

"Is my company that bad?"

"Yes, actually."

"Fair," he says. "I'm certainly no Roxy."

"Nobody is," I say.

"How long have you been friends?"

"Since primary school. Mrs Spalding used to line us up for lunch according to surname, so I was always stood behind Roxy. One time, Ross Walsh put a daddy longlegs in her sandwich, and I stopped her from eating it. I threw her lunchbox at him, so I shared mine with her."

"Brought together by the gods of the alphabet and sandwiches."

"Don't," I say, shuddering. "I'm waiting for her to realise our friendship was a total fluke and she'll leave me for someone better."

"You don't think that?" he says. My shoulders slump as I blink at him. "Why do you think that?"

He looks down at me, such sincerity in his eyes, and I suddenly have to offload before I internally combust.

"So . . . the plan was for Roxy and I to go to the same uni: Bristol. She's studying forensic science, and I'm going to study linguistics."

"Right . . ." coaxes Fake McKinley, but I think he knows where I'm going with this.

"That's the plan. Or *was* the plan," I say. He smiles at me, so I just go for it. "I didn't get in. Roxy doesn't know."

"Shit, Eliza. I'm sorry."

I haven't spoken to anyone about this apart from my parents (who, by the way, are being equal parts patient and firm with me), because the moment I consider life without a daily guarantee of Roxy in it, my chest becomes incredibly tight, like there's a Hexle Hag sitting on top of me, trying to suck my dreams out through my nose.

Fake McKinley squeezes my arm, but I can't look at him.

"Is there anything else you want to do? Anything else you're good at?"

I shrug and look around the room.

"This? But I don't think I can make a living following Damon Van Schwartz around the globe."

"What about the writing?"

"Writing?" I say, frowning.

"Roxy told me what a good writer you are."

"Did she?"

He nods. "Our time spent together was mostly her telling me how much she wants you to win the competition or the things she loves about you. She sent me some of your fan fiction, but I've not read it yet. Sorry."

It feels like he's hugging my heart. I'm still amazed that Roxy and I fit together in the way that we do.

"She said you haven't written any in a while."

"I haven't." My head turns involuntarily in Charlie Chamberlain's direction. "But I've had this idea for a new fantasy thing, a totally new character. I think."

"That's cool. I was always terrible at writing."

"I kind of love it. The comments and reactions I got on

Wattpad were so cool, and now with this new idea I just get, I don't know . . . excited imagining how someone might feel about what I've made up, in my brain," I say, surprising myself. "Other than this, I think it might be my happy place."

"Could you study writing? At uni?"

"Maybe? I guess? My mum really wants me to do the uni thing because it *'was the best time of her life'*," I say, sighing.

"You're not into it?"

"I was when I thought it would be like an extended weekend with Roxy, but now I'm just kind of . . . numb about it," I say. "I have a couple of other uni options, but I really don't . . . my parents want a decision when I get back."

"No pressure," he says.

"Exactly. Dad's not stuck on uni but he says I'm not allowed to *'lie around like an unemployed herbert'*."

"Who's Herbert?" he asks, laughing.

"No idea. But I know he's right. I can't roll myself into a duvet Swiss roll and exist like that for ever. As appealing as it sounds."

He smiles at me, and despite the utter turmoil my soul is in right now, shovelling this shit off my chest takes the pressure off my lungs a little.

"My grandad used to say, find a job you don't hate, as long as you spend the rest of your time doing something you love."

"Sounds so simple," I say.

"He was retired." We watch someone pick up a bracelet, check the price, then move on quickly. "What about that course. The *Vampire Falls* writer one?"

"Gloria Hannigan?" I say, then shake my head. "I'd never get on that, especially the residential. They pay for the accommodation in Ireland, but you have to get yourself there. And that's if she even selects you." I've looked at the course outline so many times, I could recite every step in the process to Fake McKinley and tell him how many Funko POP!s it would cost to enrol (clue: *a lot*). I slide down in the chair, my back hurting. "Anyway . . . where's doing a writing course going to get me?"

"Didn't you say writing was your happy place?" he says, frowning at me.

"Yeah."

"Is there any better place to get to than that?"

I open my mouth to tell him all the better places I can think of, but he smiles at me, knowing I can't name any.

"That's good," I say, nudging him with my shoulder.

"I know," he says, nudging me back. "I'm very pleased with myself."

"Can we talk about something else now?" I say, suddenly feeling very drained.

"Yes," he says, standing up, "because I've had my eye on these."

He leans over the table, picking up two helmets that I recognise from the battle scene in the season three episode, "We Are All Of Blood". Intricate snakes circle the eye holes and I'm again blown away by Dorothy's talents.

"Put it on," he says, putting one in his lap then holding the other over my head.

I couldn't feel more like hiding inside a helmet right now

so it's actually the perfect thing. I nod and pull my hair out of the way, and he slides it on, the nose guard sitting over my nose. I peer through the eye holes at him.

"Oh yes," he says, nodding at me then carefully putting his on.

We pick up swords and pretend to strike each other, then someone stops in front of our table, frowning at us over the top of their phone.

"Eliza?"

"Roxy!" I say, looking at her through one of my eye holes. "You're back."

"What . . . why are you . . ." she says, blinking from me to Fake McKinley, then around the room. She shakes her head and lets out a long sigh. "Please, just tell me that's not stuck on your head."

My heart lurches then I feel a release as Fake McKinley gently removes my helmet. Roxy smiles. Phew.

"Say goodbye to your friend. You need to get ready for the next part of the competition. There's some paperwork, apparently."

"But I'm minding the stall with . . ." I say, looking round at Fake McKinley.

He beams at me, still wearing the helmet, and holds his sword out in front of him.

"I release you, Eliza," he booms. "You may depart with Roxy."

"You two are so weird," says Roxy, smiling at us both with the same fondness one might have for a one-eared, incontinent dog.

CHAPTER THIRTY-SEVEN

JAWFAIN

(flutters around cell and lands on Viggo's shoulder)

VIGGO RASSMUSSEN

Thank you, Jawfain. I needed that.

Vampire Falls. Season six, episode nine –
"All Together Now"

"What are they calling it again?"

Roxy pulls the competition paperwork out of her backpack and frowns at it.

"*Fallers Forever,*" she reads. "You have to sign this waiver then give it to one of the Headset People," says Roxy.

"A *waiver*? It's not UFC, for god's sake." I blink at Roxy. "It's *not* UFC, is it?"

"No, Eliza, it's not UFC," she says.

I sign my life away, then sit back and rest my head on my bestie's shoulder, a position lots of us have adopted in Conference Hall A. A flame of hair catches my eye. Vivian, Charlie Chamberlain and Sadie are in the front row – VIP seats arranged by Damon Van Schwartz himself. I allow myself a little eye roll at the backs of their heads and Vivian turns around. She probably saw the eye roll with her own third eye. Sadie looks round then jumps up and runs round the chairs over to us.

"Eliza, look!" She plonks herself next to me and flicks through her phone, then holds up a slightly blurry photo of me from last night. "I took loads of photos. I'm getting this one printed. I'll send you some."

"Thanks, Sadie," I say, scooching closer and smiling as she scrolls through the photos. "Did you enjoy it last night?"

She nods until her head nearly pops off her shoulders.

"I liked yours better than Vivian's, but don't tell," she says.

"Thank you," I say, crossing my heart. "I won't."

I look over at Charlie Chamberlain, surprised that he's looking right at me, his arm resting on the back of his chair. For some reason, I feel like I'm back on that stage again, the spotlight shining down on me, and I've forgotten why I'm there.

I gesture to Sadie.

"*She OK with us?*" I mouth.

"*Of course,*" he mouths back, nodding.

He smiles, as if he's waiting for me to say something else, but I hadn't planned on a follow up, so I just sort of look back at him and feel very conscious of my face. I don't think he's blinked once. Are we doing a staring competition? I probably shouldn't look away or breathe, just in case.

Felix walks on stage, and we all look up at him. Thank goodness.

"Morning, everyone."

Roxy frowns at me. Felix has the amazing ability to be the

centre of the convention without being the centre of attention. He's low key, but this morning he just seems kind of . . . low. Something's missing from his voice.

"The judges really enjoyed last night's performances, and I know the audience did too. Our competitors were *fang*tastic."

Pause for clapping. I watch Vivian to see how she responds to the attention from those around her. As suspected; with ease. I guess she's used to it. I need to look around at every single person to acknowledge the praise and file it away in my catalogue of emotions to refer to at a later date and remember how it feels.

"We're working through the scores from the judges, plus our notes on the audience response for each competitor. But now, on to this round of the competition. Here," he says, stepping to the side as the spotlight illuminates behind him, "we have three coffins. A member of your team must stay in the coffin for as long as possible."

I glance at Sadie and Roxy, giving them a little shrug.

"Easy," I say. "I'll have my phone."

"You will not be allowed your phone," says Felix, even though he can't possibly hear me from there.

I shrug again.

"Still easy. They can't stick us in there and not allow breaks for the toilet."

"There will be no comfort breaks."

I swallow.

"Snacks?" I say, hopefully.

"Snacking is not permitted in the coffins," says Felix.

"What *is* this hell?" I say, shaking my head.

"This is a test of your love for *Vampire Falls*," says Felix. "Competitors, you need to decide which member of your *tomb*, sorry, *team*, has what it takes to stay locked up in the shadows for the longest."

Chatter erupts from the audience and this time I'm not enjoying all the looks, which are basically *rather-her-than-me*.

"So, you're getting in the coffin, right?" I ask Roxy.

"You're hilarious," Roxy says.

"Well, I can't ask Dorothy, can I? Not with her hip." Dorothy is a few rows behind us. Snoring. She's sitting next to Fake McKinley, who waves. "Although . . ."

Roxy looks over her shoulder then pulls me back round.

"You are *not* scooping up a sleeping Dorothy and sticking her in a coffin," she says, jabbing me with a finger.

"Fine," I say, rolling my eyes.

"Maybe Fake McKinley'll do it for you?" says Roxy.

"You think?" I say. Dorothy has slumped over so she's resting on his arm. "I'm not sure he'd even fit."

Charlie Chamberlain waves Sadie over. She jumps up and turns to us.

"Will you be at the party tonight?" she asks.

"Yes," says Roxy. "Are you dressing up?"

Sadie nods, her eyes sparkling.

"We're coming as Beryl and Livius, you know, the psychic brother and sister from season four?"

It's gorgeous seeing a new fan fall in love with the show. My heart swells in delight for everything she has to come. The merch, the spoilers, the Thursday nights when a new episode drops on Netflix. It's all part of a fan's journey.

"Yeah, we know who you mean," I say.

"Is this your favourite theme of the weekend, Sadie?" asks Roxy.

Sadie shakes her head.

"My favourite is the karaoke party. I mean, I think it will be."

"Really?" I say. "Isn't it Ghosts and Gargoyles?"

"Yeah, but not because of the dress-up, I mean because of the singing. Charlie told me how much fun it is."

I nod. He came to the convention on a day pass one year. Mum waited patiently for all of us to have a go on the karaoke before driving us home. When I say all of us, I mean Charlie and Roxy because I could never sing in front of real people. Drums, yes. Swordplay, yes. But singing out loud while a bunch of people stare and judge my horrendous voice. No thank you.

"He's right, Sadie. It is good fun," says Roxy.

"I can't wait," she says, her eyes wide. "Then I'll be a real fan."

"You are a real fan, Sadie," I say.

"Not until I've completed my first convention," she says, her face serious and hopeful.

Roxy and I look at each other, and I'm glad to see she also has a little tear for Sadie's burgeoning obsession.

"OK, I better get back." She throws her arms around me and squeezes hard. "Good luck, Eliza. I know I'm on Vivian's team, but I secretly want you to win really. Don't tell."

I nod as she turns and runs off, unable to confirm that I won't tell because I will definitely cry if I try to speak.

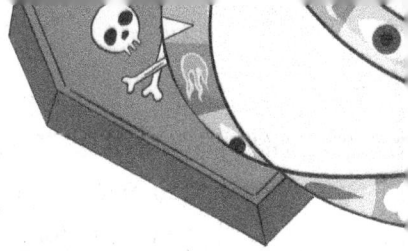

CHAPTER
THIRTY-EIGHT

JULIANA THE DEMON HUNTRESS

This is for the blood of my parents!

Vampire Falls. Season four, episode ten – "Finally Here"

I'm so glad you're dead when you're in one of these for eternity.

Roxy attempts to massage my shoulder muscles, which is impossible because they are currently the hardest substance on the planet right now. Someone should probably contact NASA. I stare at the chasm of shadows and anxiety, aka the coffin, and squeeze Jawfain. A Headset Lady comes over and ushers us up to the stage.

"You can do this," says Roxy, following me up the steps. "You never get to be alone with just you and your thoughts, so think of it as a bonus."

"Why are you making this more terrifying?" I say, gaping at Roxy. "Who wants to be alone with themselves and their thoughts?"

"Serial killers probably," offers Dorothy. "And plumbers."

Roxy looks over her shoulder at the other contestants standing in front of their coffins.

"Focus, babe. I heard Rashawn does scuba diving. Vivian

isn't going in; claustrophobic apparently." Wow. So, she is human then and not a cyberbabe created to destroy us all. "Charlie's going in for her and he's OK with small spaces. Remember when he hid inside the sofa bed, and we watched an entire episode of *Vampire Falls* before he jumped out."

I glance at Charlie Chamberlain, remembering how he suddenly emerged from the sofa like some kind of Ikea zombie. Roxy and I screamed and screamed until he'd fully clawed his way out wearing his McKinley mask. Mum was in on the whole thing and just carried on making Thursday night burritos.

"I remember," I say, watching Charlie Chamberlain do that neck stretch thing athletic types do before the big game or whatever. He's wearing a pair of grey joggers and football T-shirt, so he looks all snuggly. Sorry, when I say snuggly, I mean he's planned for comfort, and not just worn the limited items of clothing from the catalogue he'd assigned himself during this weekend.

"Like I said, you can do this, babe," says Roxy again.

I give her what my nanna would have called a *chewing-shit* smile and look back at the coffin. Whatever joker set this up has laid a plastic skeleton wearing the Full Moon Diner uniform inside each one.

"Maybe you should have worn something less . . . tight," says Fake McKinley.

My baggy *Blood is Forever* T-shirt is fine, but my jeggings are, let's face it, half a size too small.

"Thank you for that observation," I say. The air con (or the impending buried alive scenario) makes me shiver.

"Maybe I should have done layers. Are coffins cold, do we think?"

"Here."

Fake McKinley steps forward, unzipping his maroon hoodie and takes it off. He's wearing a (tight) white T-shirt underneath. Headset Lady's eyes widen, and she fans herself with her clipboard.

"Thank you," I say.

"May this hoodie bring you the clearest of thoughts and emptiest of bladders," he says, putting it round my shoulders.

I stick my arms in the oversized sleeves. It completely swamps me, but I wonder what washing powder he uses as it's so soft.

"Very cute," he says, pulling the hood over my head. I laugh and smack him away. He tugs the golden hoodie toggles, nodding at me. "Good luck."

"Is it just us or are we all getting in the coffins?" says Charlie Chamberlain, his eyes flicking between me, Fake McKinley and Headset Lady.

"Right. Yes," says Headset Lady, shaking herself free of Fake McKinley's muscle trance. "Time to say goodbye to your friends."

"For ever?!" I blurt.

"Just for the duration of the competition," she confirms.

Team Awesome hug me one by one before descending the steps and sitting in the front row. Headset Lady looks at her clipboard, nodding as she digests the information, then smiles up at us. She has a nice smile. I'm glad I got to see it before I die.

"Once you're in, we'll put the lids on. As with the other heats, there are points for each place – so we won't tell you if anyone comes out; not until the final person remains. Anyone need the toilet before we start?"

"Yes! I mean, no," I blurt, looking at the other two for guidance. They offer me nothing. Mind games. "I don't know."

"You can't take that in with you, I'm afraid," Headset Lady says.

I look down at Jawfain then clutch him to my chest. Headset Lady shrugs, then Roxy runs up the stairs and takes him from me.

"Take good care of him," I say, putting my hand on her cheek.

"I will," she says, then heads back to her seat next to Vivian and Fake McKinley.

"OK." Headset Lady sticks the clipboard under her arm. "Please step in and make yourselves comfortable."

We all step inside our coffins. I sit down then shuffle until there's enough space for my legs to stretch out. I shove the skeleton over and lie back, propping myself up on my elbows.

"H-how will we get out?"

"Just push the lid off and step out. Quietly though, or your competitors will hear you," says Headset Lady. "If there's an emergency, just ask for help. They're made to keep sound to a minimum, but we can hear you if you speak up, don't worry."

"I'm sorry, why are we doing this?" I ask in a panic. "Coffins have nothing to do with vampires."

The other two look round at me. I realise the absurdity of what I've just said, but I'm slightly panicking, OK?

"You don't have to do this if you don't want to," offers Charlie Chamberlain.

"Who says I don't want to do it?" I frown at him then lie back. "I can't wait to do it. Lying in coffins is actually my favourite thing to do so I feel sorry for anyone who thinks they can beat me."

"OK then."

His voice floats from the other side (not literally) and I watch the stewards lower my lid down. I take a few deep breaths and close my eyes. Just focus on Comic Con, Eliza, you can do it.

CHAPTER THIRTY-NINE

JULIANA THE DEMON HUNTRESS

I will never forgive you, for as long as I live all my lives.

Vampire Falls. Season two, episode seventeen –
"Dead Moon"

My Trip to San Diego Comic Con and Megan Nicole Jefferies. ROUND THREE.

I open my eyes. The lid is on but thankfully it's not as dark in here as a real coffin would be, I don't think. I can actually see everything clearly, including the skeleton I'm sharing with who's facing away from me.

"Rude."

I try to rearrange him but I can't quite manoeuvre my arms, so I just frown at the back of his head instead. I reckon it's a he. I'll call him Frank. My left bum cheek is going numb, so I roll onto my side until I'm kind of spooning Frank. Not that I've ever spooned anyone before. Great, so my first experience of intimate spoonage is with a life-size plastic skeleton. Brilliant.

"Have you done this before?" I whisper to Frank, putting my arm over his waist.

He doesn't answer. He's such a good listener. I peer at the side of his skull, where his ear would be. I wonder if it's an anatomically correct skeleton but never listened properly in biology, due to it being on a Friday which is the day after *Vampire Falls* episodes drop on Netflix. My hand twitches. The desire to grab my phone and check how many bones a skeleton has is overwhelming. I wonder if I'm addicted to my phone. My hand twitches again, desperate to check the signs of being addicted to your phone. God, this is boring. I wonder how long we've been in here.

"How long's it been?" I call into the ether.

A pause, and a headshake. I can tell when people are shaking their head or rolling their eyes at me without looking. It's a gift.

"Thirty-eight seconds."

"What?!" I turn to Frank, shaking my head. "It's been at least five minutes."

"Sounds like you can't hack it," says Charlie Chamberlain, his voice clear but turned down a few notches.

I glare in the general direction of his voice, which happens to be the back of Frank's head.

"I was merely assimilating information," I respond.

"Will you be assimilating information for the duration, or will you be competing in more of a quiet way?" he asks.

"I'm sorry," I snap, "I didn't know they'd made you the chief invigilator."

"They did actually."

"Well, good for you, I guess. Something else to stick on your bulging UCAS form."

"Um, hi?" Rashawn clears his throat. "Do you guys, like, know each other?"

I turn and look at the other side of my coffin. I'd forgotten Rashawn was here too. I open my mouth to respond but Charlie Chamberlain gets in first.

"We're friends."

"*Used* to be friends," I correct him.

There are a few beats of silence before his voice materialises again.

"Used to be friends then," says Charlie Chamberlain.

I turn back to him quickly.

"Why did you roll your eyes when you said that?" I say.

"How could you possibly know I rolled my eyes?"

"Well, did you?" Silence. "Knew it."

"Maybe you should stop talking to save oxygen in your coffin," says Charlie Chamberlain.

"Guys, focus," says Rawshawn. "You used to be friends but now you're not? Is that correct?"

The way he says it sounds so final and simple, and I wonder why I've spent so much time turning it over in my head when that's what it is. We used to be friends but now we're not. I wait for Charlie Chamberlain to answer.

"Correct," he confirms.

"So what happened? You're both here, so you must have that in common," says Rashawn.

"He's only here because of Sadie," I say.

"Who's Sadie?" asks Rashawn.

"His sister. Who is adorable, despite her bloodline."

"Right," Rashawn says. "And the sister is a Faller, but

you're not, Charlie?"

"He used to be," I spit.

"I'm capable of responding for myself thank you, Eliza." He clears his throat. "I still watch the show."

"No, you don't," I snap.

"Just because I don't watch with you, doesn't mean I don't watch it, Netflix police."

I frown at him. Well, not him, at Frank.

"OK, I think we're starting to unpack something interesting here, guys." I imagine Rashawn looking at us over his glasses. "You used to watch it together?"

"He'd never heard of *Vampire Falls* until I showed it to him."

"Right, so you're his sire? That's big, guys."

Sire is what fans call the person who introduced them to the show. I try to shrug but the coffin is making my shoulders numb. Charlie answers for me anyway.

"She was. Sired over a tray of chicken and chips."

I swallow. I was certain when we'd stopped being friends, he'd erased all memory of our friendship, including his entry into it. I can't believe he remembers what he was eating that day.

"Chicken and chips?" asks Rashawn.

"Never mind," says Charlie Chamberlain.

"Perhaps The Kinnuix brought you this weekend, Charlie," says Rashawn, referencing a destiny-spinning demon from season three, "and we're all grateful it did otherwise DVS would literally be dead right now."

I roll my eyes. Not Rashawn too. Surely the Charlie Chamberlain fan club has enough members.

"Are you rolling your eyes in there?" says Charlie Chamberlain.

Does he have the gift too? I prop myself up on an elbow.

"Damon Van Schwartz coughed on a mint, and Dr Cullen here intervened with a couple of claps on his back. It wasn't a big deal."

"I performed the Heimlich. Do you know how hard that is?"

"Oh, you *performed* it?" I do air quotes inside my coffin. "I didn't realise it was a *performance*. Your greatest yet, no doubt."

"It's dangerous if you don't do it right. You could break someone's rib."

"And thank goodness you did it right because you came to the rescue and made yourself the hero of the convention. Excuse me if I don't give you a standing ovation but I'm lying down in a coffin."

"Whatever, Eliza. Maybe just stop talking to me. It's what you're best at."

"*Oh*," says Rashawn, (probably) nodding in his coffin. "Now we're getting somewhere. Why'd she stop talking to you, Charlie?"

I hold my breath, waiting for Charlie to say something, but after a few seconds Rashawn's voice floats through the darkness again.

"I've over-stepped. So sorry, guys. Obviously sensitive. I'm studying therapy and counselling at uni, and getting carried away," he says. "Message received."

I turn towards Rashawn's voice and take a breath.

"We just . . . grew apart," I say.

"OK, I hear you," says Rashawn, his voice soft. "But why the beef? People who grow apart don't snipe like you two.

There's more, isn't there?"

"I think we both just . . . changed?" Charlie offers.

I turn and glare at Frank.

"Excuse me – I did not change, Charlie Chamberlain. I am still the lovable nerd I was when we became friends. You're the one who changed. You're the one who swapped the *Falls* for football. And Vivian."

"Vivian?" repeats Rashawn. "Oh, the impossibly hot redhead roller-skating one? This is making sense now."

I turn back to Rashawn's coffin.

"What do you mean, *it's making sense now*?"

"Maybe I shouldn't get involved, hun," he says.

"You've been probing us for the last forty-five minutes; you *are* involved!" I point out.

"It's been two minutes and sixteen seconds," clarifies Headset Lady.

"*What?*" I wail. Is San Diego actually worth this? "Hell. This is actual hell."

"Did you two hook up or something?" says Rashawn, his voice low.

"No!" we both shout in response.

"OK, OK, just . . . *something* happened. I can sense something between the two of you and it's more than just *change*."

"She pushed me away and she pushed me out."

"You didn't need us any more," I snap. "You had a whole football team of bros and dudes just waiting to worship you."

"*Because* you pushed me out. I literally had nobody."

"Why'd she push you out, Charlie?" asks Rashawn.

"I didn't push him out! I didn't push you out, Charlie," I snap.

"You ghosted me," he says. "You ignored my texts and phone calls. You removed me from the *Falls* WhatsApp group. You blocked me on everything. I came round to your house and your mum said you weren't there, but I could see the light in your room."

"Because *you* blanked *me*, Charlie. You ignored my messages; you wouldn't answer my calls."

"For, like, a week," he says.

"It was one of the hardest measures of time I ever had to exist through, Charlie," I say, my voice wobbling. "Doesn't matter that it was just a week."

I don't mention the devastation of him choosing Vivian over me, and I don't tell him that I spent way more than a week crying myself to sleep. Or that I didn't tell Roxy just how deep the crack in my heart was because I didn't want her to know that our friend had hurt me so badly.

"Charlie?" says Rashawn, his voice calm. "Do you want to respond to that?"

"I'm sorry," he says, but I don't know if he's just saying it because of Dr Rashawn. "I freaked out, OK? I thought everything would change and I'd lose you, then it did, and I did."

I lie in the darkness, the pain of his looks of indifference compared to his face lighting up when he saw me still squeezing my lungs.

"You broke my heart, Charlie. I knew it would get broken one day," I say, clasping my shaking hands together, "but I never thought it would be you breaking it."

"So, you feel like Charlie broke your trust. Is that right, Eliza?"

I nod, and somehow they both know.

"I fucked up; I realise that," says Charlie Chamberlain. "I realised, like, a week later but you wouldn't speak to me. I tried to reach out to you, but you'd made up your mind and it was like we'd never happened. Do you know how that made me feel? Do you know how lonely I was? You had Rox, but I had nobody."

"You were fine with your new friends," I say.

"Because I *had* to be. I *had* to go and make new friends. The worst thing . . ." He pauses and I blink at Frank, wondering what he's going to say. Charlie Chamberlain, not Frank. I haven't got cabin fever yet. "I didn't want to lose you as a friend but that's exactly what happened. You punished me by taking that away because you knew how much it would hurt."

"*I* punished *you*?" I repeat, tears pricking my eyes. "How can you say that? How can you say I hurt you, Charlie? All you've done since then is make fun of me. How do you think that makes me feel?"

"It's just banter, Eliza."

"Using my favourite thing to make me feel shit about myself isn't banter, Charlie."

"I was just messing around?" It comes out as a question, like he's not sure if he was or not. I'm not sure either. "It was the only . . . it was . . ."

"It was what, Charlie?" says Rashawn. "Tell her."

"It's the only interaction I get with you. We used to make

fun of each other all the time . . . I just . . . I just miss messing around with my friend."

I thought lying inside a coffin was torture, but hearing Charlie Chamberlain saying all this is worse.

"But you just laugh when your mates do it. When Vivian does it."

"When has Vivian ever made fun of you?" he says.

I spin round to look at Frank, the shadow of sentimentality retreating in the wake of instantaneous rage.

"All the time! I've seen her whispering to you about me. She hasn't stopped since she got here. I don't know why you had to bring her."

"What's Vivian got to do with this anyway? I thought we were talking about us?"

"We're not talking about us," I say, chewing the inside of my cheek.

"Fine, ignore this conversation just like you ignored me. Shit, Eliza, when did you get so cold."

"Cold?" Tears spring in my eyes as I blink at Frank. "How can you say *I'm* cold? You didn't . . . you didn't even contact me when my nanna died, Charlie. I'm sorry you felt pushed out, that I pushed you out, but I thought you would, despite how things had changed."

I'm glad of the darkness and the privacy as my face completely crumbles and I don't know if the tears are for Nanna or for Charlie. Maybe they're for both.

"Eliza," Charlie Chamberlain says, his soft voice sending a little crack tearing through my left ventricle.

"Forget it," I say, trying to keep control of my voice.

I take a deep breath and search my pockets for a tissue which, of course, is fruitless as I hadn't planned on having a meltdown inside a coffin today.

"I . . . I . . ." Charlie Chamberlain's voice is quiet, like it's tiptoeing towards me. "I came to your house, Eliza. Of course I came to your house. I wouldn't have . . ."

I lift my head, waiting for the rest of his words.

"What?"

"You were asleep, and your mum said you'd been awake all night, so I didn't want to . . . I just . . . I wanted to . . . but I left what I'd brought and . . . maybe I should have waited but it had been so long, and your mum was upset. I didn't want to intrude."

I swallow, blinking at the back of Frank's head, then press my cheek against the cool, white plastic. We don't say anything for a while, and I let Charlie Chamberlain's words swirl around the fake coffin dust and paint fumes.

"*Guys,*" sniffles Rashawn. "Eliza, I'm sorry about your nanna."

"Thank you," I squeak, also sniffling.

A sliver of light slips into the coffin as my lid lifts and a hand emerges holding a travel tissue.

"Thank you," I say to the hand.

"You're welcome, love," says Headset Lady.

I dab my face and blow my nose, then lie back. My chest feels lighter, like I've dropped something I've been carrying around for ages. Or let it go.

"Charlie, I . . ." I pull myself up onto my elbows a little and look down at Frank. "You're right, I . . . I did push you out of our friendship. I shouldn't have done that, but . . . I'm sorry, OK? I'm sorry for what happened, and I'm sorry I pushed you away. Most of all, I'm sorry that I don't have you any more; I'm sorry you're not a part of my life. You were my favourite part of my life for a while. I miss that, and I miss you. That's what I'm most sorry about."

"Don't you want to know what he brought you, Eliza?" whispers Rashawn after a while.

"Huh?"

"He said he brought you something when he came to your house."

I look round.

"What did you bring me, Charlie?" I say, waiting for him to respond, but there's nothing. "Charlie?"

The competition doesn't seem as important suddenly, and I sit up, pushing the coffin lid off to the side. I blink in the light then find that Charlie's lid is also at an angle and his coffin is empty. I look up at Headset Lady.

"He left," she says.

"When?" Rashawn and I ask in unison.

Headset Lady looks down at me, her eyebrows tilting up in sorrow.

"Just before you told him you're sorry, and that you miss him. Sorry, love."

I nod and look around. There are still quite a few in the audience, including my lot and Vivian and Sadie, who're all frowning at me. Roxy looks over her shoulder at the double doors, so I guess Charlie Chamberlain is long gone. I sigh and look back at his coffin.

"I'm so sorry he wasn't here for all that, Eliza," says Rashawn, "but I guess that makes me the winner now, though, right?"

CHAPTER FORTY

COX THE OBSERVER
*The answers are right there in front
of your stupid, distracted, mortal eyes.*
BUD LEROY
(looks up from phone) What he say?

Vampire Falls. Season three, episode twenty –
"It's Always a Mary"

"What did he say though? He looked upset when he got out," Roxy says, smooshing my face with a damp and cold sponge. "We could hear mumbling, but we couldn't make out what you were saying."

After the coffins, I looked for Charlie Chamberlain in the lobby, the coffee shop, the restaurant – but I couldn't find him. I don't know what I would have said to him anyway, but I figured something would come when I saw him. I'm not usually lost for words, as you know.

"Not much," I say, not sure why I don't want to tell her exactly what he said. "Just the usual Charlie stuff, I guess."

"Charlie?" she says, straightening up and looking at me in the mirror. "You never call him Charlie."

"I always call him Charlie. It's, like, his name, Roxy. Have you bumped your head?"

"Sorry to burst your bubble, babe, but you always call him Charlie *Chamberlain*, like he's a villain." She dabs make-up into the crease of my nose. "Or a superhero."

"Do I?"

"You do," Roxy says. "Right, writing time's over. Close your eyes."

I click my pen off and close my notebook, but my fingers itch to get back to scribbling down the ideas that have been bubbling inside my brain for the last couple of days. I didn't realise how much I missed that feeling.

I close my eyes and flinch every time the sponge touches my skin. For the Vampire Apocalypse party, we're in the Taylor High soccer strip, but slightly bedraggled so we look like we're in search of human brains.

"I wish Iris was here," I say.

The dabbing stops and I risk opening my eyes. Roxy's blinking at me, the sponge frozen in mid-air.

"Do you?"

I nod. "She's much gentler."

Roxy frowns and smears make-up over my eyelid without warning. I guess I asked for that.

"Right," she says, rubbing strawberry smelling hair wax through her fingers. "I'm not spending ages on hair as we have headsets apparently."

"What've headsets got to do with a zombie apocalypse?"

"It's a silent disco, babe," she says, tweaking my hair. "Should be cool."

"Really?" I say, not convinced. She picks up the eyeliner. "I don't think zombies wear eyeliner."

"These zombies do," she says, turning to me, the applicator poised in her hand. "Wings will look cool against the grey. Come on."

I turn my face to her and look up.

"If we get to room together at Bristol, I can do your make-up when we go out, babe." I daren't move as she comes at me with the eyeliner wand. "Stop pulling away."

"I'm not."

"You are," she snaps.

"It's my reflexes. I can't help my reflexes, Roxy."

She blows a piece of backcombed hair out of her face then looks around.

"Try to relax," she says, leaning over and picking something off my screwed-up duvet. "Hold this."

She throws my Jawfain cuddly onto my lap and I squeeze him. Fiddling with his ears always calms me down.

"Keep your head straight, and close your eyes," says Roxy.

I don't think nodding is permitted so I just close my eyes and focus on Jawfain's fur between my fingers.

"That thing's like your comfort blanket. You're nine."

"Hey," I say.

"Didn't say it was a bad thing. He's cute. I wish I had one."

"I'll get you one for your birthday," I say. "We can be Jawfain twins. Where'd you get it?"

"Get what?" she says, lining my other eye.

"Jawfain. You got him for me when . . ."

I grip Jawfain's ears hard as something falls into place.

I look round at Roxy, causing her to smear a line across my cheek.

"For god's sake, Eliza," she huffs.

"Sorry, I . . ."

My voice trails off, retreating to a year ago. Even though I'd been awake most nights leading up to it, I remember that afternoon. I'd just woken from a nap when Dad knocked on my door and told me Roxy was downstairs. I peeled myself out of bed and went down to find her waiting for me in the hallway. She squeezed me tight, and we had a few tears together before she had to get back. It was Mum's turn to catch up on the sleep she'd lost at the hospice, so after Roxy'd gone, she wasn't awake to tell me the gift bag I'd found right where Roxy had stood in the hallway wasn't actually from Roxy, but from someone else.

"You didn't get this for me?" I ask, knowing the answer.

Roxy glances at Jawfain, still annoyed, and shakes her head.

I look down at Jawfain, his cute face smiling up at me as if to confirm what I've just realised. I was so tired from the nights we'd spent at the hospice, and the next week was such a blur I mustn't have thanked Roxy for the gift, so she couldn't have told me it wasn't from her.

And I couldn't have known who it was actually from.

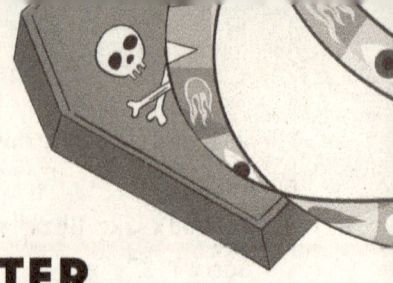

CHAPTER
FORTY-ONE

ORION FENIMORE

You're alive.

LILA MURPHY

So are you. Well, kind of.

Vampire Falls. Season one, episode twelve –
"Masquerade Brawl"

Roxy and I walk out of the lift into what feels and looks like an actual zombie apocalypse (though the lifts wouldn't be operational, of course). We look at each other and smile, then she loops her arm through mine and we head into the flesh-eating mob.

The undead are everywhere; squeezed on sofas drinking through straws so they don't smudge their make-up, waiting at the bar whilst talking to intrigued non-zombie and non-convention (and probably alarmed) hotel guests. There's even a couple carrying an over-tired zombie toddler.

People ask us for selfies, and we of course oblige, hanging out our tongues because that's how zombies roll. Roxy delights everyone with a few keepy-uppies with a blood-splattered football, flicking it up in the air and catching it in the crook of her neck. I don't know if I've mentioned this before but shit, she's cool.

We go to the bar, and I order us a couple of beers. Beverages in hand, we head towards Conference Hall A.

"Whoa," says Roxy, putting her hand on my arm and slowing. "How weird is that?"

I look around, wondering what she's talking about, and then it hits me. Or it doesn't hit me. There's no music coming from inside the hall. We head through the doors and everyone's wearing headphones, behaving (and sounding) like there *is* actual music playing even though all we can hear is a weird out-of-tune hum. It's like behind-the-scenes footage of a scene at The Purple Nightcap, with people acting like there's music blasting, but there isn't any.

"Hey!"

Fake McKinley beams as he stops in front of us and takes off his headset, Dorothy clutching his arm like he's offered to help her cross the street. He's dressed as the science teacher who was sadly eaten by his entire chemistry class when he accidentally created a zombie virus in school. As you do. The only reason I know that's his costume is because he's wearing a faculty name tag: bespectacled Mr Marian was near retirement and hunched over from years of marking papers. Fake McKinley just looks like Clark Kent. A Henry-Cavill-if-he-had-a-beard, Clark Kent.

"Hey, guys. Excellent costumes," says Roxy, looking him and Dorothy (who looks amazing as Venefica the witch with a crown of finger bones and a long red cloak) up and down. She turns to me. "Who are you looking for?"

"Huh?" I say.

"You keep looking around for someone."

I swallow, realising that I *am* looking around for someone.

"I'm just . . . looking at the costumes." I clear my throat and point to my ears. "So, how do they work then? The headsets?"

"I'll show you!" says Fake McKinley, a huge smile on his face. "You get them from the front and when you put them on it's like being at a club, but you choose the DJ."

We follow him across the dance floor and Dorothy breaks off and joins everyone shuffling around to music I can't hear. Someone lurches at me suddenly, their face contorting as they mouth unknown song lyrics and clap their hands. Their friend grabs them, and they bounce up and down together. It very much feels like walking through a, you guessed it, zombie apocalypse but without the threat of having my flesh consumed.

Fake McKinley beckons us over to a table filled with headsets, all with white lights blinking on them. He picks one up and hands it to Roxy. She puts the headset on, frowning as she flicks the dial round. The light on the side of her headset moves through a rainbow of colours until she stops at red. Her face lights up and she puts one hand to her ear and nods to her song choice.

She shimmies into the middle of the dance floor where Dorothy is already jiving around, throwing her arms in the air. I laugh at the sight of Roxy towering over tiny Dorothy, but my heart feels warm. This is what conventions are all about for me. Doesn't matter who you are: if you love *Vampire*

Falls, you're welcome to party with us.

"Here," says Fake McKinley, holding a headset to his ear and turning the dial. "You can see what DJ other people are listening to by the colour of the light."

He frowns as the lights change colour, then his eyes twinkle and he puts the headset over my ears. My headspace is immediately filled with music. He puts his back on and bops along, completely out of sync with the disco beat going off inside my head. It's weird, and it's fun, and it's freeing, and I can't help but smile.

I turn the dial to see what else there is. Everyone dances around me as I move through each channel until, there it is, the perfect song. I close my eyes and lift my hands. The guitar intro sends me right into my favourite *Vampire Falls* scene.

Lila and Orion spend most of the episode apart, fighting demons and preventing an apocalypse. Orion arrives at the Vampire Ball, desperately looking around the dance floor, and just as the guitar starts, in walks Lila. She's dressed for the ball (despite having just fought to the death), but Orion's in his signature hoodie and jeans combo (with an eye mask, even though he's a ghost; we'll let the continuity team off the hook for that one though). Lila lifts her green ball dress to reveal she's still wearing her trusty Doc Martens.

They make their way towards each other, weaving through all the other ballgowns and tuxedos, the guests oblivious to almost being on a real vampire's menu. They meet and begin to dance, the traditional vampire courtship taught to them by Viggo, one hand held up close as they move into one another, looking deep into each other's eyes as they step side to side, closer, then further away.

It's the reason I've never had a boyfriend, never really kissed anyone, not that I'm inundated with offers. That's what love and romance looks like to me, and nobody could ever live up to it.

The music lifts me above everyone and everything, and I smile as I twist and turn, imagining Lila and Orion dancing together. I pull my headset off to check the colour of my light – yellow – then put it back on, just as I notice someone off the dance floor watching me, tapping their hand against the wall in time to the music in my head, their headset light the same colour as mine.

Charlie smiles, the kind of smile I used to live for in the common room. He puts his beer down on the table, then leans over Sadie whose nose is almost pressed against her phone. She nods and he ruffles her hair then looks back at me, his eyes sparkling with the joy great music brings.

Charlie weaves between people on the dance floor, tapping his hand on his leg along to the beat in his head, and in mine. My heart flutters as he gets closer. Is he *actually* doing this?

Are we doing this?

He's a few metres from me now, and magically a path clears in front of us, just like it does for Orion and Lila. We step up to each other, until there's barely any space between us, and move round to the left, then turn to the right. The song's chorus tiptoes up my body, caressing my skin.

He lifts his hand until it's eye-level, and I do the same.

Our palms press together, and the fifth of November explodes through my entire body. Reluctantly, I move my hand to the small of my back, and he does too, *because we are doing this.* I step back and forward, then lift my other hand so our palms come together.

There are those fireworks again.

All the zombies have melted away and it's just me and Charlie together. His eyelids are heavy, and his smile is sweet and content, like he's just woken from a dream. I bite my lip, knowing what's coming next, and slowly his fingers clasp over mine, pulling me into him. His body feels warm, and he looks over every inch of my face. I breathe in, and my heart instantly recognises his aftershave. It smells of vanilla and sweet orange, of touching knees, crumpled little notes, and fingers brushing in the popcorn bowl. It smells like Charlie.

His hand moves to the small of my back, and I freeze. I don't care that I have a slash across my chest or that I'm wearing a football strip. All I know is that I'm here with Charlie, and I've missed him. He unfurls his fingers from mine and I panic that he's pulling away, but his hand moves up to the side of my neck, gently, then tucks my hair behind my ear.

We're doing this. We're actually doing this and I—

The most unlikely scenario has the audacity to catch my eye and I step back from him, turning to look properly so I can confirm my eyes are playing a bizarre, inappropriate prank on me.

"What?" I whisper.

I pull my headset off. Charlie says something, but my attention is very much on the two people wrapped around each other in the shadows next to the control booth.

Two people, smiling and twirling each other's hair, headsets dangling in their hands.

Roxy and Vivian.

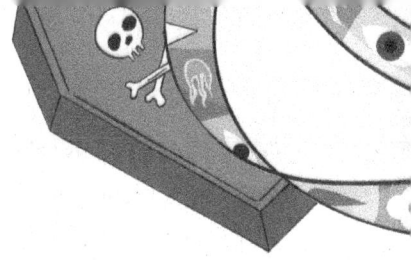

CHAPTER FORTY-TWO

BUD LEROY

I guess it was a little out of left field.

LILA MURPHY

*A little? A little?! I think you need
to adjust your quantities, Bud.*

Vampire Falls. Season three, episode fourteen –
"Reckoning and Beckoning"

The quiet of the dance floor clarifies the scene. My best friend and the person I've been at odds with all weekend, smiling at each other, the flashing lights making it look like Roxy's brushing Vivian's hair over her shoulder in slow motion.

"Eliza?"

Charlie's voice goes from confused to *oh-I-see-what-you're-seeing* by the third syllable of my name. I shove my headset into his hands and go over to the clandestine couple, the few drinks in me maybe making it more of a *storm* than a walk. Vivian notices me first and takes a quick step away from Roxy. Roxy looks round, her flirtatious smile dropping from her face the moment she sees me.

I stop in front of them, not really sure what I want to say, what I want to accuse them of, so I just look at Roxy. Vivian speaks first, tucking her hair behind her ear.

"I'm just going to . . ."

She walks off, leaving Roxy and me at the edge of the dance floor together. Roxy puts her hands up, as if she's surrendering.

"Before you say anything," she says. I fold my arms and stare at her. "It's not what it looked like."

"What was it then?" I snap. Roxy shakes her head a fraction, her eyes flicking towards Vivian. I back away from her. "You know what? I can't. I literally can't deal with this."

Roxy grabs my hand and tries to pull me round, but I shake her off, so she hurries in front of me.

"Eliza, don't," she says. I stop and fold my arms again, but I can't look at her. "Eliza, come on. It was nothing."

I wring my hands together and look round. Vivian has sat next to Sadie, which is probably a smart move. Charlie's at the table as well, pretending not to watch us. I turn back to Roxy.

"Nothing? I know your moves, Roxy. I know the up-close bit and then the hair push bit. I know what it means. I saw you do it with Iris." I shake my head, my eyes widening. "Oh my god. *Iris*. How could you do this to her?"

"I'm not," she says, tension creeping between her eyebrows.

"You're not what? Betraying her?"

Roxy watches a couple swinging their way past us, then she turns back to me and folds her arms.

"Don't act like you give a shit about Iris. This is about you, not her."

"Excuse me? I do give a shit about her," I respond automatically, although it's a pretty harsh (and unexpected) accusation. "It's about both of us."

She shakes her head and smiles, but not a Roxy kind of smile. I've never seen this kind of smile on her before. I don't like it.

"Have you for one second wondered why she isn't here this weekend? Why I've been on the phone constantly?"

"Yes, I . . ." I pause, thinking back to Roxy telling my why Iris couldn't come, but I can't remember. "You didn't tell me."

"I didn't tell you, or you didn't ask? The thought hasn't crossed your mind, has it? If you'd thought for a split second, *hey, I wonder where Iris is,* the question would have been out of your mouth. But you didn't."

"Why are you turning this round on me?"

"I'm not, babe! I'm just telling you things aren't as clear cut as you make them out to be." Roxy shakes her head. "You've had the whole weekend, but you've been so obsessed with Charlie and Vivian and this fucking competition you just didn't think about it. Charlie did. Charlie *and* Vivian both asked where she was."

The mention of their names makes my cheeks flush and I'm angry with myself for letting them have such an effect on me, but I can't seem to navigate through our conversation. I clench my shaking hands and clear my throat, trying to steady my voice.

"When have you been speaking to Vivian?"

Roxy rolls her eyes and shakes her head.

"What exactly is your problem with her? She hasn't actually done anything to you, Eliza."

"She hates me."

"How does she hate you? Didn't she help you on stage to enter the competition? Hasn't she posted a load of gorgeous photos of you? The reason you don't like her is because she's made everything different, and you can't stand change."

I rub my forehead, unable to process a universe where Vivian isn't my enemy.

"So . . . where *is* Iris?" I ask.

A flicker of sadness flashes across Roxy's face and she looks at the floor. I finally put the pieces together and just want to embrace her, so she doesn't have to say it out loud.

"We broke up."

"What?" I reach for her hand, but she steps away. "I'm so sorry, Roxy."

"Are you?" she says, looking away from me.

"Of course I am! It's just, since we arrived, with Charlie being here and—"

"Fucking Charlie!" she says, pressing her fingers against her temples. "You're not the only one in this hotel with a broken heart, Eliza."

She's just below shouting level now, and she's shaking a little. I've never seen her like this before, and it's the worst thing that's happened over the whole weekend, probably even the duration of our friendship.

"I don't have a broken heart . . . I . . ." I say, desperately trying to stop this from finally happening.

"You're not the only one who lost him, babe," she says,

glancing at him. "I miss him too. I miss us."

"I don't . . . I mean, I . . ." I start, searching for the right words.

"You guys kissed, then he messed up. He realised he messed up, but you've been punishing him ever since. Can't you see you're punishing yourself too? And me? You hold everyone up to these insane standards so it's impossible for anyone to live up to them."

I shake my head and blink away my tears. Roxy's right, I know she's right. Charlie ghosting me was worse than if we had never kissed at all, so I pretended it didn't happen. I pretended *he* didn't happen, and I did the very same to him.

"It's easier for you to hate him than to admit you were wrong too. And the crazy thing is that you're *still* obsessed with him, but you won't admit it." She looks at me, her face cold. "Obsessed with Charlie and this fucking competition."

I blink at her, wondering how to close this floodgate, or if it's a good idea to try.

"The competition is for us. We've always wanted to go to San Diego."

"Yes, but it's not about San Diego any more," she says, getting louder and louder. "Because you're up against Charlie and Vivian, you're taking the whole thing personally."

"No. No, I just want us to go," I say, shaking my head and biting my lip, "to go to a convention one last time, together, just us, to go and be *Vampire Falls* fans. One day we're going to be here or . . . or hang out together for the last time, and we won't even realise it."

Roxy's face softens and her voice dials down a couple of notches.

"What?"

"And this could be it," I say, my voice cracking. "And I can't miss any of it, I can't miss a single second with you."

"We'll still do this when we're at uni, babe," she says, rubbing my arm.

"We can't . . ." I say, shaking my head, a mess of tears and snot bubbles. "We can't because . . . because I didn't get in!"

The failure bursts out of me, but I don't feel any less heavy now I've shared it with her.

Roxy's eyebrows pinch together, and she steps forward.

"What? Why didn't you tell me?" she says.

"I don't know," I say, my chest tight.

"So, what are you going to do?" she asks. All I can do is shake my head. "It'll be OK, babe. We can sort this out."

"No, we can't, because there's not going to be a *we* any more!"

I turn away but she grabs my arm.

"Hey, don't run away, Eliza."

"Why not? That's what Charlie did; that's what you're going to do."

"Don't be silly, babe."

"I'm not being silly!" I snap, snatching my arm out of her grasp. "This is . . . it's just . . . not cool, Roxy."

She calls my name, and it sounds so loud and exposed in the quiet of the silent disco. I walk away from her, unable to stop myself looking at Charlie and Vivian who look at me with such pity in their eyes, I could scream. I stop at their table, my hands shaking as I wipe the tears from my face.

"Eliza?" Charlie says, standing up from his chair.

"W-why did you have to pick her?" I say, barely able to get the words out.

His eyebrows pinch together and he looks at Vivian, who's fiddling with her phone in her lap, then back at me. Sadie's wearing a pair of cat headphones now and doesn't look up from her phone.

"I . . . I didn't pick her, Eliza," says Charlie, lights strobing across his confused face from the party that I couldn't feel further away from. "She picked us."

Charlie, Vivian and Roxy, who's now coming over, watch me, wondering what's next for this latest Eliza meltdown.

"That's not what I mean," I say, shaking my head and turning from them.

Charlie starts to come after me, but Vivian grabs his hand and whispers to him. I run past the dancing, away from the party, away from Roxy, and Charlie and Vivian, and through the doors of Conference Hall A, not sure where I'll stop but that I'll be alone when I get there.

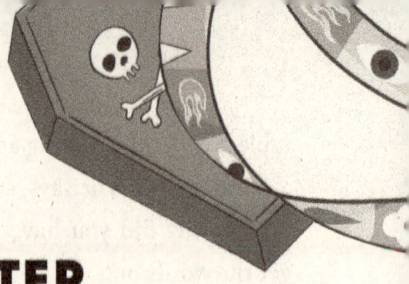

CHAPTER FORTY-THREE

LILA MURPHY
It can't get any worse though, right?
JULIANA THE DEMON HUNTRESS
Why must you tempt fate in this way?
Immortal Fortiana simply cannot resist.

Vampire Falls. Season four, episode eleven – "Come Out"

I didn't sleep last night. I spent half the night waiting for Roxy to come in (she didn't, but she did message to say she was fine – no kiss), and half replaying our stomach-churning argument. Plus, another quarter thinking about dancing with Charlie. Yes, I know that doesn't add up to a whole thing, but I don't really feel like a whole thing right now. Fractions are the least of my worries.

I haven't seen Roxy this morning, and I don't know what I'd do if I did. I suspect she's lying low because she knows that, and she knows I'll be processing. We fell out once because of Bud Leroy's new love interest (the casting and the storyline was *all wrong*, especially so soon after they killed off Kayon O'Keefe. Bud and Kayon is my, and most of the fandom's, OTP) and I didn't speak to her for two days. Roxy refers to such fallouts as '*Eliza's stages of stubborn ass-ness*' and I can't disagree.

But we've never argued like this before. Like, not ever. It makes my tummy hurt when I think about what she said, but I've realised my leaning on her had become an unspoken expectation. I thought we sort of slotted together, but maybe it's become a bit one-sided. I don't know. I'm just trying not to think about it – the argument, her finding a replacement for me at uni. It's so strange without her brushing breakfast crumbs off me or pointing out my wardrobe malfunctions, but I need to get used it.

"Remember, guys: a warrior is always ready with their weapon."

I sigh and attempt a transition from slumped to ready, as Chip Rodrigo, *Vampire Fall*'s stunt co-ordinator and ex-Marine, circles us, tweaking our weapon positions or correcting our stance. I contemplated going back to bed after breakfast, but I'd already paid for the weapons workshop, and actually, holding a double-bladed Megna sword replica might be what I need in my life right now.

The workshop is in the same room as the photos yesterday. There's plenty of floorspace for footwork, and high ceilings for swinging swords around. Stewards hurry in through the door on one side and out the other and attendees wander through, watching Chip demonstrate the moves because he's a pro, and also, an absolute hulking mass of muscle, protein and, from the veins on his neck as thick as my pinkie, steroids.

"Hold your weapon, tight. It's always wet during battle: either rain, or the blood of your enemies," booms Chip.

Everyone in the group giggles with their partner, trying to hold a serious battle face as they brandish their swords. Everyone apart from me, because my true partner isn't here. My stomach lurches. I bet she's with *her*. Probably planning their wedding.

"Well, I'm not being a bridesmaid," I grumble.

The two girls to my side exchange a look then step away. I forget I can't say things out loud if Roxy's not here, especially if I'm holding a weapon.

"First, guys, show your respect with a nod of the head, but don't take your eyes from theirs," says Chip, the overhead lighting making his bald head shine. "Good . . . er, you, with your hoodie on inside out. Where's your partner?"

"I don't have one. I'm alone. She left me."

"Oh dear," he says awkwardly, concerned I'm about to cry. Let's not rule it out, Chip. "No problem: I'll buddy up with you."

Great – I'm partnered with the teacher. He claps me on the back, and I almost go flying. His hands are almost the size of large Domino's pizzas. Maybe even family size.

I suck in some air and try to focus as Vivian sashays in, looking like a character from a fantasy computer game. Uh. Am I not safe anywhere? I look her up and down. Roxy's always joked about how hot Vivian is but apart from that, what is there? It's not like they have anything in common. Apart from being tall. And liking *Vampire Falls*. Vivian seems pretty loyal to her friends, I guess, which Roxy is. Or was.

Next, of course – thanks, universe – Charlie Chamberlain follows Vivian into the room. My stomach lurches at the sight of him and I brace myself for Roxy appearing next. They're like cockroaches; one appears and the rest soon follow. If cockroaches were blessed with perfect bone structure, flawless skin and glossy hair. But Roxy doesn't walk in, so my shoulders relax maybe 0.04%. Chip steps back, assuming the ready position, his eyes shining with fury and intent.

"Remember, keep your eyes on your opponent's weapon. Ready . . . one!"

Half the group step forwards, mimicking Chip's move. I try to keep my eyes on him, but Charlie has caught up with Vivian and she's turned round to him as moves in close to her.

"Two!"

I glance back and copy the next step, moving to the side and pulling the double-blade down to my side, then look back over at them.

Vivian folds her arms and blinks at Charlie like he's divulging something of great importance. I clench my fists around the sword as I watch them, their mouths set in serious lines. Vivian actually has a tiny line between her eyebrows. Charlie nods then looks around the room, his eyes stopping on me. Vivian looks over too, then puts her hand on his arm and leans in, whispering something.

I'm not a professional lip-reader but I know when someone's saying my name.

"Three . . . AARGH!"

"What?" I say absent-mindedly, glaring at Vivian as I move back from the third position. Everyone's looking at me now, some with their hands over their mouths. I turn back to Chip, who's dropped his weapon and is clutching his nose, blinking down at me. "What happened?"

"You hit me in the nose!" he groans.

"I . . . I . . ." I say, looking from him to the others, vaguely aware of the accusation but more focused on what Vivian was saying about me. "Sorry, I . . ."

"You were growling!" he whines, a steward appearing at his side with a wad of tissues.

I know this is one of those moments where Roxy would reel me in, but Roxy isn't here, so I storm over to Vivian.

"What are you saying about me?" I demand, my hands shaking.

"Nothing, Eliza," says Charlie, stepping back a little. "We were just—"

"I saw her say my name," I say, my voice wobbling. "What did you say about me?!"

Vivian looks down at me, biting her lip. A display of guilt if ever I saw one.

"She didn't say anything, Eliza."

"I'm not stupid," I snap at Charlie. "I *saw* her."

Vivian shakes her head and puts her hand on Charlie's arm.

"I . . . I overheard something," says Charlie, looking everywhere apart from at me. "More than once. From the stewards. The guys backstage."

"About *me*?"

He shakes his head and rubs the back of his hair, then looks at Vivian.

"Just tell her, Charlie," she says, her voice soft.

"I can't," he says, looking at the ground.

"Tell me what?" I say.

Vivian slowly takes the double-bladed sword from my hands, then Charlie nods at her and looks back at me, his brown eyes empty, like the bottom of a well. "They've been saying . . . this is the last *Vampire Falls* convention, Eliza."

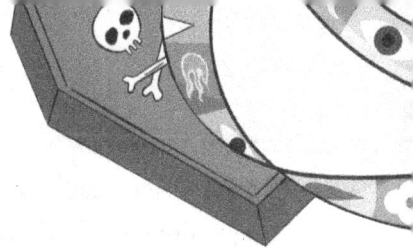

CHAPTER FORTY-FOUR

BUD LEROY

I don't feel anything, Lils. What's happening to me?

Vampire Falls. Season five, episode twenty-two –
"Can't Be Real"

"What do you mean," I say, "*this is the last convention*?!"

I *thought* I'd lowered my voice, but I had not. I'd done the opposite of lowering. The room pauses and turns my way, murmurs of confusion or upset, but even though I've just said the words out loud, I feel nothing. I'm obviously dead inside because what do I have to live for if this is actually true and my convention and these people and these actors aren't here waiting for me, once a year, arms wide open?

People in the workshop overhear and fire questions at Charlie, who of course doesn't have the answers they want. Suddenly, the room swirls into a maelstrom of noise and heat, and I lean over, putting my head in my hands.

"Are you OK?" someone asks, a gentle hand on my back.

I peek through my fingers. It's Vivian, but I have few options right now.

"I feel sick," I groan.

"You gonna vom?"

I shake my head, but she hands me a bottle of water. The questions and voices suddenly turn up a notch and I look from my braced-to-puke position. Felix has just walked in. He spots me, tilts his head to the side as he takes in my current status, then gives me a little wave.

"Eliza, I've been looking for . . ." he starts, heading towards me.

He slows from his usual jaunty walk and his smile slowly drops from his face as he realises the noise and upset he's walked in on is directed at him.

"Sorry, what's this . . ." he starts, but Vivian steps forward and puts her hands up for quiet.

She gets it.

"Is it true, Felix? Is this the last VF convention?"

Felix blinks at her, his mouth opening and closing like he's considering different words then deciding against them, until finally his eyebrows angle up above his glasses and he deflates. I straighten up and try to focus on him, but I feel dizzy.

"I'm afraid it's true," he says, nodding.

The noise in the room starts up again and Felix looks from face to face, unable to answer any questions at the rate they're being thrown at him. Charlie Chamberlain steps forward.

"What happened, Felix? I mean, I've heard some stuff but . . ." he says, shrugging and looking around.

"I'm sorry . . . I'm sorry, truly," he says, putting both hands up in surrender and sighing. "Believe me, nobody wants this less than I do. Ultimately, this is a business, and

I've been forced into this decision because of a number of factors, all to do with money. I was going to make an announcement tomorrow but . . ."

He doesn't have it in him to even finish his sentence but looks at us all, chewing the inside of his mouth. Suddenly, he starts nodding and holds his hands out like he has some kind of offering.

"But I'm not totally out of the game: I'm partnering up with Dragon Events to work in a wider range of conventions."

There's some nodding and murmuring around the room and Felix swallows a nervous lump as he smiles tightly. People ask him when Dragon Events will announce guests and what the venue will be, until a loud noise cuts through all the interest in the shiny new convention."BOOOO!"

"Stop it," hisses Vivian.

"Was that *me*?" I say.

Vivian nods.

I totally knew it was me, I just couldn't hold it in.

"Honestly, guys, they've got some excellent guests lined up already, including some of the OGs from *Vampire Falls*, but I'm really excited about some of the *fresh blood*, pardon the pun."

Felix pauses, his face hopeful when he gets a few claps from around the room. I put my hands behind my back in case they suddenly clap together of their own accord, and someone mistakenly thinks I'm on board with this change of direction, because I don't know if I've made this clear, but I AM NOT.

"Thanks, guys. I knew you'd be supportive."

Not me. I'm not supporting Felix's non-*Vampire Falls*

venture one bit. This is the worst thing that could possibly happen, on top of all the other worst things that have happened.

"Where are you going?" asks Charlie.

"To my room," I say, shaking my head. "To pack."

Maybe I'm the only true fan here or maybe this weekend means more to me than everyone else, because nobody else looks as though their entire life has just shattered to pieces. I turn away, slinging my bag on my shoulder, and slam right into a wall. Or it feels like a wall before I look up and see Chip Rodrigo standing right in front of me.

"Well?!" he says, but I don't know if he's talking to me because he's pinching the bridge of his nose and tilting his head back.

I look round, and shrug.

"Well, what?" I say, barely able to muster words.

He flinches as he looks down at me briefly, then tilts his head back again.

"You gave me a nosebleed!" he says.

"Well, *they* gave me a nosebleed as well," I snap. Doesn't Chip Rodrigo realise my entire life has fallen apart in less than twenty-four hours? Surely a bloody nose is a hazard of the job? A wave of misery crashes over me and I look up at him, trying to blink away tears. "A nosebleed in my heart!"

"Eliza," says Vivian, reaching out to me, but I shrug away from her claws.

"That's it. I can't, I . . . I'm leaving."

I rush to the door, vaguely aware of someone calling my name but I have no interest in talking to Charlie or Vivian or anyone who has recently given me a heart nosebleed, which I know sounds ridiculous but now I've said it I have to stick with it.

"Eliza, wait, please," calls Felix, but I don't stop because he, too, is on my list. "Wait. It's about the competition."

The competition? I sigh and turn to look at him.

"What about it?" I say, crossing my arms. "Is it cancelled? Was it a fake competition for a reality show about obsessive freaks? Have I been disqualified for being overly attached and emotional and stubborn and incapable of processing any form of change, Felix? Is that what's happened?"

Felix's eyebrows pinch together over his glasses and he wrings his hands together. He steps forward and shakes his head.

"You came second. We're announcing shortly but I couldn't let you just leave without knowing you get to have coffee with Damon Van Schwartz. I mean, isn't that brilliant? Congratulations, that's every fan's dream!"

"Yeah," I say, feeling like a balloon losing the last of its helium. "Brilliant."

CHAPTER FORTY-FIVE

LILA MURPHY

I just feel like everything around me is crumbling.

BUD LEROY

And I really want to unpack that with you,

Lils, but everything around us is crumbling.

This crypt is literally crumbling RIGHT NOW.

Vampire Falls. Season three, episode ten

– "Kiss Your Death"

I wander aimlessly, my heart sinking further as Felix's news snakes its way around the attendees and follows me through the hotel. There are a few tears, a few shocked faces mourning our precious weekend, but most people seem placated by Felix's new venture.

Not me. I feel hollow, like my very core has been swept away by the death of this weekend, my convention, losing the competition to Vivian (Felix didn't have to say it, but it's obvious she's the winner), and Roxy. All of it. I can almost hear my name floating away as I slope round a corner.

"Eliza! Eliza?"

I look round, realising that someone *is* calling my

name rather than my feelings of desperation manifesting themselves. Fake McKinley jogs down the hallway towards me.

"Hey," I manage.

A couple of Fallers run round the corner, shrieking that they're about to miss their autographs and he pulls me out of the way. Their carefree laughter and excitement lingers in the hall, even as they disappear around the corner.

"Are you OK?" Fake McKinley says. "I've been looking for you."

He looks down at me, his thick eyebrows pulled together. I heave a massive sigh and shake my head.

"I'm sorry ... I ... everything is ..."

Another small group stampede round the corner and we step back, letting them past in a flurry of excitement. The noise and the fans and the corridor all press down on me, and I feel like there's too many people but I'm all alone and I ...

"Hey," says Fake McKinley, his voice gentle and calm. He takes my hand and squeezes it. "Let's get out of here. I know a place."

I automatically start to protest, wanting solitude so I can really wallow in my aloneness, but the warmth of his fingers around my hand is nice because it's a feeling other than the despair that's about to overflow. I nod, then follow him down the corridor. He pulls his phone out, sends a couple of messages then puts it back in his pocket.

It feels like we walk the entire length of the hotel until we finally stop at some double doors, where everyone's favourite independent adjudicator, Dimitri, waits.

"Hey, man," says Fake McKinley, bumping Dimitri's fist, "thanks for this. Appreciate it."

"No worries," says Dimitri, tapping the security panel by the door with a card attached to his belt.

Fake McKinley holds the door open and nods me through the doors, and chlorine floods my nostrils. Our footsteps echo off the tiled floor and walls of a short corridor, then we walk through another door to a decent-sized swimming pool. It's such a shift in the environment I've been absorbed in over the weekend, that I forget my entire life has fallen apart.

Just for a second though.

"Come on," he says.

I follow him round the pool to a row of white plastic sunbeds.

"Won't we get in trouble, being in here?" I ask, checking the corners for cameras.

Fake McKinley shakes his head.

"Dimitri's cool. He let me in the other day. The pool's being repaired or something; it's been off limits for months."

"I didn't even know there was a pool," I say.

"You going to sit?"

I nod, and walk over, lowering myself down slowly. I don't need a comedy style collapse and trap situation right now. The plastic is hard and unwelcoming, but the quiet and the still water calms the storm that was brewing inside me. Mildly. Fake McKinley sits opposite me and clasps his hands together as he watches me settle.

"I'm so sorry you didn't win, Eliza. You smashed the

cosplay; the judges must have been out of their minds."

"How did you . . .?" I say, frowning.

"I sort of overheard Felix talking about it after they screened 'Music, Maestro'. I now have 'Everyone Hates McKinley' stuck in my head."

"Oh . . ."

Normally the very mention of a song from the musical episode would be enough for me to launch into a performance, but *oh* is all I have right now. "

"Coffee with actual Viggo Rassmussen though; you must be pretty psyched?" asks McKinley.

I wait for that to resuscitate my soul, but there are still no signs of life. McKinley frowns and steps closer.

"Eliza, are you OK?"

"Yes," I blurt, shaking my head.

"Very convincing," he says, smiling. He leans forward, tilting his head. "Did something happen with Roxy as well?"

"How did you know?"

"I've never seen the two of you without each other for more than ten minutes," he says, "apart from the time you got stuck in the chair."

My heart twists at the memory, realising that Roxy had to leave me stuck in the chair because she was on the phone to Iris. I look at him and nod.

"But it's more than that, right?" he says. I nod again. "I heard Felix's news about the convention. I'm really sorry. That's a lot for you."

"Thanks," I manage.

"It's him as well though, right?"

"Felix?" I say, wondering why I should add Felix to my list of woes.

"Charlie."

His name makes my stomach flip. I blink at McKinley, Charlie's confused face when we nearly kissed last night blurring my vision. I bite my lip and nod again.

"What happened?"

"Nothing," I say, shrugging. "Everything."

"You want to talk about it?" asks Fake McKinley.

I blink at him again, then look down at my hands. Do I? What would I say and where does it all start? How did I let this competition get so out of control that I didn't notice my best friend was going through a break-up? Or, let's be honest, was it actually me that was out of control? For once in my life, I don't think I have the words to even start exploring how I've messed things up so badly.

"It's cool," he says, taking my non-response in the way I need him to.

Fake McKinley holds his hand out and nods at a very appealing spot next to him. I take a deep breath, grab his hand and let him pull me across.

"Is it OK if we just sit?" I ask.

He nods, then shuffles round a little so he's facing away from me and looks over his shoulder.

"May I suggest leaning?" he says, his smile open and inviting, just like his presence. "I highly recommend it."

I nod and try a smile, then turn myself round so we're facing away from each other, just like we did after I got myself stuck in a chair and he was having an anxiety attack. I lean back against him, and his warmth gives my body the support to surrender to the fear that's been clawing at me since I lost Charlie, since I was rejected from Bristol, since I found myself in Vivian's voluptuous shadow, and since my argument with Roxy. I'm so tired I can't fight the sorrow of losing the most important friendships of my life any more.

"Surprisingly good, right?" says McKinley.

I nod, grateful he's there, taking my weight, but I can't stop a wretched sob escaping my heart. It bounces off the tiles and the walls, so it's like I'm crying in surround sound. Suddenly, Fake McKinley's brick wall of a back is gone and I'm all alone and I panic, crying harder, but a split-second later I feel him with me again. Not back-to-back any more, but he puts his arm around me, pulling me into his shoulder as I cry and I cry and I cry – for the convention, for Roxy, and for Charlie.

For all of them.

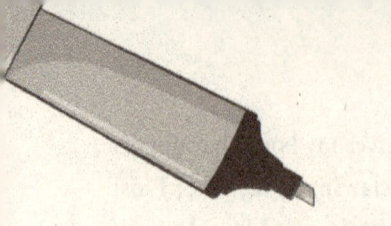
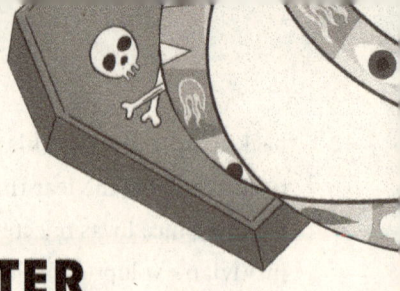

CHAPTER FORTY-SIX

VIGGO RASSMUSSEN

No! Jawfain?! Get him out of there!

Vampire Falls. Season five, episode two –
"Two Heads Are Better Than None"

As I hadn't expected to have a one-to-one with my hero today, I've just gone with my scheduled Sunday clothing which consists of grey jogger bottoms, a *Vampire Falls* hoodie and my red Vans. By Sunday it's usually all about comfort, and that's what my soles and my soul are craving right now.

I turn down the corridor and let out a long sigh. Honestly, I thought I'd be more excited at the prospect of coffee with Viggo Rassmussen himself, but I can't snap myself into full superfan mode, not when there's a part of my heart missing. If Roxy were here, we'd be holding hands and running down the corridor, then we'd do a jumpy dance. I took her jumpy dance for granted.

Felix is outside a meeting room, rubbing his forehead as he looks at his phone. He looks up and smiles at me, barely, and shoves his phone into his back pocket.

"Hey, Eliza," he manages. "You're here."

Shadows under his eyes and a chin full of stubble show just how much these weekends take out of him. I kind of don't blame him for making a change.

"Hey, Felix. Thanks so much for this."

"Not at all," he says, waving my thanks away. "Thank you for being such a big part of our final weekend. It means a lot."

He looks at me, his eyes brimming with such sadness I almost launch myself at him for a hug but instead he knocks on the door. Voices come from inside and it opens.

"Hi there," says Debbie, a Californian smile on her face. "Mr Van Schwartz is excited to meet with you, Eliza."

Felix's smile falters as he looks at his phone again, then starts backing down the hallway.

"I'll leave you with Debbie, Eliza," he says over his shoulder. "Enjoy yourself."

"OK . . ." I call after him, but he's already disappeared round the corner.

I look at Debbie for an explanation but she's still smiling at me. She seems to be in permanent smile mode. Her cheeks must ache.

"If you'd like to come in?" she says.

"Sure, I . . ."

I hover in the doorway, certain I can hear someone crying in the distance. Wondering if it could be Felix and if I need to unholster that hug, I look down the corridor, but Sadie runs round the corner, her face blotchy and streaming with tears. I don't know what's happened, but the sight of a crying Sadie splits my heart in two. I open my arms as she gets closer and she falls into me, squishing her face into my shoulder.

"Sadie? What's the matter?" I say, looking over her for injuries. "Are you OK?"

She tries to speak but just sobs louder. I squeeze her back, waiting for her to find her words until Charlie runs round the corner. A mix of relief and tension confuses my body as our eyes lock, and he stops a couple of steps from us.

"Sadie, I know you're upset but please don't ever run away from me like that," he says.

She clings to me tighter and hiccups something into my chest, like she's seven years old again and doesn't understand why she can't watch the lady with the sword tell off monsters with us.

"What did you say, Sadie?" I say, frowning at Charlie who just shakes his head and shrugs.

She looks up at me, her huge eyes spilling over with tears.

"The . . . the . . . karaoke p-p-party is c-c-cancelled," she manages, squeezing her eyes closed.

"What?" I say, shaking my head. "Felix wouldn't do that, not for the last convention. He knows what it means to us."

"And Ch-Ch-Charlie says we have to l-l-leave today!" Charlie puts his hand on her shoulder, but she shrugs him off. "I *hate* you, Charlie!"

"I don't understand," I say. "What's happened to the party tonight?"

I stroke Sadie's hair, as Charlie looks over his shoulder then leans into me. Child is suffering trauma, yet my skin still sparkles as boy closes the space between us. God, I'm pathetic.

"Apparently the karaoke guy hasn't shown up," says Charlie.

"How do you know?"

"Sadie has made me sit in the green room and all the other off-limit sections the entire weekend. I heard a couple of Felix's team stressing about it. The guy isn't answering his phone and Felix has already paid him."

"Can't they just do another silent disco?" I ask.

"The sound guys are halfway to Newcastle with all the equipment. I heard there's literally zero money left. Apparently, Felix put everything into this weekend. He's skint. Most of this has run on the goodwill of the guests, *especially* . . ." Charlie nods towards the open door. I look round. Damon Van Schwartz. "Apparently, Damon thinks a lot of Felix and loves doing this so much he talked all the other actors into coming without an upfront fee. Felix isn't making a penny, and now the karaoke guy hasn't shown up."

"So," I say, totally relating to Sadie's eleven-year-old meltdown, "the final, *final* convention party isn't happening?"

Charlie shrugs. I look at him and swallow.

"But why are you guys leaving early?"

"What's the point in staying?" He tries to shrug again, but his shoulders have tensed up. "It's not going to end how I . . . how she wanted it to."

Charlie puts his hand round my back and for a moment I think he's going to hug me, but instead he takes Sadie's hands and unfurls her from me. She's just snivelling now, worn out from the crying.

"C-can I have a piggyback?" she asks, looking more like the little girl I first met nearly five years ago.

Charlie assumes the universal piggyback position, and Sadie manages to jump up, pressing her head against

Charlie's shoulders. I tuck her hair behind her ear, and she blinks at me, her bottom lip wobbling a little.

"Sorry, Sadie," I say, as Charlie carries her away to pack up her unfinished weekend.

I watch them disappear, then Debbie's voice pipes up beside me.

"Shall we?"

Shall we what? I wonder for a second then I sense that I'm close to a forcefield of greatness and never-ending talent, and I remember why I'm there. Damon Van Schwartz stands next to Debbie, looking at me with his slushie-blue eyes.

"Sorry, I was on my cell, and honestly, I couldn't bear to see the kid like that." He shakes his head, his hand on his chest. "Anyway, let's do this. Eliza, right?"

I nod and follow him into the small meeting room. We sit at the end of a long table with a few headshots of him fanned out.

"Charlie's swinging by again before he goes, right?" Debbie nods, and Damon Van Schwartz looks round at me and smiles. "What would you like? Debbie is happy to head out and get our drinks."

"Oh," I say, looking at Debbie. "Iced latte, if that's OK?"

"Sure," she replies, her tight smile suggesting it's very much not OK and she thought her coffee fetching days were behind her. "Usual for you?"

Damon Van Schwartz nods and Debbie hustles from the room in a cloud of Chanel. He slides the headshots towards me.

"A gift for you, Eliza. All signed, of course."

"Thank you," I say. "I think I'll give them to Sadie."

"Oh, she has one of each already," he says, smiling, "and

I gave Charlie a Falls folder too."

"That's kind of you."

He waves his hand and shrugs.

"After what Charlie did for me," he says, "it was the very least I could do."

I nod, remembering that moment on the first day and how much I hated Charlie for muscling in on my big fan weekend. It feels like a million years ago.

He clasps his hands together and looks at me over the top of them, one eyebrow raised.

"May I make an observation, Eliza?"

"Um, yes?" I say, still waiting for my excitement to bubble up and wreak havoc, but it can't find its way to the surface.

"As an actor, I'm very much a watcher of people," he explains, waving his hands around. "I notice things that others wouldn't. How people wear their emotions on their face, how they carry it on their shoulders. That sort of thing."

I nod. Face and shoulders. OK.

"I'm also an excellent listener, but when I say that I don't mean listening with my ears. I mean, listening with *this*."

He points at the buttons on his black shirt. I lean in, looking for a secret listening device until I realise he's pointing to his heart.

"OK . . ." I say.

"What is the relationship status between you and my good friend Charlie? Because the three times I mentioned his name since you got in here, I saw something on your face."

My hand flies up to my face, worried I've still got flakes of pecan pastry on my cheek or something, but again, I realise what he's saying.

"Really?"

"Yes, really," he says, leaning forward. "You two have a connection, right?"

I shake my head.

"Connection maybe isn't a word I'd . . . I mean, we used to . . ."

I jump when he slams his palm against the table, just as Debbie swoops back in with our drinks.

"I knew it! You can't hide that kind of history. Charlie kept talking about you, and I just *knew* it. I know what to listen for to get the hidden story, Eliza. Didn't I say I knew it, Debbie?"

"You did," she says, gently setting his cup and saucer down, the smell of peppermint tea wafting over the table.

She plonks my plastic takeaway cup on the table with such disinterest that it nearly tips over.

"Thank you," I say, grabbing it with both hands (I'm still wary of milky drinks).

Debbie settles in the chair next to Damon Van Schwartz and looks at her phone. I watch him dunk the teabag around the cup, then clear my throat.

"Ask away, Eliza," he says.

"How'd you know I wanted to ask something?"

"Told you. I listen from *here*," he says, pointing to his chest again.

"Um, did Charlie really talk about me?"

"He did," he confirms.

"What did he say?" I ask, the tips of my ears getting hot.

"Usual stuff. Complaining about you. How annoying you are," he says, his blue eyes twinkling.

"Oh. That's not very encouraging."

"Oh, but don't you see, Eliza. It is. It's more than encouraging."

I cross my arms, not really sure how Charlie grumbling about how irritating he finds me can be a positive thing.

"Sorry, I shouldn't pry in your personal business, I just love to see people connect." He leans forward, putting his elbows on the table. "What else would you like to ask me?"

"Is it true the karaoke party isn't happening tonight?"

He glances at Debbie then takes a sip of his tea.

"I kind of meant something about me or my process, but OK," he says. "Yes, I'm afraid it is. Poor Felix. That guy loves all of you nearly as much as I do."

He puts his tea down, and ordinarily I'd be thinking of ways to steal his used teabag, but all I can think of is poor Sadie. I look down at my hoodie; there's still a little wet patch of Sadie tears. I can't believe the *final* party of the *final* convention isn't happening, and we're all going to be left sort of . . . hanging.

"I can't believe it's coming to an end like this," I say, shaking my head and blinking back tears.

Damon Van Schwartz frowns and sits back in his chair.

"What?" he says, looking round at Debbie, who's still smiling but also raising her eyebrows. "Who told you it's ending?"

"You just told me," I say, frowning at him and Debbie.

"*I* did not just tell you *Vampire Falls* is ending," he says, putting both his hands up.

"*What?!*" Apparently, I've just jumped up and knocked

my chair back. The room spins and my throat feels like it's closing. "*Vampire Falls* is *ending*?"

"Mr Van Schwartz did *not* say that," says Debbie, putting her hands on her hips. "You're putting words in his mouth."

"That's exactly what he said," I say. "He's putting words in his own mouth."

"Guys, guys, please," Damon Van Schwartz says, trying to blind me with his perfect smile. "Whatever you think you might have heard . . ."

"You *just* said it," I repeat.

"Whatever you think I *may* have said, is *possibly* classified information only to be officially shared at a time when the network sees fit."

I stare at him, a bit of worry tilting those perfectly threaded eyebrows upwards, and I sigh, exhausted. I lift my chair back up and slump onto it, my legs unable to take the weight of any more bad news or breakups or arguments.

"Why?" I ask, imagining Sadie's face when she hears that her new favourite thing is coming to an end.

He shrugs and shakes his head, wistfulness glistening in his eyes.

"Everything changes, Eliza. If you try to fight that, you just end up alone." He stares at the carpet and takes a sip of tea, then he's back in TV star mode by the time he puts the cup down on the saucer. He claps his hands. "Let's get back to business. It's not every day you get to have coffee with a Hollywood star, am I right?"

"No," I say, shaking my head. "It's not ending like this. I won't let it."

Damon Van Schwartz glances at Debbie, exchanging an unspoken code for when a fan is about to go Annie Wilkes on him, but they don't need to worry. I'm in a room with my favourite actor from my favourite TV show and he's just dropped a bombshell, a heartbreaking, life-altering bombshell, but something else occupies my core right now. All I can think about is how tightly Sadie held on to me as she sobbed; the best weekend of her life coming to a crumbling, disappointing end. And then it hits me.

"She doesn't think she's a real fan until she's completed her first convention," I murmur, standing up slowly.

"Are you OK?" asks Debbie, edging towards me like I'm a wild horse.

"No," I say, looking at her. "No, I'm not OK, but I know how to make it better."

I head to the door.

"Where are you going?" asks Damon Van Schwartz. "You haven't touched your coffee, and we wanted a few fun selfies for Insta."

"Sorry, I can't," I say, gathering up the headshots (well, he did sign them especially for me).

Damon Van Schwartz looks at Debbie, then nods and stands up.

"You go to him, Eliza," he says, tapping his chest. "You go to him, and you tell him."

I walk to the door, turn back and nod, but this has nothing to do with Charlie, like Damon Van Schwartz thinks.

This is for her.

CHAPTER FORTY-SEVEN

VIGGO RASSMUSSEN

For goodness' sake, Lila!

You must get out of your comfort zone!

LILA MURPHY

But it's so comfy in there.

Vampire Falls. Season one, episode four – "Bury Me"

Of all the people I expected to find Vivian sitting with, Dorothy was not one of them. I take a deep breath, smooth down my hoodie, because apparently appearances are important to me now, and I walk over to their sofa. Vivian's looking down, smiling at Dorothy as she finishes her story.

"... and she said, 'I've never even seen that corset!'"

Vivian throws her head back and laughs, putting her hand on Dorothy's shoulder who looks delighted. They both look at me.

"Hey, Curly. You OK?"

"Hi, Dorothy. Kind of."

"What do you need? More fire breathing?"

"Not this time." I bite the inside of my cheek, wondering how the hell I'm supposed to navigate this. "It's actually

Vivian I wanted to talk to."

Vivian's eyes widen for a split second, then she crosses her longs legs and raises an eyebrow.

"I'll piss off and leave you to it," says Dorothy, holding up her hands so I can pull her up from the sofa.

She shuffles off towards the coffee shop, and I turn to Vivian. She's wearing over-the-knee velvet boots and a striped jumper dress. She looks like she's advertising the sofa, whereas I look like I'm advertising cold and flu medicine. She blinks at me, her perfect eyebrows getting higher and higher.

"Sit down or something then. You're hurting my neck."

I nod and sit down, sprawling backwards. The sofa's lower than I thought. I clamber into an upright position as Vivian watches me and smiles.

"Er . . . congratulations, by the way," I say, amazed I manage to get the words out.

"Thank you," she says, quietly and reserved, not at all the way I'd say it. "That's not what you wanted to talk about though, is it?"

I shake my head, and she clasps her hands over her knee.

"What can I do for you then, little one?"

"Well," I say, taking a deep breath. "I kind of hoped you'd help me with something."

"*Help* you with something? Don't you want Roxy to help you, whatever it is? You're a little team, or whatever." She clears her throat and looks around the lobby. "Where is she anyway?"

I stiffen, even though I'd prepared for this.

"I don't actually know. We haven't spoken today. She didn't

come back to the room last night."

"I know," she says, biting the side of her thumbnail, her green eyes wide. "I mean, nothing happened but she needed somewhere to stay so . . ."

"Fine," I say, rubbing my forehead. "I mean . . . it's none of my business what she does."

"Of course it is," she says, frowning. "Isn't she your bestie?"

"Yes, but . . ."

"Aren't you like a mama bear when it comes to you and yours?"

"Huh?"

"I mean, isn't that why you hate me?" she says. "Because you're protecting your friends?"

"What?" I say, my head spinning. "I don't hate you, Vivian."

I say the words, but they couldn't sound more unconvincing.

"Lies, lies. Everyone hates me – or they love me – I totally get it though," she says, shrugging.

"You do?"

"People – *some* people," she says, looking me up and down, "make their mind up about me before they've given me a chance. *Some* people like to put other people in neat little boxes. A box for nerds. A box for jocks. A box for hotties. Do you know why *some* people do that?"

I shake my head.

"Self-preservation. So they can stay safe in *their* box. Sometimes though, they don't know what's in the other boxes until they've opened them. Maybe they've misjudged what it says on the outside."

"OK . . ." I say.

This conversation isn't going the way I thought and it's making my brain hurt.

"Do you get what I'm saying?" she says.

"No," I say, *totally* getting what she's saying.

She smiles and inches forward on the sofa.

"Look, I'm not here to get between you and Roxy, or you and Charlie," she says, her full lips in a serious line. "I actually think you seem fun."

"Then why do you call me *bitch* all the time?"

"I call everyone *bitches*," she says, waving her hand dismissively. "I'm terrible with names."

"Oh," I say.

"Look, when I offered to help Charlie out with Sadie, he said you'd be here and we could end up hanging out. I mean, he got that *totally* wrong. *Boy*," she says, rolling her eyes. She's right there. *Boy*. "But I can see why he wanted to."

Again. This conversation has gone off the tracks.

"You can?" I say, blinking at her.

She nods. "You're ridiculous; it's adorable."

"*Is* it?"

"It's been so much fun," she says, smiling and nodding.

"*Has* it?" I ask, wondering what convention she's been at.

"I've never been to a convention," she says, her eyes sparkling as she looks around. "I had no idea it would be this cool. The competition, the cosplay, the people. Getting to know Roxy." She smiles wider when she says her name. "Seeing Sadie fall even harder for the show. And Dorothy! I mean, where did she come from?"

We both turn to see Dorothy in the middle of the foyer

juggling some fake oranges for the queue outside the coffee shop. She throws one up high, spins round, then catches it in her mouth.

"Nobody knows," I say, gobsmacked.

We turn back to each other, and Vivian reaches forward and flicks the toggle on my hoodie.

"I've had the best time with you guys," she says, smiling, "and even though I have total hair envy, I've really enjoyed our fun little rivalry."

Fun?

"Really?" I say, my mouth hanging open.

"Really," she repeats.

Her phone vibrates and she picks it up. There's barely a frown line on her forehead, whereas I've already got a perma-line from being constantly livid at the world. But I *think* I have good hair, so swings and roundabouts. Getting a compliment from Vivian has boosted me in a way I didn't know I needed. I kind of don't blame Roxy for wanting to kiss her.

"Charlie's asked me to help with Sadie." She puts her phone in her bag and gets up. "She's in the middle of an eleven-year-old breakdown."

"You better go."

"Didn't you want to ask me something?"

"It can wait," I say, mentally checking the time and knowing it can't really but Sadie, and Charlie, need her. "Good luck."

"Thanks," she says, shrugging. "Been through a million of these with my brother and sisters."

"How many do you have?"

"I'm the oldest of five."

"Whoa."

This explains the winner-takes-all mentality.

"Yep. It's why Charlie asked me along. To be honest, she's been a breeze. I'm so glad I came."

Her eyes twinkle as she recalls the weekend, and her smile is like a prize to anyone watching. I *promise* you I'm not in love with her, but I can see what Roxy sees. The redhead has layers, but I've been stuck on the first one.

"Good."

"Just come by my room in a bit and we can talk then?" I nod and she turns away, calling over her shoulder. "Later, bitches."

"Later, bitches," I respond, falling under the spell of Vivian, despite myself.

CHAPTER FORTY-EIGHT

MCKINLEY THE PESSIMISTIC WEREWOLF

I know that's what you all call me!?

Vampire Falls. Season two, episode sixteen –
"Come Back Moon"

The final panel is always bittersweet. Felix brings the guests on stage and they usually share a running joke from the weekend or mention a cute baby they made friends with. And we all laugh and feel warm, knowing that we've had a weekend of loving our favourite show and its stars, along with other Fallers who get who we are and what we're about.

This time though, it's more than bittersweet. It's bitter*sour*, if that's a thing. Firstly, I'm sitting in the hall alone. I've spent most of the day in Vivian's room (a sentence I never thought I would say, believe me), where I witnessed a true genius of people management and manipulation (same thing?) at work (no more brackets, I promise). Roxy was already in Conference Hall A when I came in, sitting near the front with Dorothy asleep on her shoulder. Fake McKinley isn't around, which is a shame because I could have done with a dose of his exuberance. We all could.

Word has spread that the karaoke party isn't happening and there's a feeling of loss hanging heavy over everyone. Packed suitcases and bags punctuate the end of the rows; I guess people don't feel the need to stay for a non-ending. I haven't told a single soul what Damon Van Schwartz told me. I can't do it to them, and also, I don't think it's sunk in because I haven't responded with an Eliza-style meltdown.

I haven't seen Charlie. I *want* to see Charlie. There's a panicky voice in my head whispering that he's already gone, that Sadie's gone too, and this is all for nothing. But it won't be. Even if they've gone, it won't be for nothing.

I tune back into the stage chat. Felix nods and smiles at Amber Anderson, then turns to the audience. You can see the shadows under his eyes from back here, but he smiles. The audience whoop and clap for him and the final panel.

"Thank you everyone, truly. This couldn't have gone ahead without you, and I . . ." His voice cracks, and the audience responds like they're at a pantomime. "I've never done this to get rich, as you know. I just wanted to bring these guys to meet you, their fans, and it's been a pleasure doing so for all these years. Things will be a little different in the future, but we'll always be *Vampire Falls* family."

"Blood is for ever!" shouts the audience.

Felix smiles and puts his hand on his chest.

"Blood is for ever," he repeats, turning and nodding to the guests as they stand up one by one, clapping him.

There's a massive, snot-filled sob. Yes, it's my own.

"Before we bring this panel to a close, we actually have one more guest to bring on and introduce to you. A sort of bonus guest."

The audience's attention is piqued. *My* attention is piqued. Roxy shifts in her seat, waking Dorothy up. This is highly irregular.

"OK, OK, guys," Felix says, waving everyone to calm down. "Damon, would you like to do the intro?"

"My pleasure, Felix," says Damon Van Schwartz into his mic. He gets up and joins Felix at the side of the stage. "Now, I heard a rumour that a couple of scenes from our spin-off show, *Midnight in Portland*, found their way onto the internet. But I know none of you law-abiding citizens would break any laws by watching it, right, guys?"

About forty-three per cent of the audience laugh.

"The new show is set in the same world as *Vampire Falls*, and features the character Stellan Denver, my half-brother. I can tell you *exclusively* that the show has been green-lit and will be premiering next fall!"

That same percentage clap their hands. They're a pretty enthusiastic bunch. Damon Van Schwartz waits for them to settle down then lifts the mic up to his mouth, and gestures to the other side of the stage.

"So now, it is an honour to introduce to you, my fictional half-brother *and* my brother from another mother, Dylan Maguire!"

Everyone looks at each other, frowning and clapping their hands, limply. How can Conference Hall A get excited for an actor sixty per cent of us didn't know existed? Nevertheless, I clap the actor, whoever he is, feeling a little bad for him being introduced to his new audience at possibly the lowest point of the weekend.

And then I see who it is.

Roxy, who's seen who it is too, spins in her seat and looks for me, shaking her head in disbelief as our eyes meet and we share a moment of true fan history.

A clean-shaven Fake McKinley, or Dylan Maguire, comes from the other side of the stage, waving to the audience. Damon Van Schwartz greets him with an almighty bear hug. I shake my head, laughing to myself as he takes the mic from Felix and turns to look at his audience. He's wearing grey joggers, perfect white trainers, and, like a cherry on top, a *Vampire Falls* T-shirt.

I smack my hands together so hard they sting. I'd give anything to be sitting with Roxy right now, but I sit up straight so I can at least see how her hair reacts. Dylan lifts the mic to his mouth and the audience quietens down, even though most of them don't know who the hell he is. But he is very handsome, and that T-shirt is *tight*, so they're willing to give him a go.

"So, I take it from that, you guys don't recognise me from the show," he says, a Californian drawl surprising me. "Does this help?"

Roxy looks round at me again, mouthing what's just popped up in my head.

He's American!

I bob my head up and down at her and she turns back to the stage, just as he pulls a pair of black-framed glasses from his back pocket and puts them on. That forty-three per cent of the audience reacts with cries of recognition and his character's name, Stellan, ripples across the crowd. The other fifty-seven per cent react to seeing a really hot guy putting on a pair of glasses. I'm somewhere in the middle.

"As my buddy Damon here just said, I play the main character in *Midnight in Portland*, the half-brother of Viggo Rasmussen."

"His more intellectual half-brother," interjects Damon Van Schwartz.

The audience laughs and Dylan throws an arm around him. We've never experienced anything like this, and it's breathtaking.

"You might have read some rumours about whether the show was going ahead, due to the lead actor," he says, pointing to himself, "having some personal issues. While I'm not going to address any of that, I admit coming straight out of college and being from a predominantly theatre-orientated background, I did have some reservations about committing to the show. I'm aware that with shows like these, and with fans like you, you're not just an actor showing up each week, but you're part of the fandom. And I wasn't sure I was ready for that."

The audience quietens, not sure they want to hear they can sometimes be a *little intense*.

"I loved the premise of *Midnight in Portland*, and I loved the production team, but I'm a pretty private person and wasn't sure I wanted to open my life up to you guys. To do *all this*," he says, waving his hand around the stage and the front row, "not after going through some personal issues."

Damon Van Schwartz puts his arm around Dylan, nodding his head.

"So, I just want to tell you what I've learnt this weekend." Everyone stares at him, waiting for him to tell us that we're too weird or vampire TV shows suck. He looks out at the audience, his eyes moving across their faces like he's searching for someone, and then they stop. On me. And he smiles. "This isn't just a fandom. This is a family."

Everyone jumps up, clapping the newest member of our extended family. Dylan beams at the audience, putting his hand on his heart, then lifts the mic to his mouth again.

"Blood is for ever!"

"Blood is for ever!" responds the audience, throwing in some whoops and whistles.

My cheeks ache from smiling and I wipe away my tears.

"Thank you, Dylan. I'm sure you'll have a few new members in your *fang* club by the time you leave."

"Thanks, guys," says Dylan, "that's all from me for now, but I look forward to a little karaoke with you later."

Felix's face drops and the audience mood shifts from jubilation to melancholia, now reminded that we only have a few hours left together before people start leaving. Felix steps forward, his face a picture of sorrow.

"Actually, Dylan, I need to officially tell everyone this is it for the convention. Sadly, the karaoke party won't be going ahead. You're welcome to stay but I'm afraid there's no equipment for a DJ or a party. I'm so sorry to let you all down."

There's a low hum from everyone now Felix has confirmed the rumour and their convention will be coming to a crumbling non-end. There's a sob from the back of the hall and I look round, feeling guilty that my heart leaps at the sound of Sadie's tears.

So, they are still here.

"Actually," says Dylan. I turn back to the stage and everyone pauses, wondering what the new guy's going to say.

"The karaoke's back on."

Felix frowns and looks round at a Headset Guy just off the stage, who shrugs back. Felix turns back to Dylan.

"Who told you that?" asks Felix.

"The redhead told me," says Dylan, gesturing to the side of the stage.

Felix goes over to Headset Guy who leans into Felix's ear, pointing over his shoulder. Then, anyone who isn't looking properly would miss it, a sheet of red hair suddenly flicks up out of the shadows, followed by a hand on a hip as Felix nods at whoever's filling him in. Everyone around me murmurs, wondering what the hell is going on, and I sit in the middle of it all, knowing that they're about to get the convention end they deserve.

Felix walks back to the middle of the stage and puts his hand up, looking a little shellshocked.

"OK, so in an unexpected twist of events, which I'm inclined to just go with, the karaoke party, our final karaoke party, is back on." He turns to the guests still sitting on stage. "I hope you'll join us?"

"Try and stop us," Damon Van Schwartz answers for all of them.

The audience erupts in applause and there's a particularly high-pitched squeal coming from the back.

"In that case, I'll ask everyone to clear the hall, I'll speak to this mysterious redhead and her *associate bitch*, and we'll be back on schedule for eight. See everyone later."

Associate bitch. I think that's me.

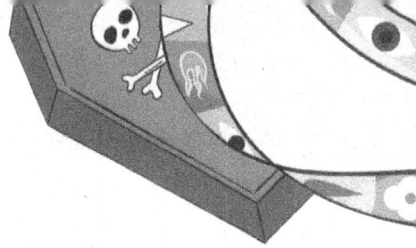

CHAPTER FORTY-NINE

LILA MURPHY

So now what do we do?

JULIANA THE DEMON HUNTRESS

*Now? Now we partake in the festivities,
my surprisingly capable friend.*

Vampire Falls. Season one, episode twelve –
"Masquerade Brawl"

Usually, although karaoke is arguably the most beloved part of the weekend, the attendees roll down from their rooms or rock up from the bar to find a standard set of flashing lights, karaoke equipment and a low-key tech guy managing the song requests.

Not so when Vivian is thrown into the mix.

When I went to her earlier, hoping we could salvage the karaoke party, she listened intently, nodding along with her fingers clasped in front of her like a mafia boss. She then leant forward and said she would help, but more than that, we would make it the final convention party we would all remember until we're old and *Botoxed up.*

She has not deviated from this self-appointed directive.

The entrance is adorned with swathes of black fabric and creeping red roses. Each time someone gets to the end of the rose adorned tunnel, a sensor triggers confetti cannons, showering squealing attendees with fake petals. The round tables are set up with black tablecloths, fake red candles flicker above shiny candelabras, and tiny fairy lights sparkle round the edge of each table.

Giant inflatable bats sit on either side of a flashing dance floor, their wings flapping around as a fan pumps air though them. There's a pop-up cocktail bar to the side, a glamorous mixologist in a burgundy velvet dress offering concoctions like Vampire's Kiss and Bloody Scary.

Conference Hall A pulses with joy and happiness.

I hurry across the dance floor towards Vivian who's at the karaoke helm. Someone dressed as Lila Murphy in the masquerade scene is on the stage, coming to the end of a classic from the musical episode. Inside the booth, Vivian moves between the laptop and control panels like a sea serpent, greeting the audience in her Britney mic, lining up songs and encouraging the singers, even the terrible ones, as she glides back and forth on her roller skates.

I mean, obviously she's wearing her skates.

She looks up from the laptop and spots me, then raises her eyebrows in question.

I shake my head, and she presses a button on her earpiece.

"They'll be here," she says, a smile softening her face.

She rolls out of the way so her assistant tech person can plug an important-looking wire in. Toby (yes, *my* Toby) is so small he slots in perfectly around a roller-skate-wearing goddess.

"Hi, Toby," I say.

"Vivian said this was your idea?" he says, glancing up from the decks.

"I . . . not really, I mean, she . . ." I start, unable to take the credit for what Vivian interpreted from my hopeful *let's-make-karaoke-happen* suggestion.

Toby raises his eyebrows and nods at me, then frowns at the switches and dials in front of him. It's the most comfortable I've seen him all weekend.

"Good for you, Eliza," he says, the tiniest of smiles nudging his wispy moustache.

I smile back at him, then turn to watch a blood-soaked Flayer demon crucify a Lady Gaga song, but everyone is here for it and the roar of applause at the end is heart-warming. Everyone around me is smiling, everyone is happy the weekend didn't just fizzle out, our final party just an afterthought.

Everyone apart from the people I really want to see.

"Hey, Eliza."

I look round at Dylan Maguire, his silhouette strobing like a star breaking through the ozone layer.

"Oh my god, you weirdo! Hey!" I say, returning his embrace. "Congratulations, or something, I guess?"

He pulls away and beams at me, gesturing to move from the speakers so we don't have to shriek at each other. He pulls a chair out for me at one of the tables, and we sit down.

"I just want to say sorry for not telling you who I am," he says, his thick eyebrows full of concern. "This was kind of a personal exercise for me, but I should have been more upfront."

"Are you kidding me?" I say, beaming at him. "This is the

most exciting thing to happen to me personally since Damon Van Schwartz sneezed on my elbow."

"Still, I am sorry, Eliza. And also: gross."

"Don't apologise," I say, shaking my head. "I'm just . . . I don't even . . ."

He laughs, putting his hand up.

"Believe me, I get it," he says, and I'm struck by how good his English accent was. He's obviously very talented. "Before I committed to anything, I needed to know I could exist in this world and this seemed like a good, if extreme, way to test myself. Damon sort of took me under his wing and told me how everything that comes with the show can be kind of intense. I wasn't sure if I could be around it all."

"Yep, I guess we're kind of a weird bunch if you're not used to it," I say, patting his arm. "So the McKinley costume was so you could move among the mortals?"

He nods, smiling.

"I thought some of you might recognise me from the leaked episodes," he says. "Thought it might help prepare for the show a little as well."

My hands fly to my cheeks, and I gasp.

"You mean you went *method*? Are you part *werewolf*?!" He raises his eyebrows but neither confirms nor denies, like a seasoned pro. "Spoilers. I *love* this."

"I said nothing," he says, smiling.

"You've decided to go ahead with the show though?" I ask.

He nods, looking around at the party.

"I'm just gonna lean into it." I can't help but smile as he repeats my own words back to me. "Seriously though, this weekend, this whole thing, hasn't been what I expected. I didn't realise a TV show could mean so much to people, and I'm excited to be a part of that. The friendships that are built because of it are unreal."

"They are," I say, tears pricking at my eyes.

"You look after each other," he says, squeezing my hand.

"We do," I say, nodding as I squeeze back.

"Thank you, Eliza. Thank you for the chair, for the crown, for all of it. You really helped me decide to take a chance on myself." He takes my other hand and looks down at me. "I hope you'll give yourself a chance too, whatever that looks like."

I swallow, unable to speak, but give him the biggest, most definite nod I can.

"Life is about connection, Eliza, and sometimes you have to let yourself reconnect."

He looks over my shoulder and smiles.

I look round just as the cannons go off, so I get to see Sadie, dressed in a blue sparkly dress, squealing at the red confetti. Roxy, stunning in goth vampire mode, spins her around like a tiny ballerina, her hand turned upwards so the confetti falls through her fingers like snowflakes. Charlie's stopped next to them, the only one not in costume, combing the petals out of his hair with his hands, but he's smiling.

They're all smiling.

I want to race over and spin Sadie around too, but mostly I just want to hide behind Dylan, so that's what I do.

"You OK back there?" he says, letting me crouch behind his sizeable frame, the gentleman he is. I nod. "Was that a nod?" I nod again. "OK, because they're coming over here."

I peek out from his side and Sadie races up to me like she's just found me in a game of hide and seek, so I just go with that. She jumps up and throws her arms around my neck, in all likelihood doing some long-term spinal damage, but I'm prepared to live with it because the joy radiating off this kid could cure most ailments.

I squeeze her back and she lets go, clapping her hands together.

"It's just like I dreamt it in my dreams!" she squeals, beaming round at us. She turns to Charlie. "Can we sing something, Charlie?"

"I don't think . . ." starts Charlie, shaking his head.

Sadie's face drops and we all look at Charlie, who has just crushed a tiny koala baby.

"I think that was a rhetorical question, Charlie," Roxy says. "It's basically mandatory to sing. It's all part of the convention experience."

"Fine," he says, semi-rolling his eyes as Sadie jumps up and down hanging on his arm. "Where's the song book or whatever."

"There's an iPad at the front; you just put in the song and Vivian does the rest," I say.

"Thanks," says Charlie, holding my gaze for a few seconds before Sadie drags him away.

"Well, hello Mr Hollywood Star," says Roxy, putting her fist out to Dylan.

He bumps Roxy's fist, a relaxed smile on his face.

"Hey, Roxy." He looks round at me. "So, the others were saying I need to sing with them, apparently."

"Yes. It's actually mandatory," says Roxy, and I'm glad for her easy chit-chat.

Dylan smiles at her.

"I better make sure they choose something I can actually sing, but I'll see you guys later?"

"Definitely," I say.

"Great," he says, giving us a little salute. "Thanks again."

Roxy and I watch him walk to the actors' table, then we turn to look at each other.

"That was unexpected . . ." starts Roxy. "Right, OK, no messing around then?"

Taking inspiration from Sadie, I have clamped myself to Roxy and squeeze her tight with both arms. I press my cheek against her spiky goth vampire top, which is incredibly uncomfortable against my skin but not as uncomfortable as a life without her friendship.

"I'm sorry," I say. She puts her arms around me and kisses the top of my head. "I'm so sorry, Roxy."

"It's OK, babe."

I pull away and grab both her hands.

"It's not. I was a twat," I say, shaking my head. "A massive one."

"Maybe medium-sized," she says, shrugging.

"I've missed you."

"I missed you too, but I know the Eliza stages of stubborn ass-ness off by heart."

I snort and wipe my nose on the back of my hand without releasing Roxy's. She grimaces but in a familiar way, like she knows she's stuck back with me now.

"I was so obsessed with Charlie being here and ruining our weekend that I actually ruined it myself," I say.

"You didn't ruin it, babe."

"I nearly ruined *us*, which is worse. I'm sorry I freaked out about you and Vivian."

"There's no me and Vivian," she says, tweaking my nest of hair. "We were just talking."

"Talking about doing naked stuff by the looks of you, but I'm still sorry. I don't know why I . . ." I shake my head, a thousand thoughts rushing through my brain at once. "I was scared of losing you. I don't want to lose any more of my people. We don't have much time left and . . ."

"We have donkey's years, babe."

I shake my head. "But you're going to Bristol and I'm not, and you'll make new friends and . . ."

"I hope so, but that doesn't stop you from being my best friend."

I shake my head. "Everything's changing."

"Change doesn't just mean bad; it can mean good too."

"I guess so," I say, looking at Dylan sitting with his actor pals.

"You, Eliza Gellar, are far too annoying and gorgeous to ever slip from my life, so whatever uni we're at, whatever convention, wherever in the world, you will always be my very best, most irritating, friend, OK?" I nod. "Blood is for ever?"

"Blood is for ever," I repeat. "I really am sorry I overracted about Vivian. She's actually really . . . well, I'm still not convinced she's human, so I don't know what she is but she's growing on me. I seem to have collected all these grudges against people who aren't in my very exclusive party of two, and I appreciate it's pretty stifling in here."

Roxy smiles at me.

"Well, I feel special to have been admitted. And it's not just the two of us any more." Roxy looks up at the stage at the owner of an incredible pair of lungs belting out "Dancing Queen": Dorothy. "We've got Dorothy now. And Fake McKinley, aka Dylan. And maybe . . ."

She turns to look at Charlie, who's looking at the karaoke iPad with Sadie. I think back to dancing with him last night and how my overreaction at seeing Roxy and Vivian together ruined a moment I've been daydreaming about for years.

I turn back to Roxy and shrug.

"I think I've blown it with him."

"We'll see. Let's just enjoy this," she says, bumping the inflatable bat with her elbow.

She squeezes me again and I breathe in her gorgeous Roxy smell, knowing that we're going to be OK, and that feeling is worth way more than coffee with Damon Van Schwartz or tickets to Comic Con with Megan Nicole Jefferies (though I am hoping our new friend Dylan can hook us up with tickets somehow. Just waiting for the right moment to ask).

Roxy heads to the cocktail bar and Vivian waves me over.

I go over and she grabs my wrist, pulling me into the booth.

"What's up?" I ask.

"Just wanted you to see it from this side," she says, turning me round so I'm facing the party. "See how much fun everyone's having?"

And she's right. The dance floor is packed, flashing a rainbow of happiness as everyone claps and sings along to Dorothy belting out the Abba classic. Old friends sit at the tables together, shouting deep and meaningfuls into each other's ears, and new friends hold on to each other, wondering when they'll get to do this again. And I'm wondering too, but right now I just want to be in it, because this is what it's all about.

I nod, and smile at Vivian, who puts her arm around me and rests her chin on top of my head, because of course she towers over me in her skates.

"This was you, Eliza. You did this for them," she says. Sadie drags Charlie past us, making him spin her round as she sings with the crowd. "She wouldn't have seen any of this if it weren't for you."

I shake my head.

"You did all of this. I mean, where the hell did you get an inflatable vampire bat on a Sunday?"

"The Halloween stuff my dad hires out was just sitting around, waiting for October. I made a call." She shrugs. "This is all you."

"I brought nothing, it was just an idea."

Vivian shakes her head and looks down at me.

"You brought your heart." She pushes away from me and twirls around, stopping in front of the laptop. "Now get out of my booth, bitch."

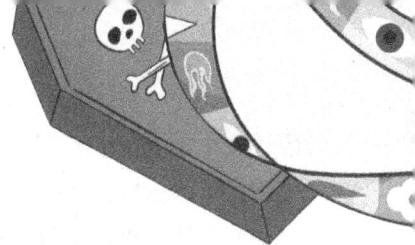

CHAPTER FIFTY

LILA MURPHY & BUD LEROY

And if we're here once I wanna laugh with you
After all there is I'll never lie to you
We're gonna smile
We're gonna deal
You're the one who sees me for real
Only silence if it's ending

Vampire Falls. Season six, episode ten – "Music, Maestro".

It's the best karaoke party of all the karaoke parties, and I'm not just saying that because I've made up with my bestie and had quite, *quite*, a lot of beers and also other drinks.

Damon Van Schwartz and Dylan insisted we sit at their table with the rest of the actors, so I've just spent the last four minutes screaming in Amber Anderson's ear about how the scene with her sister makes me cry every time I watch it. I know sitting with civilians probably isn't how she'd like to spend a Sunday night, but she doesn't show it, and before that she grabbed my hand and told me she was seething I didn't win the cosplay, which, to me, is better than getting full marks. Apparently, she threw a glass of water in another judge's face in an act of frustration and '*to sober him the hell up*'.

Sadie, unbelievably, is still going, weaving around the chairs to chat with everyone. They all respond like the professionals they are, giving her their full attention before she loses hers and moves on to the next person. Charlie watches her every second, smiling as he nurses his soft drink and hugging her back every time she goes to check in with him.

Felix looks way more relaxed than we've seen him all weekend, and I smile at him as he heads round the table and crouches down by my chair.

"Eliza," he says, both hands across his heart. "I can't thank you enough for what you've done tonight."

"It wasn't me," I say, shaking my head. "Vivian did all this."

"But you wouldn't give up," he says, his mouth set in a serious line.

"I . . . just wanted everyone to have this, Felix."

"I know," he says, nodding as he reaches into his inside pocket. "I don't know what your plans are, but if you're looking for very, *very*, badly paid work with terrible hours, these guys are looking for good, passionate people."

I frown at him then look down at the purple business card he's handed me and read the gold type.

"*Dragon Events*?"

Felix pulls himself up, nodding at me.

"Think about it," he says, smiling at Damon Van Schwartz who's waving him over to do a shot. "I said about the bad pay, right?" He wanders over to Damon before I can respond and Roxy comes back to the table, biting her lip to keep from smiling after spending the last twenty minutes talking to Vivian. I put the card in my pocket and decide to tell her about Felix later.

"I think the DJ fancies you."

"Course she does," Roxy says, taking a swig of her beer. She waves at Sadie. "Think your song's up next, Sadie."

Sadie gasps and waves Charlie up, her eyes wide with excitement. He looks back at her, very much not mirroring her excitement, but pulls himself up.

"What did you choose?" asks Roxy.

"I don't know." Charlie shakes his head. "I let her pick."

"Up next is beautiful Sadie and her averagely handsome brother, Charlie," announces Vivian.

Everyone applauds Charlie and Sadie as they head up to the stage, one slightly more enthusiastically than the other. The applause doubles when the song title comes up on the screen. Called "With You" but known to Fallers as the *Death Duet*, Lila and Bud sing it together after a Kweticca demon temporarily stops both their hearts, causing their lives without each other to flash before their eyes. They slope into the diner afterwards and order two Kitchen Sink Burgers, and by the end of the scene they're on the Full Moon Diner counter, singing together in a perfect moment of lightness after we all thought they'd been killed off.

Charlie holds Sadie's hand, and she looks up at him, holding her microphone up ready. The lighting around them changes through a few colours before it settles on blue, matching Sadie's dress. Nice touch, Vivian. The intro starts and we all quiet down, settling back in our seats to enjoy. I look back at Roxy.

"I love this song," I say.

"Me too. Can't wait to see ..."

Roxy's face crumbles from happiness to concern when the intro is over and the first line of the first verse should be sung, but it's not. Sadie's frozen on the stage, her wide eyes looking out at everyone as the mic shakes in front of her face.

"Oh no," I whisper, my hands over my mouth.

Everyone at the table – everyone in Conference Hall A – holds their breath, willing poor Sadie to find her voice and sing her heart out and enjoy the moment she's been waiting for since she arrived here. But there's nothing, and I can see her lip wobbling, even with Charlie kneeling down and trying to coax her out of her stage fright. I can't watch.

I look at Vivian, sure that she has a plan or another song lined up, but she's facing away from the stage, staring down at her laptop in concentration. Suddenly, unable to watch the terror on Sadie's face any longer, someone jumps out of their chair and rushes up onto the stage, leaning into Sadie's mic and squeezing her hand as they pick up the lyrics to the song.

That someone is me, apparently.

Sadie looks round at me, her eyes sparkling with almost tears, but the shock of having me singing next to her seems to shake her from the on-stage nightmare. She takes a breath and bites her lip, holding the mic up a little higher so I can stand a little straighter. I sing the words without taking my eyes from hers, and not just because I know the words better than the pores on my nose, but because the colour is coming back to her cheeks and she's almost smiling again.

I get to the end of Lila's part and I wink at Sadie. She nods and we both look at Charlie, who sings Bud's part next. I try to unfurl my fingers from her hand but she squeezes tighter, so I stay where I am and we watch Charlie mess up the lyrics. He looks down at her and waggles his eyebrows, and she laughs at her brother then hands me the microphone.

The audience claps along with the song, and I nod my head to the beat, smiling down at Sadie as I come in with my lines, then Charlie joins me and we're singing together, both of us looking from the screen to Sadie, whose face is a picture – so happy that she looks like she could channel everyone's elation and float above the stage. She still manages a big smile as she grits her teeth when I fail to hit the high notes, and Charlie sticks his fingers in his ears pretending he can't bear to hear my voice. I mean, obviously he's pretending.

We come to the end of the song and everyone at the VIP table is standing, cheering Sadie's name even though she didn't manage a word, and Roxy and Dylan wave at us like proud parents. I hug Sadie then glance at Charlie. He's watching me, his smile the same as it was the first time he walked into my living room and he fell in love with *Vampire Falls* all those years ago.

And I fell in love with him.

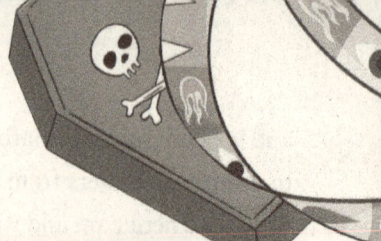

CHAPTER FIFTY-ONE

JULIANA THE DEMON HUNTRESS

It's not goodbye. In Megna we say, until our next battle.

BUD LEROY

*Kind of pessimistic, Jules. You've been
spending too much time with McKinley.*

Vampire Falls. Season one, episode twelve –
"Masquerade Brawl"

"I'm so glad I'd written *driving tomorrow* on my hand, so I'd remember not to do shots," says Roxy, flashing me faint ink on the back of her hand. "I'd feel like absolute shit right now."

I glare over her full English, trying not to barf at the smell of brown sauce (is she a middle-aged builder? Gross) and rub my forehead.

"Hmmm," I manage.

"Do you? Feel like absolute shit, I mean?" she says.

"*I* do," confirms another voice.

We both look up at Vivian. She lifts her sunglasses and places them on her head. She may feel like absolute shit, but she does not look like absolute shit. She's stunning as usual. Makes me feel like absolute shit. I mean, if I didn't feel like that already.

"Hey," says Roxy, her face brightening.

Vivian sort of scrunches her nose and smiles at Roxy in greeting. It's cute. They're cute.

"Packed and ready to go?" asks Vivian.

I nod. We said goodbye to Dorothy and Dylan after swapping contact details with both of them. Dorothy asked Dylan to drive her to the railway station and he obliged, carrying her luggage out to his hire car. I think she may have been asleep for his big reveal and still not actually know who he is.

The restaurant is nearly empty now and the few that remain scroll through photos of the weekend or look over their signed merch. I still haven't told anyone what Damon Van Schwartz said about this being the final season, and I don't think I ever will. I know how much people love this show and I can't be the one to break their hearts.

"Are you leaving now?" I ask, looking at Vivian, then glancing, again, around the restaurant.

"Yeah, but I had to come say bye to you bitches."

She smiles down at me, and maybe it's nostalgia for the final convention or the belief that by touching her she might transmit some of her beauty to me, but I stand up and give her a big hug, before sitting down very quickly due to the restaurant spinning of its own accord. Weird.

"Are you driving back with Charlie?" asks Roxy.

"He and Sadie left earlier," says Vivian, glancing at me. "I got the train here anyway."

Knowing that Charlie is no longer in the same building as me makes my body overflow with sorrow, and it takes everything I have left not to rest my cheek on the white tablecloth and go to sleep.

"Are you OK, babe?" says Roxy, stroking my hair, as apparently, I *didn't* have enough of whatever it was to stop me doing just that.

I nod, and neither of them need to quiz me any further. Last night was about the convention, about making sure Sadie got the ending she wanted, that we would remember the final night of the final convention being the best ever, so I didn't really get a chance to talk to Charlie properly. It was impossible to talk properly over all the singing, and once Sadie had got her confidence, she dragged him up to sing practically every other song of the night. Every time I looked at him, he was already looking at me, smiling. I'd planned on saying goodbye this morning. Saying more than goodbye; saying sorry, and all the things I wanted to say since I lost him.

I pull myself back up and reach into my onesie pocket, pulling out a folded piece of paper ripped from my notebook. I hold it gently in my fingers, careful not to tear or rip it as if I'm holding my very own heart. I look up and they're both watching me. I hold it out to Vivian, who frowns but reaches for it.

"If you see Charlie, will you give this to him?"

"Of course," says Vivian, gently putting it in her bag.

"Thank you," I say, giving her what I hope is a genuine smile, and not a *I-think-I'm-going-to-barf* grimace.

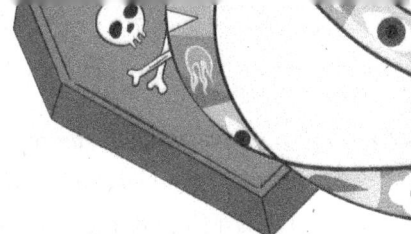

CHAPTER FIFTY-TWO

VIGGO RASSMUSSEN

Humans never fail to surprise me.

Vampire Falls. Season three, episode seventeen –
"Signs of Life"

There is nothing worse than post-convention blues. Apart from being forced to listen to the football team's playlist in the common room, whilst suffering a very serious case of post-convention blues.

Nothing has changed at school. Roxy and I sit in our socially assigned spot by the vending machine, and everyone else hangs in the sections they always hang in, no clue that we've had the best and most emotionally charged weekend of our lives and that I learnt more about myself over those few nights than I have in any of these classrooms. Vivian waves at me from her spot on the sofa and I wave back, taking a quick look around the common room before I turn my attention back to Roxy.

"You liked it though, right?" she asks.

She's scrolling Vivian's Insta, going over the photos from the weekend.

"Liked what?" I say.

"Liked what," she repeats, shaking her head, then looks at me. "*Midnight in Portland*. I've been talking about it for the last five minutes. You watched it, right?"

I nod.

"And? What did you think?"

"I'm too blue to think."

She shakes her head and looks down at her phone again. A paper aeroplane, courtesy of the lads in the corner, hits me between the eyes. Welcome back to reality, Eliza. I open it up to find an extremely graphic drawing of me and Viggo doing it. It's actually quite good; I almost feel bad screwing it up.

"You loved it," says Roxy. "You're just too stubborn to admit how beyond right I am about it."

"That is correct," I say, putting my head on her shoulder.

I close my eyes for a few seconds and let the banter of the common room wash over me, before sitting back up and looking around, my eyes lingering on the football team in the corner.

"I haven't seen him all morning, babe."

I don't answer because I don't need to. The final convention has left me feeling empty, and I think the idea of Charlie was keeping me moving forward. But I've not seen or heard from him since karaoke, and I know this because I've checked by phone approximately sixteen thousand times an hour.

"Do you think Vivian gave it to him?" I ask.

"I don't know, babe," says Roxy.

I close my eyes and resume my previous head-on-Roxy's-shoulder position and wonder if we can just stay like this for ever and then she wouldn't have to go to Bristol, and I wouldn't have to exist in a world that doesn't have new episodes of *Vampire Falls* in it. I must be falling asleep as the common room buzz gets quieter and quieter, like someone's turning the volume down on each little clique, and the music too. I really am dreaming when Damon Van Schwartz's voice floats across the common room.

"*Don't cry, Lila. Save your tears for when you really need them.*"

But then Roxy says my name, and she doesn't normally make an appearance in this specific dream. She's usually in the one where we've robbed Tesco and we're trying to get away on a rice pudding moped.

She grabs my wrist so hard it hurts. I gasp and look down at her fingers digging into me.

"Get your pointy talons off me; you're cutting off my circulation," I say, looking between my poor wrist and her face. "What's wrong with you?"

"Oh. My. God," she whispers, shaking my arm on each word.

I realise the common room has actually gone completely silent and it's not just in my head. I look up at what Roxy's gaping at.

"Oh. My. God," I repeat.

Actual Damon Van Schwartz is standing on one of the benches by the common room doorway, in full Viggo Rassmussen costume. Guyliner, everything. I think I need to say that again, because I might be having an out of body experience.

DAMON VAN SCHWARTZ IS IN MY COMMON ROOM.

"*I'd given up too, Lila. I didn't think I had any hope left.*

But hope is a funny thing; it's a snuffed-out candle, leaving a curl of smoke in its wake. That tiniest red dot just needs a little breath to reignite it and the flame flickers back to life when your back is turned. It dances in the dark and says I'm still here."

He steps off the bench, puts his hand on his hip and walks past the year twelves, who may not be *Vampire Falls* fans but have seen him in *Engine Failure* or *Only Ever*, so they gape as he glides past, nodding at them, and even doing a few fist bumps.

I turn to Roxy, who stares back at me with an equal amount of *what the fuck is happening* written all over her face. Damon Van Schwartz stops in front of the vending machine and breaks character for a split second when he spots me and winks. He looks over his shoulder, just as someone else follows him. Roxy and I look round, and she squeezes my arm, covering her mouth with her other hand.

Charlie stands in the doorway of the common room, dressed in Orion's signature hoodie, just as he was the first night of the convention. Roxy half gasps, half laughs. Charlie clears his throat, and I can hear the nerves in his vocal cords. He walks to the middle of the common room, not looking directly at anyone apart from one person.

Me. I'm the one person.

I bite my lip and goosebumps bubble across my flesh as Charlie walks past Damon Van Schwartz who claps him on the shoulder.

"I'm back, Lila, and I've been thinking about you and what you said. It's all I've been thinking about, even when I thought

there wasn't a way back," he whispers. "*I know I infuriate you because you say I think I know it all, but that's because I do. I've been dead a long time and I've seen a lot of stuff, before internet and TikTok were a thing.*"

My eyes brim with tears as I take his words in. *My* words, from the final part of the *Vampire Falls* fan fiction I scribbled down before breakfast yesterday. I look at Vivian, who has her hands clasped under her chin as she smiles back at me.

She did give it to him.

"*I know that sunsets really pop in the fall because the air is clearer. I know how to kill and bury a Clopwyck witch, so she won't reanimate and seek revenge. I know that my eyes are the exact same shade of green as my mother's.*"

I bite my lip, as Charlie conjures a small laugh and sob hybrid from inside my heart.

"*But there* are *things I don't know, things that I don't ever want to know,*" Charlie, as Orion, says, his eyes locked on my face. "*I don't know how my soul would exist without the possibility of a sunset with you next to me. I don't know if the buzz I get at the sound of your name would be replaced with the numbness I had before I met you. I don't know how I would pass the lonely hours of wakefulness, without our conversations and your expressions on repeat in my head. I don't know how I could live a life, this life, without you in it. I don't* want *to know.*"

Roxy's hand moves from my arm, and she pushes me up so I'm standing. I fold my arms, conscious of everyone staring, but I don't look away from Charlie – I don't even want to blink because I don't want to miss a single second of this surreal moment so I can play it over in my head for the rest of my life. "*I can't not be us, Lila, I can't not be around you. I don't know how to be me without you. That thought is what kept me swimming upwards from the depths of Halxja for eternity, or until Viggo found me.*"

He looks back at Damon Van Schwartz, who winks at us. Roxy moves away so I'm standing alone, everyone else in the common room forming a semi-circle around us, moving in as Charlie gets closer to me.

"*Can we be us again, Lila?*" Charlie says, swallowing a lump of nerves down as he pauses, then steps forward and takes my hand. "*Whatever that looks like? Can we? Can we do that?*"

Something falls from my cheek, and I realise I'm crying. I wipe my face with the back of my hand and I blink at Charlie, more tears brimming over. He bites his lip, waiting for me to answer. Roxy is next to Vivian, who is ugly (finally!) crying right now. I smile at my friends then look back at Charlie. I'm filled with such overwhelming love for him, for our friendship, our past, our TV show and our lost years, that I feel like I'm going to burst. I take a deep breath and squeeze his fingers and fall deep into his eyes.

"*Yes,*" I whisper. "*We can.*"

Charlie smiles and pulls me into him. He puts his hand on my cheek, and I can't remember if it's from my scene or a real episode or who cares because right now everything else has disappeared and I'm pressed up against Charlie Chamberlain, his lips on mine, and I feel it everywhere in all of my body for the rest of time.

The common room cheers and he pulls me closer, smiling against my lips as we both try to ignore the audience for the most amazing and embarrassing moment of our friendship, until the cheering is drowned out by the guitar intro to Lila and Orion's theme on the common room speakers. We pull away for a moment in surprise, and I spot Vivian with her phone, still in tears but absolutely beaming at me as she turns up our song.

Because Lila and Orion's theme will now for ever be Eliza and Charlie's song.

ONE YEAR LATER

MIP CON BITCHES

Vivian

One more sleep bitches! @Roxy don't forget my boots I left at your house. Need them for cosplay Saturday night.

Roxy

I won't (love those boots) 😎

Has everyone seen the party themes? Pretty lame.

Eliza

They're always lame.

Roxy

Oh you are alive then.

Eliza

What?

Roxy

You missed Friday FaceTime babe ☹

Eliza

Sorry! Couldn't get away, Felix had me on line-up reveal for Coven Con. Someone got overwhelmed and fainted.

We've all been there.

Roxy

Don't stand me up next time.

Eliza

Vivian

Stop hogging the GC bitches.

Did you hear from Dylan @Eliza

Eliza

My best friend and MTV award-winner Dylan Maguire you mean?

Roxy

😳

Vivian

😳

Eliza

He got us all upgraded!

Roxy

AMAZING!!!

What time you think you'll get there?

Eliza

I literally fly back from my writing course at Penrose Hackett the night before.

Did I mention prize-winning author and screenwriter Gloria Hannigan handpicked me for her writing residential?

Roxy

You might have mentioned it babe.

Eliza

Kay.

So I get back from Ireland, sleep eight hours then Charlie's picking me up.

Vivian

Did your writer lady like the story you wrote about me btw?

Eliza

It's not about you, Vi.

Vivian

A kick-ass redhead who glides around as if she's on skates?
She's me. You're welcome, bitches.

Eliza

Charlie

We'll arrive at 11.

Eliza

We have to get coffee on the way.

Charlie

You have mentioned several times. I am aware of this.

Eliza

It's tradition.

Charlie

It's not tradition if it's a new convention.

Eliza

It's a new tradition then.

Charlie

That doesn't make sense.

Eliza

You don't make sense.

Roxy

You two are weird.

Eliza

Love you too.

Vivian

Got to go.

See you tomorrow, bitches!

Roxy

See you bitches.

Eliza

Bye bitches.

Charlie

Bye.

Eliza

@Charlie!

Charlie

What?

Eliza

Say it then.

Charlie

Bye bitches 😳

Toby

Guys!

Finally told Mum and she's cool as long as I share with Charlie.

Toby

Guys?

Eliza

Good for you Toby 😀

ACKNOWLEDGEMENTS

When I tripped through the revolving doors of my first *Buffy the Vampire Slayer* convention, I felt like I'd arrived at the mother ship. Just like Eliza with *Vampire Falls*, I'd found the Georgia-shaped space I'd been searching for, and now I feel that way about the book community. I wouldn't have got here without some amazing people in my weird little corner, so strap yourself in for a long list of gratitude.

My fabulous agent, Lauren Gardener. You had me at 'I got stuck in a chair once' and I'm so glad you did. Thank you for loving and understanding Eliza, and for tuning into my brain. Callen Martin, thank you for insisting the readers know what Charlie Chamberlain smells like. The amazing Hazel Holmes, thank you so much for your enthusiasm for *Foes and Cons* (and *Vampire Falls!*) – I'm so glad to be part of the Fox & Ink family. Thanks to Kathy Webb for the editing journey and for swooning over the ending, Nicki Marshall for her amazing proofreading superpowers, and Antonia Wilson for PR and marketing. Thanks, also, to Chloe Seager and SCBWI for setting the competition I entered with what became the first chapter of *Foes and Cons*, and Lina Langley for pointing me in the right direction.

Can we just take a moment for the cover? I can't express my love for Trisha Srivastava's incredible artwork and Amy Cooper's bold cover design – thank you, both, for bringing my characters to life and giving *Foes and Cons* such an eye-catching cover.

Cynthia Murphy, thank you for believing in me even when I didn't anymore. I'm eternally grateful to Wattpad and Luke for bringing us together (hi, Luke!). Josh Winning, thank you for always listening and knowing what to say, and for giggles and beers in the Ipswich sunshine.

Julia Tuffs. Although you're shorter than me, I felt like I was looking *up* at you when you gave me *The Pep Talk* at Waterstones in January 2023. *We have to do the work* – and we did. A hundred words became five hundred, and then a thousand, and then some more, until it was done. I don't think I'd have finished this book without your daily check-ins, and I'll be forever grateful. Dude, you are awesome.

For a long time, I felt like a fraud because I thought I'd never be published again, but a bunch of book people made me feel like there was still space for me. Thank you to all the lovely authors I've chatted to at launches and conventions, the Goodshippers, the UKYA Discord gang, and Chelley Toy and Point Horror Book Club.

Close Encounters et al. Bub Chahal and Russ Myers, thanks for letting me waltz around the shop like I own the place, and allowing me to be the main character from my own book by supporting your convention. Katy Glover, you get a separate, special thank you from those two because you're my absolute fave, and because you brought Sarah L. Miles (also a fave) into my life. I'm so grateful for all you've done to support me.

Thank you to everyone who gave me a space to write: Sarah and Sarah (aka Fairygod-Sarah and Regular Sarah) at your kitchen table, Josh in your lovely home, and Dad, for cups of tea at the desk (and for letting us host *Buffy the Vampire Slayer* on Tuesday nights back in the day).

I also need to thank my daughter who endured two-hour-long ballet lessons even though she hated them, but it meant I could write in the car every Saturday. I should also thank my son, who's the best at insisting I take breaks from the screen. And Kirk Seymour, of course and always, for making it work. Love you all, marvellous much.

Foes and Cons is about belonging, among other things, and now that you've read this story, it belongs to you, reader, so thank you for choosing it. I hope it helps to fill the you-shaped space you've been looking for.

HAVE YOU EVER WONDERED HOW BOOKS ARE MADE?

Fox & Ink Books is an award-winning independent publisher specialising in Children's and Young Adult books. Based at the University of Lancashire, this Preston-based publisher teaches MA Publishing students how to become industry professionals using the content and resources from its business; students are included at every stage of the publishing process and credited for the work that they contribute.

The business doesn't just help publishing students though. Fox & Ink Books has supported the employability and real-life work skills for the University's Illustration, Acting, Translation, Animation, Photography, Film & TV students and many more. This is the beauty of books and stories; they fuel many other creative industries! The MA Publishing students are able to get involved from day one with the business and they acquire a behind-the-scenes experience of what it is like to work for a such a reputable independent.

The MA course was awarded a Times Higher Award (2018) for Innovation in the Arts, and the business, Fox & Ink Books, was awarded Best Newcomer at the Independent Publishing Guild (2019) for the ethos of teaching publishing using a commercial publishing house. As the business continues to grow, so too does the student experience upon entering this dynamic master's course.

www.foxandinkbooks.com
www.foxandinkbooks.com/courses/
foxandink@lancashire.ac.uk